DYSTOPIAN EXPRESS

DYSTOPIAN EXPRESS

EDITED BY
ROBIN BLANKENSHIP
AND
F. L. HALL

Hydra
Publications

Hydra
Publications

Table of Contents

FRIENDING

By
Gregory L. Norris

The numbers on Kane's screen jumped up by three—a good sign, but hardly the bonanza he'd anticipated, especially following his speech regarding the taking of chances and the discovery of. "Friends and neighbors you didn't even know you had!"

That signature line had notched him close to 30,000 'likes' in the first minute following the broadcast, and was initially offered up on T-shirts and coffee mugs, landing a call from a marketing agent convinced she could make them both rich—based upon the final outcome, of course. But interest appeared to have fizzled as quickly as it ignited, given the latest trending report: three new friendings two hours after his time in front of the camera. Kane's heart resumed its gallop; not that it had slowed, but the big jump in numbers and friends had at least offered promise.

He paced the cubicle as much as the tight confines carpeted in somber industrial gray allowed. With so many eyes watching, he knew it wasn't good to appear overly nervous, any more than it was wise to flash even the remotest glint of smugness for the cameras—and the world—to see. The seconds dragged past with maddening slowness. His next glance at the screen showed another two friend requests. The little silver and teal icons of human silhouettes on the monitor perked him up. But the rush of emotion soon darkened, for six more of his new friends had unfriended him.

A shiver tumbled down Kane's spine, curiously hotter than cold. He attempted to swallow, only to discover his mouth had gone completely dry.

"Please," he whispered, knowing the cameras caught that, too.

The danger of appearing too desperate wouldn't help, nor would constantly looking at the results on the cubicle's screen, which Kane did anyway. A window on the big monitor displayed his name—fourth from the bottom. Drop into the Lowest Three and…

"With time to vote running out, we'd like to remind viewers that they, through the power of social media, can make a difference—all the difference—in the lives of the unpopular, the unattractive, and the friendless," said Rance Rollins, host and announcer. He then urged the viewing audience to vote with their hearts, not their prejudices.

Another dozen viewers friended Kane, whose live-feed played out on the screen directly following Rollins' update. But in the final minute, more than fifty unfriended him—what they referred to in the industry as, 'The Shadenfreude Guillotine'. Harm-Joy activity, he knew, always ran rampant during the countdown. Though not spoken of during Kane's briefing, he understood from rumors that the Guillotine ran deep with scandal, with popularity often bought out by those who could afford it as the seconds evaporated.

His name and the one beneath leapfrogged. Kane Eskridge slipped from fourth to third, below that all-important teal and silver line.

His heart pulsed. A foul metallic taste blossomed across his tongue. Lowest Three. Kane shook his head and attempted to speak, only no words emerged. He willed his feet to move—Run! Just run!—but at first they refused to cooperate. How many security checkpoints existed between the cubicle where they'd taken him and the outside? He'd counted at least eight. And those were the ones that were visible.

Kane tipped a look back at the monitor. His palsy broke.

"He's running," Rollins announced, the glee clear in his voice. "Oh yes, as expected, the first of our Lowest Three appears to be headed for a last-minute attempt to escape. Maybe, it's a desperate ploy to cobble extra numbers as we reach zero in four…three…two…"

Kane shuffled out of the cubicle, aware of the leaden weight of the new shoes the network had bestowed upon him, along with the crisp, tailored suit. The tie attempted to choke him. The clothes must have been designed to constrict, thus strangling the wearer where he stood, Kane thought.

But that was never their solution. A small mob of men dressed in black appeared ahead of him, blocking the corridor. They were all attractive, in perfect shape, tall…no doubt popular despite the feral glints in their eyes.

Kane whispered a plea for mercy. Rollins' voice boomed in response, "Kane Eskridge, you have been judged as too ugly and unpopular and, as such, too abnormal to live."

The men, he saw, all clutched ceremonial hammers. More approached from behind. They formed a circle around Kane, waited a second or so for the cameras to catch up, and then they swung.

Republic of Masks

By
Josh Brown

It didn't start as a way to divide social classes. No, it started as something quite different. People actually began wearing masks out of fear that their privacy was becoming compromised, something that was supposedly protected under the Fourth Amendment of a previous government. Surveillance cameras and facial recognition software became the norm; they were everywhere, from every corner of every block to the vest of every soldier, law enforcement officer, fireman, teachers, construction workers, and even postal carriers.

So people began wearing masks. There was no law against it, wearing a mask in public. It started as a small, rebellious movement. Kids, they said, trying to make a statement against the "the man." But the fad caught on, and spread like wildfire.

Certain businesses started to ban the wearing of masks inside their establishments, but that had little effect and did not last very long. People were content to place an order for their groceries and other wares online and have them delivered for a small fee (the delivery drivers themselves usually wearing brown or yellow balaclavas).

So, those businesses that did ban the wearing of masks quickly reversed themselves. I suppose that's where it began, really. Holding a true "if you can't beat them, join them" mentality, department stores and scores of entrepreneurs looked to cash in on the fact that every household in the country wanted (needed?) masks. They began to manufacture masks by the boatload. There were big masks, little masks, fancy masks, casual masks—masks for all occasions. Soon, it was no longer acceptable to wear a simple balaclava or three-hole "ski" mask. One needed a mask for the office. A mask for working out at the gym. A mask for a trip to the movie theater. A mask for a Sunday drive. A mask for your next date, and another one to slip on later should your date extend into the bedroom after hours.

The surveillance cameras became irrelevant, forgotten about really, and eventually they were phased out of the new government's homeland security program. Cameras on those soldiers, law enforcement officers, firemen, teachers, construction workers, and postal carriers had been replaced by masks.

Teachers wore a certain kind of mask as they taught in classrooms. Firemen wore a certain kind of mask, able to connect quickly to oxygen tanks should they need to rush into a burning building. Doctors, nurses, and health-care officiants wore a certain kind of mask. Judges and lawyers wore masks. Law enforcement officers wore a certain style of mask—a blue-and-black half mask with large eye-holes as to not obstruct their view. Even street gangs and members of organized crime wore masks that identified their allegiances.

What started as a push for privacy and anonymity became just the opposite—a method of identifying one's self and letting the world know who you are and what you stand for. Young kids would spend long countless hours customizing his or her mask in an effort to individualize. Certain attributes quickly came in and out of fashion for these masks—half masks, full masks, domino masks, masks with bright colors, muted colors, beads, certain sayings or slogans etched or scrawled across them. There was even a "retro" movement for a short time in which teenagers again wore simple balaclavas. Masks were no longer worn exclusively in public; they were worn in privacy of one's home as well, at all hours, even during sleep.

Criminals, killers, thieves, convicted felons, rapists, child abusers, were issued court mandates to wear a certain type of mask identifying them as the bottom-feeders of society. These masks were permanently bonded to the wearers' skin for the rest of his or her life, and any attempt to tamper would result in instantaneous death. In fact, some criminals attempted removal knowing that death was imminent in doing so, preferring to die rather than go on condemned and branded as a disgraceful and deplorable individual for the rest of their lives.

By the time the fourth world war came to an end and the United Nations of America had established their new government, the absence of a mask on one's face was considered a social faux pas—undignified, tactless, and quite embarrassing. Everyone wore a mask, from the very highest of upper society, to the lowest. Newborn babies were given their mask immediately after the umbilical cord was cut. People were buried, or cremated, in their mask.

Government officials and the upper echelons of noble society became prone to wearing very intricate masks in public. These masks, almost exclusively half-masks specifically, were usually very large and intricate, with gilded scrollwork and inlaid gems. In any given city, state, or societal construct, the masks of specific high-ranking families were well known among the public. Anyone attempting to wear a mask that identified with a family that was not their own, or outside of their social status, ran the risk of a swift and harsh punishment.

Such as it was that the masks soon became the downfall of the government and the doom of society. Sudden, violent, and vicious—civil war erupted. The Clutterbucks, a prominent and powerful family of the southern region of the republic, in vast majority control of the nation's dwindling oil supplies, became at odds with the Midwinters, another prominent and powerful family, dominant of the northern regions, and in control of the republic's water supply. It was said that the Midwinters had been developing an engine that operated on nothing but water. Their team of scientists had created a fuel cell that could separate the atomic bonds between the hydrogen and oxygen atoms, then recombine them to release energy. The innovation was a breakthrough, but there was still problems in fully applying the technology to engines (lubrication of the engine was still an issue), and therefore, vehicles of any sort.

Should such an innovative invention come to fruition, however, it had the potential to render oil useless, as water could then be used as fuel not only for the human body but also any mechanical contraption powered by humans. The days of oil were coming to an end, literally and figuratively, and as such the Clutterbucks became desperate.

Someone in the masked guise of a Blackwell (another prominent family who found their fortune manufacturing microprocessors) attempted to murder the patriarch of the Midwinters, in broad daylight, in a public space. The would-be assassin's attempt was foiled, and the nefarious character turned out to actually be a low-ranking and distant cousin to the Minstrels, a family knows for having close ties to the Clutterbucks. The Blackwells retaliated immediately against the Minstrels, who in turn enlisted the help of the Clutterbucks for protection. The Midwinters sat back and watched the three families destroy each other until the time was right, then struck all three at once, obliterating the Minstrels completely and taking control of both the oil and microprocessor industries from the Clutterbucks and Blackwells in doing so.

The balance of power shifted to severely to the Midwinters that they became a sort of royalty, and their influence on government was such that their eventual attempt at a coup proved successful. The United Nations of America was no longer a republic by and for the people. It was now a full-blown monarchy. The patriarch of the Midwinters, now effectively known as King Miles Midwinter, issued a decree relating to national security. Addressing his cabinet of Dukes and Barons, the King of America declared he would sign into law a bill that declared each and every family, rich and poor, to register the design of their hereditary heraldic mask, and thus be identified with design of said mask going forward. Alterations may be applied for, but were not guaranteed.

The public outcry was enormous. The people rioted in the streets, setting fires and raising mayhem. They eventually rebelled against their masks throwing them into the fires and shouting things like "Unmask for liberty!" or "Real face, real power!"

Soldiers were deployed and given orders to use lethal force against any such rioter, as riots and protests were declared illegal long before the onset of the third world war. More than two point five million protesters across fourteen cities mercilessly lost their lives. Soldiers simply threw dead bodies, riddled with bullet holes, atop their own riotous fires, there being so many bodies they didn't know what else to do with them.

The new Midwinter monarchy now ruled with fear, and the decree soon came down that anybody not wearing a mask would immediately be put to death. No trial, no judge, no pleading one's case. Just death. Also put to decree was that each individual's mask, again, no matter social status, would be equipped with a camera, so that the law-enforcing body of the new monarchical government could be aware of a citizen's comings and goings at all times. The theory was sound: If you commit a crime, the government was watching. But also having lunch? The government was watching. Taking a shower? The government was watching. Making love to your spouse? The government was watching.

The Midwinter court then leveraged their majority interests in the microprocessor industry to begin manufacturing such cameras, and also began placing public surveillance cameras everywhere. The intention being, in addition to every single registered mask, to place a camera on every corner of every block, on high-tech satellites in in space, on the uniform of each and every soldier, law enforcement officer, and public official, and, eventually, inside every citizen's own home.
Masks were mandatory, but privacy, as it is, was illegal. Any individual or group attempting to seclude themselves, or information about themselves, would be subject to punishment of death. Leave your mask on, they said, and in doing so, let the world know who you are.

Greater Good

By
Jeff Provine

The agents of the Greater Good came for Will Dagny at nine o'clock in the morning. He knew they were coming. He thought about filling the house with gas from the stovetop and rigging a match on the door. Then he thought about flooding his house ankle-deep in salt water and running in a line from the circuit breaker. In the end, he just sat in his recliner and did Sudoku puzzles.

They knocked and introduced themselves. It was formal and polite.

Dagny didn't move.

They gave him a warning to come out.

Dagny set his puzzles aside, stood up, and walked to the back of the house. Just as he came into the kitchen, the front door exploded inward. Dagny heard the battering ram hit the floor, followed by heavy thumps of boots. The pack of agents spread into the house barking orders, codenames, and call-signs.

Dagny opened the kitchen door and began walking into his backyard. He admired his high-end gas grill and the lounging chair he built himself out of pine lumber. He'd made and eaten a number of masterpieces here: steaks, burgers, one time a whole roast pig. He ate them slowly, looking out over his lawn and redbud trees he'd trimmed to be nearly identical. The trees and lawn had grown shaggy as summer turned into fall, but he didn't care anymore.

"There!" a voice muffled by a black visor and helmet called.

They grabbed him as he was opening the back gate to walk out into the alley.

~*~

It had been years since the Greater Good took over the old county courthouse. Much of the building was the same: same block walls, same purpose of judging the people, same air of legal mystery. The real change could only be seen in the mural above the front steps. The predatory, oppressive symbols of the eagle and stars had been chiseled away. The blind woman with the scales still stood nobly there. She was joined by the new icons: the faceless Many whom the woman served and the multi-armed, leech-mouthed Parasites, whom she cast out.

The woman raised her sword and towered over all other images.

The agents of the Greater Good pulled Dagny from the back of the windowless van and shoved him up the stone steps. The courthouse was packed. Its lobby stank of cleaning fluids and too many bodies in one place. A line of panicked defendants stood with two black-masked agents flanking each. Quick-mouthed lawyers buzzed up and down the hall. Dangerous defendants wore chains on their wrists and ankles. Others held their own wrists while their knees shook.

It was Review Day, six months after Audit Day, what had been Tax Day, April 15 on the old, inefficient calendar. More vans pulled up, adding bodies to the mass, then left to find more defendants. Dagny, like the rest of the wretches, hadn't been able to prove in six months that they were contributing members of society.

The man in line in front of Dagny caught his gaze. He was grizzled, probably only in his forties, though years of hard living in his face and gray-patched, sleep-spiked hair made him look twenty years older. Chains hung from his hands down to his ankles. The man's blue eyes were almost vacant; his young lawyer nervously shifted his weight from one foot to the other. Dagny wondered what the older man had done during the revolution. He looked like he could have withstood all the pepper spray in the country from the National Guard before the Natties joined the overthrow of the One-Tenth Percent. His lawyer would've barely been out of middle school then. Did he remember those days at all?

The line shifted forward. Someone else's review was finished. Dagny stood still until the agents had to push him forward.

A man in a dark blue suit walked up to him carrying a plastic digipad. Without looking up, he asked, "William Townsend Dagny?"

Dagny cleared his throat. "Will."

"Right," the man replied. "I am your appointed attorney for your Review. It is my duty to—"

Dagny interrupted him. "I choose to represent myself."

The lawyer paused. He looked up from his notes written over pre-printed court documents. He stared at Dagny. "What?"

"I choose to represent myself."

The lawyer's eyes flicked to the agents at Dagny's sides. "Sir, I must recommend that you—"

Dagny shook his head slowly. "I choose to represent myself."

"You do understand," the lawyer began to argue, "that I have a great deal of knowledge about the Code for Good. I've won forty cases over my career, already one this morning. Yours is an easy case. You work hard at a good job; your record isn't that bad. I could…"

Dagny let him speak. He had nothing better to do while the line slowly progressed. When the lawyer's rambling finally ended, Dagny said again, "I choose to represent myself."

The lawyer's eyes widened and then narrowed. He looked at the agents again. They stood still.

The lawyer leaned forward. In a softer voice, he said, "Listen, you'd really be doing me a favor. I'm behind this year. I had some parties that got a little out of hand and a little… wasteful. We're halfway to the next Audit Day already. If I don't do enough pro bono Reviews, I'll be in that line, too!"

Dagny shook his head.

One of the agents bumped Dagny's arm. "Just take the man's help."

Dagny looked at the agent, but he couldn't see beyond the heavy padding, the helmet, the belt loaded with nonlethal weapons. Somewhere under that black visor, there was a person. He probably meant well. Most people probably meant well; they probably always had, no matter how bleak things got.

Dagny was sick of good intentions. "I'm going to represent myself. If you don't stop talking, I'm going to tackle you and take a bite out of your throat."

The agents grabbed Dagny's arms.

Dagny pulled and chomped air in the lawyer's direction. He gave a toothy smile. "How easy would my case be then?"

The lawyer didn't smile. He fumbled with the screen on the digipad and finally dropped it. When he stood back up with it, he held out a stylus. "You have to sign."

Dagny reached out a hand. One of the agents grabbed it with a leather-gloved iron grip. Dagny looked at the black visor, then slowly took the stylus and signed the dismissal form. The lawyer took his stylus back and hurried away.

Dagny turned back to the line. He was close to the courtroom now. A gavel banged, and he heard the words, "You are sentenced to two hundred fifty hours of community service and a two percent donation of property."

Applause rang through the court. Review Day drew a crowd, just like a public hanging.

The line shifted forward again. The man in front of Dagny stepped inside to an alcove, leaving him with a clear view of the courtroom through the door.

It was still much the same it had been before the revolution. The walls were made of marble panels surrounded by ornate woodwork. It must have been grandiose in its day; now it was clean but gradually falling into disrepair. Ripping it all out would have been a waste of taxpayer money.

An older lawyer began his case defending a young man who sat at the table before the high judge's seat. The young man leaned back in his seat, as if disgusted that he had to be here. He was dressed in the height of teen fashion: ballooning pants, faux-diamond chains, and a clear plastic shirt to show off his tattoos: a mixed theme of jungle animals and flames. His hair was painted red and carefully molded into two little devil's horns, very fashionable.

Dagny overheard a mumble from the crowd, "If he'd spent half the time doing something productive instead of on his hair, he wouldn't be here."

The audience ranged from a gaggle of old women to young mothers with restless babies to men who looked like they'd just walked in from the street. Some came to campaign for loved ones, others simply to enjoy the Review. Television had never been the same since the Enlightening Entertainment Act censored anything glamorizing negative behavior. People craved watching gossip being made.

"...so, your honor, I beseech you to see in your good judgment the potential of this young man," the lawyer summed. He waved a hand back at the pointy-haired young man, who gave a superior, scoffing huff.

The judge looked down from his seat. He was bald and wore glasses, nondescript as an egg wearing black robes. He looked more like an accountant than a judge.

That's fitting, Dagney thought.

The judge raised a finger. "I do recognize potential, yet I do not see how anything could come of what I see in front of me." He pointed the finger at the devil-head. "You were notified of your lacking six months ago on Audit Day. What have you done since to contribute?"

The kid shrugged and looked away.

"As noted in my report," the lawyer explained, "he has been sidetracked from studies or work due to his mother's illness."

"Yes," the judge said. He shuffled papers. "This illness that has not been documented and did not prevent the mother from having her own positive Audit?"

The lawyer nodded. "The family felt it would be a waste of societal resources to visit doctors, as all she needed was restful care when not working. She has been a great inspiration to young Mr. Howards here."

The judge paused a moment and then ordered, "Howards, stand up."

The devil-head loudly pushed his chair back and swung his shoulders to stand, as if he had to cast off a huge weight. He stood tall and danced a little to stretch.

When he was finished, the judge asked, "What do you do for your mother?"

"Well, see, I," the devil-head began. "I, like, get her breakfast made… and sometimes when she comes home, she's tired, so's I stay with her and get her things if she needs 'em."

"And what do you do with the rest of your time?"

The lawyer's eyes momentarily went wide. He stepped forward and opened his mouth to answer for the devil-head, but the judge waved him off.

The devil-head scratched himself. "Well, y'know, I'm workin' on improving myself… I exercise and read… stuff, and I'm thinkin' about putting an album together. And my friend Jimmy, see, he can get me on stage down at the Owl sometime… when my show's ready."

"So you're a musician?"

"Totes yah."

"I see."

The judge sat back and shuffled his papers into a neat pile. "Albion Jeremiah Howards, you have failed your Review in accordance with your lackluster record following your Audit. In appreciation of your wishes to be a musician, I hereby sentence you to one month of Reeducation and nine months in an appropriate Trade Institute, following a test for your aptitude." He banged his gavel.

The courtroom buzzed. Several people applauded. Others murmured.

The lawyer shrugged and walked back to his briefcase as if the boy ceased to exist.

The young devil-head threw up his hands.

"Yo, no, man, listen!" he cried. "I don't need none of that! I can do my own thing, see? I don't steal no more, either!"

Agents dragged him away, and Dagny turned. He couldn't look.

Even closing his eyes, he could still hear the rumbling approval from the crowd.

His own agents pushed him forward into the waiting box. The grizzled man in line in front of Dagny passed him. Under his uncombed beard, his lips were pressed tight. Dagny nodded to him, but the man didn't react.

The court came into session, and the man's young lawyer stepped forward. "Having been convicted of murder, my client has made an appeal that society has been improved because of his actions."

Dagny blinked. In murder trials where self-defense was clearly out, saying the victim was a detriment to society was an increasingly common plea. The Greater Good could do it, so why not citizens?

The judge sighed. "Bring the Audits."

Bailiffs appeared with piles of papers. The judge dug through them, finding the final analyses. He read one, looked up at the grizzled man on trial, and then read the other. He put both down.

"While I see your point, it is shown that the victim did pass all but two of his yearly Audits. The Greater Good is robbed of a fair bit of merit. What will your client do to make up for that?"

The young lawyer shifted. He looked back at the grizzled man who sat motionless. "He is volunteering for the Service Camps."

A murmur rolled through the crowd.

The judge banged his gavel. "A lifetime in the Service Camps. Good record of contribution may lead to appeal in another Review. Further detraction from society may result in execution or exile. You will reap what you sow."

Soft applause rang through the crowd. The grizzled man was taken away by the agents, still mute and staring. Dagny felt as if he had just watched the man die. In his place, there was a robot made of meat working for the Greater Good of the Many. He didn't know the man, didn't know what he had done, but he mourned him.

"William Townsend Dagny," a voice called.

Before Dagny could move, the agents grabbed him and pushed him to the front of the courtroom. They stepped back, and he was alone in front of the judge, who suddenly towered over him. Behind him, he could hear the soft rumbling of the crowd, like the ocean's shore with unseen might he couldn't fathom.

He began to feel woozy.

"Mr. Dagny," the judge called.

The words brought him back to the courtroom. He set his jaw.

The judge looked over papers and scratched his bald head. "Mr.

Dagny, I must confess I haven't seen a record like yours before. In April, your Audit was returned only slightly negative. Usually, a person sees this as an opportunity to make some adjustment and become a productive member of society."

Dagny remembered that day. The forms had come in the mail, print-outs that took account of the impact his life had on the world around him. He wasn't a bad person, but apparently he wasn't good enough.

Sabrina had left him, saying she couldn't be with someone who couldn't even pass the Audit. She had packed her things and stormed out. Her shrill cry of "loser" still rang in his head. He had been left there, alone with the paper that showed precisely all the things that were wrong with him.

He never hurt anybody, but then he never helped people either. He really just preferred to keep to himself. What did it matter if he didn't donate to charity? So what if he liked to eat too much meat while watching contraband movies? It was his own damn life!

"Following Audit Day, Mr. Dagny," the judge continued, "your record becomes terrible. A number of traffic violations, noise complaints, terrible nutrition requiring future medical visits, wasteful consumption, and your financial records show no signs of tipping or contribution."

"I know," Dagny said. "I'm done with society."

The ocean roared up behind him in a gasp.

The judge pulled off his glasses. "I'm sorry?"

"I'm done," Dagny told him. It was a phrase he had said a hundred times in his mirror. Saying it before the judge was so much purer and more powerful.

The judge snorted a short laugh. "You can't be 'done' with society. We are not islands unto ourselves."

"Maybe we are," Dagny said. "Maybe we're all just individual islands, close together but never really touching. Maybe we've started ignoring the water. Maybe we're imagining bridges that aren't there, and then we make ourselves build more."

The judge cleared his throat and sat up higher. He put his glasses back on. "Mr. Dagny, you're saying very dangerous things. Let me remind you that, before the revolution, there were men who thought they could put themselves above society. Executives rotted companies from the inside-out, bankers stole, politicians schemed against their own countrymen, and advertisers lied to sell poison. The Many rose up and cut off these Parasites. We made the world a better place."

Dagny shook his head. "I'm not trying to put myself above

anybody else; I'm trying to get out from under the Greater Good."

A collective groan burst from the crowd. People started whispering and even talking outright. The judge banged his gavel. It did little good.

Dagny shouted over the noise. "I'm sick of having to spend every moment thinking how I'm going to affect society! I'm sick of numbers adding up to tell me I'm a bad person! I'm so sick of it all… I want out! I request a sentence of exile!"

The crowd suddenly became still. The judge's gavel hung in mid-air, frozen in shock. Dagny felt a weight lift from his chest.

"Nobody has ever chosen exile," the judge told him. He looked to lawyers. "Can someone even choose exile?" They shrugged and began to dig into their digipads.

"I choose it," Dagny said. "I'll go to the island; I'll take care of myself. I'm done with your society."

The roar started again. The judge banged the gavel until they were quieted. "No one chooses exile! You're an architectural engineer, Mr. Dagny. Society invested in you, and you have a job that benefits society."

"I quit. If you make me go to work, I'll design bridges that collapse."

"You'll lose all right to your property!"

"They're just chains." Dagny shrugged. "I won't be told what to do any more."

The judge arched his neck, visibly struggling to swallow. Whispers still rolled through the courtroom. Deep down, nobody was happy trying to keep everybody happy.

Dagny almost smiled. He was making his point.

The judge loudly cleared his throat. He banged his gavel once. "In light of… lack of precedent, I hereby sentence you to… six months of Reeducation with evaluation following."

Dagny gasped. He snapped the chains on his wrist and shouted, "No! I want exile! I want out!"

The judge ignored him and began shuffling papers.

Dagny grabbed the chair the devil-head had sat in. Before the agents could get to him, he threw it at the judge. It fell short, smashing against the heavy wooden desk. The judge ducked and rolled off the platform. Screams broke out in the courtroom.

The agents grabbed Dagny and pinned him. He felt the bite of a tranq-needle in his back. His limbs began to feel heavy as he struggled. The world started to go black around him.

"I want out!" Dagny tried to scream. His voice was already weakening to a whisper. "I want out."

"It's all part of the Greater Good, buddy," one of the agents told him.

"I want out," Dagny repeated, and then he succumbed.

An Unfettered Life

by
C. Bryan Brown

Bobby McFreddy sat at the Ray's rickety old kitchen table, fingers laced together on top of his old, worn leather briefcase. His expression—teeth exposed, arms rigid and knuckles white, eyes wide with shock—was that of a man who'd just waded into an ice-cold swimming pool up to his testicles. In that single, frozen moment, man often wondered whether getting wet at all had been a good idea and a decision was made to either run, high-stepping and screaming, back to the deck or just dive in headfirst. When Mrs. Ray signed her name on the Purify America privacy release, Robert decided to dive.

Mr. Ray sat to Bobby's left, reading the newspaper. He plucked a cigarette from the ashtray and snorted in disgust. "Listen here. Them damn liberal politicians want to make abortion legal."

"They do that now and again," Mrs. Ray said. She sat across from him, slowly working a puzzle in a crossword book.

"Damn fools. Ain't ever going to be legal again. Next thing you know, they'll want to outlaw public executions. Bad for the economy." Then, when someone knocked on the door, "Get that."

Mrs. Ray stuck the pencil between the pages and shut the book, pressing on the cover to make sure it stayed closed. She left the room and returned a minute later with a man in a blue double-breasted suit that cost more than a year of Bobby's rent. He sat in the last wobbly chair and the wood protested with a chorus of high squeaks and groans. Once seated, he put his briefcase (much newer than Bobby's) on the table, and manicured hands popped the latches. He arranged several brochures and loose papers in front of the Rays. He closed the briefcase with the smallest flourish of his arms and produced wide, white smile along with a hand for Mr. Ray.

"Mr. Ray," he said as they shook. "As I told your wife, my name is Sam, and I've been assigned to finalize your Purify America application."

"Yep. Nice to meetcha."

Sam turned to Bobby and gave him a curt nod. "Robert McFreddy?"

Bobby nodded.

"You have the requested financial data from the state?"

"Yes," he replied, gripping his briefcase a bit harder.

"Good," Sam said and turned his attention back to the Rays. "Thank you for meeting with me today. Free time is precious, especially with a disabled child at home. As you know from reading our website, the Purify America program is a way for you to make a lot of money and, at the same time, help preserve the integrity and future of our great nation. Do you have any questions for me?"

Mr. Ray, a thin, balding man, leaned forward, and grabbed the brochure. He made the motions of reading through it, but he turned the pages too fast; his dirty fingers left black and brown smudges on the glossy corners. At one point his eyes bulged, as if poked from the inside of his skull, and he coughed, showed something to Mrs. Ray. She nodded her head appreciatively, patted her husband's hand.

"You say the procedure is painless?" she asked Sam.

"Yes, ma'am. It's done by injection in a climate-controlled room, similar to how we disposed of criminals twenty-five years ago, only guaranteed pain free; they were never sure back then. It's quite peaceful. They just go to sleep. We wouldn't think of putting our Purify America volunteers in front of a firing squad or under the guillotine. That's reserved for the criminals, where it helps the television ratings. Those candidates eligible for our program are special and we wouldn't dare treat them as anything but."

"My Gwillam is a sweet, sweet boy."

"I'm sure he is, Mrs. Ray. Kind and gentle, too. But the fact remains that Gwillam's mental and social handicaps mean he'll never be capable of performing even the most basic survival skills such as shopping, paying bills, or working."

"Well, that's not entirely true. He works," Mrs. Ray said.

"Delivering papers three days a week with his father isn't a job, Mrs. Ray. At least not one he'd be capable of performing on his own. You barely get by on your salary and what your husband makes delivering the paper."

Lines crept across her brow. Mr. Ray, who had moved to the second brochure (populated with colorful pie and bar graphs depicting ages, monetary units to be spent and saved, those to be invested) cared little for the ongoing conversation. A two-page layout, in the center of the book, provided various Purify America luxury packages. Bobby saw a montage of pictures: a family on vacation, a couple standing in front of a house with a SOLD sign, a man taking his new sports car for a spin.

"It says here that we can take a lump sum or payments," commented Mr. Ray.

"That's correct; it's like the old state lotteries. We designed Purify America with ease and convenience in mind. It's like having your cake, and eating it in a chilled bowl with slightly melted vanilla ice cream. It's as American as apple pie."

"How long does the whole process take?" Mr. Ray asked.

"Would you believe less than a day? We have your financial worksheets, the dependent health worksheet, and now your privacy agreement. Mr. McFreddy has the required financial data from the state. If you decide to sign Gwillam up for the Purify America program, I'll run the numbers and give you the amount you qualify for. If we're still good, you'll fill out the parental rights paperwork and the Purify America contract."

"And what do those papers do?" Mrs. Ray asked.

"The first one surrenders your legal, parental rights to Gwillam, which are then reassigned to Purify America through the contract. It's an abbreviated adoption process where you give up custody and the government takes it. Unlike with an adoption, however, we pay for what you're giving up. After that, I'll you have sign the monetary disbursement agreement.

"I'll take all this information to the office, key it in, and update your file. It takes the computer a few hours to generate the final release forms, calculate your actual payout, and print your check. I bring that back to you tomorrow, we take Gwillam, and it's over."

"Are we allowed to be with him?" Mrs. Ray whispered. "You know, when they do it."

"No, ma'am."

"But he's my son."

"Mrs. Ray, while Gwillam more than qualifies for this program and you can use the money to buy any of the beautiful things in our catalog, pay off your mortgage, or perhaps spend it on something completely different, the bottom line is that we are terminating his life. And while not having creditors bother you or being in the warm tropical sun and away from the miserable Ohio winter are wonderful things for you to pursue, watching the injection may cause you to regret signing on the dotted line, and once you sign, there can be no regrets. We wish to avoid any possible unpleasantness. We want your happiness to be uninterrupted and complete, so it's not allowed."

And, Bobby thought, he's technically not your son anymore. Forgot to bring that up, didn't you, Sam?

"That sounds reasonable to me," Mr. Ray stated in a tone that indicated the subject was closed. "How much do we qualify for, Sam?"

"I can have that information for you in a few minutes," Sam said. "Mr. McFreddy? I'll need the state's data now."

Bobby unlatched his briefcase and produced the three pages of numbers. Sam's fingers danced through them and he withdrew a half-completed worksheet and a pencil from his own briefcase. He copied several numbers from the state's papers to his own, did some quick calculations, and filled in a number at the bottom of his sheet. He turned the worksheet toward Mr. Ray.

"Gwillam is eight," Sam said. "He attends the Sunday Center, and that care is discounted through the federally funded Kids Without Hope program. The Sunday Center also receives additional federal money—through another program—for each disabled child. These programs will cost us approximately eighty thousand dollars from now until the time Gwillam is eighteen.

"His medical insurance is through Medicaid. State run, but also a recipient of federal funding. We've also estimated his medical expenses when he becomes eligible for Medicare. While that's many, many years off, it's still a computable expense. Here you'll see graphs for housing, continued education, and basic living expenses such as food, clothing, and other incidental items. If I may point your attention to the center graph, this red bar indicates our total estimated expense for Gwillam through age seventy is four point seven five million dollars."

"So we qualify for how much?" Mr. Ray repeated.

"Forgive me for rambling; it's the comprehensive training," chuckled Sam, blinding them with his white smile. "Your bottom line is right here. Please remember that this is just an estimate, but it's usually accurate to within ten thousand dollars."

Gwillam's parents leaned forward and read the number Sam's perfect, white nail tapped. Mrs. Ray sucked in a deep breath while Mr. Ray cleared his throat, reached for his cigarettes. He lit one and peered at the man through the pall of smoke.

"A quarter of a million dollars."

"To do with as you please."

"And we get this check tomorrow?"

"I'd be back before lunch."

Mr. Ray glanced over at his wife. She took his hand, squeezed, and gave an imperceptible nod of her head. Mr. Ray drew the papers close.

"Do you have a pen?" he asked.

Sam reached into his inner jacket pocket, extracted a gold pen, clicked it open, and handed it over all in a single, practiced movement.

"Am I needed anymore?" Bobby asked.

"No," Sam said.

Bobby crept away from the table, briefcase tucked under his arm, and strolled back to Gwillam's bedroom, where the boy had spent the last few hours building a metropolis out of interlocking blocks and wooden logs. More than twenty-five thousand blocks covered three-quarters of the floor. Towering skyscrapers of red and blue, houses of white and green, streets of gray, all glittered in Bobby's eyes. Four way stops protected small children on the streets, a freeway system cut across the center of the metropolis to ease traffic, and a purple-tracked rail system in the yellow-bricked industrial section carried goods to the entire city. Bobby doubted most architects could conceive such a simple and effective design. The boy added more blocks at an alarming rate, his eyes flicking from piece to placement without hesitation. Some part of Gwillam's brain worked overtime, which probably kept the other, more essential parts from waking up.

And for that, kid, you're going on a permanent vacation.

Bobby recalled Senator Brody's speech that introduced the United States to his Brody Bill and, when the dust settled, the creation of Purify America.

The Senator had given a speech that, near the end, stunned the audience: "Ever since the Trade Center bombings forty years ago, we've been working towards the goals of freedom, safety, and perpetuation. The toppling of those same towers in 2001 only strengthened our resolve. North Korea's nuclear strike in 2016 hastened our activities.

"We've closed our borders to guarantee our safety.

"We've rewritten our beloved Constitution to better protect only our most necessary freedoms.

"And now, I present to you the Brody Bill, which will serve the goal of perpetuation. We will ensure the future of America by removing the elderly, the physically and mentally damaged, and the terminally ill from our society. Only then can we truly be one nation under God."

Senator Brody believed in the 144,000, a number that didn't include niggers, kikes, spics, gays, lesbians, Goths, the elderly, the handicapped, or red-heads. The bill didn't have any ready-made solutions for the majority of the minorities he despised, but it was hailed as a perfect first step to erase as much of the elderly and handicapped from society as possible. The Brody Bill floated through the House and Senate opposed by only six votes between the two. The president, who was known to fancy himself as part of some master race, signed away the lives of a million Americans on national television amongst smiles, handshakes, and other fanfare.

The bill was voluntary for anyone over the age of eighteen, though that was hardly worth mentioning since the advertising enticed the elderly to use the money as an inheritance for their children or, if they wanted, they could postpone their injection for thirty days and use the money to round out the last few items on their bucket list.

It wasn't even fair, not really. Outsourcing had killed the American employment market and those non-specialized jobs that that remained—restaurant, factory, janitorial—didn't pay enough to support a family of three much less a family with a handicapped child and the amount of money being dangled in front of these people was an illusion of prosperity. Families signed up by the hundreds to turn their handicapped kids into cash once Purify America was setup.

Bobby ran a hand through his short dark hair, knowing if his son were still alive, Bobby could be watching his grandchild instead. Children needed to be protected, not sold or sacrificed for the Greater Good. They were the Greater Good.

"He's always been a good a builder," Mrs. Ray said. She'd snuck up behind him. She sniffled, her cheeks wet, eyes red-rimmed.

"Yes, he has been," Bobby agreed. "He's gifted."

She nodded.

"Mrs. Ray, I want to take Gwillam to the park, if that's okay."

"I don't know, Bobby. I want to spend some time with him."

"I understand that. I just thought you might want a couple of hours … you know, to prepare yourself for the last night you'll have. It won't be enjoyable for Gwillam if you're crying the whole time. I don't believe that's how you want to spend the time, either."

A sob hitched her throat upward and she covered her mouth with her hand.

"Drink," Gwillam said without looking up.

"Sure thing, buddy," Bobby said.

"I'll get it," Mrs. Ray said, laying a hand on Bobby's arm. "He enjoys the park. Can you keep him entertained for two hours?"

"Piece of cake."

"Thank you, Bobby. Just have him back before dinner. We'll have family time right after."

"Sure, Mrs. Ray. Family is important; the most important thing."

Mrs. Ray gave Bobby a queer look and her face pinched together in anguish, eyes lost in the skin folds of her forehead, her cheeks newly formed lakes as she fled down the hallway toward her bedroom, Gwillam's drink forgotten. Mr. Ray appeared from the kitchen and stared after his wife.

"What the hell was that all about?" he asked.

"I'm not sure," shrugged Bobby. "She asked me to take Gwillam to the park for a few hours. She's upset and wants her last night with him to be more than tears."

"I poopied," Gwillam said as he put another brick in place

Mr. Ray regarded the sprawling city of blocks, the detailed streets and neighborhoods, the downtown skyscrapers that were brick miles away.

"I poopied," Gwillam repeated.

Mr. Ray snorted. "Fucking unreal. Change his diaper before you take him."

Mr. Ray walked away shaking his head, and Bobby picked Gwillam up and took him to the bathroom.

~*~

The early afternoon sky turned to steel as Bobby led Gwillam toward the park. Bobby straightened his blue tie, smoothed out the threadbare, polyester blend pants. His wrists jutted too far beyond the cuff and when he flexed his arms, the coat tightened across his shoulders, threatening to rip at the seams. The pants rode up in the back enough that he pulled the fabric out every few minutes to avoid creating a sweat stain. He hated it, but the suit was the only acceptable business attire he owned. After his meeting with Sam, seeing that smooth operator's outfit, Bobby didn't mind it so much anymore.

Gwillam took Bobby's hand as they walked. Two blocks from the park, Bobby turned them into an alley alongside an abandoned mini-mart, whose barred windows were black eyes staring out at a cold, dead city. Months of accumulated trash decorated the alley in negligent chic and the astringent stench, deep and stomach churning, was worse than piss on your fingers and old shit in your pants.

"Well," Bobby said. "I just can't let them haul you off. I'd be no better than them and I just couldn't live with myself. At least I can try to save you.

"I don't know where we're gonna go or how we're gonna survive, but I'll think of something. Just ain't right; it's legal murder. Killing people because they're old or handicapped and too expensive to keep around. A better America? Bullshit!

"You just wait and see, Gwillam Ray, if it's a better America. I reckon once you get older you'll understand more than most, even if you can't tell us about it. Did you know they say you're the closest thing to God's eyes we have? I don't know about any God, but I do believe you're pure."

Gwillam plodded along silently beside him. The boy's eyes never stopped moving; they shot in all directions, afraid they'd miss something. Every so often he'd make a noise from the back of his throat.

Bobby took them to the train depot, which was only a fifteen minute walk from the Rays' house. He hoped to board a train in the next hour or so, before they were missed. Bobby ignored the transients' requests for money as he pulled open the double doors that led into the terminal. He never understood why the homeless gathered at the train stations. Maybe the sight of so many people leaving gave them hope they'd escape their own tainted lives someday, or maybe they just believed people who could afford the train had more money to spare. Bobby descended the stairs into the turmoil.

The station roared with the high-pitched sound of steel wheels on steel rails; the noise grated into Bobby's inner ear until his brain rattled against his skull. The ceiling—an arched monstrosity painted in rainbow stripes—towered over them. The gathering crowds waved their briefcases and computer bags, the weapons of choice in this modern age, and they polluted the air with their shouted curses, all part of a half-hearted suburban battle cry against the corporations, the government, and the injustices of life in general. Their shuffling, offbeat footfalls played historic drummer boy to the screeching and hissing, train-wheel bugler.

Gwillam came to an abrupt stop at the bottom of the stairs and clapped his hands over his ears, shrieking louder than the symphonic cacophony around him. Bobby stared, horrified, as people made a wide path around them. Sweat trickled down Bobby's nose as he dragged Gwillam to a shop and purchased earplugs. Gwillam's hands were concrete blocks and Bobby had to yank them down one at a time to get the plugs in the boy's ears. Once installed, Gwillam's screaming wound down to a hum, as if trying to match the pitch of the incoming trains.

He pulled Gwillam to the nearest ticket window. The ticket lady (though girl was more accurate, she wasn't more than twenty) raised an eyebrow at them, though she continued to smile until a line of drool fell from Gwillam's bottom lip. Her lips turned down and she cleared her throat and looked away, nose wrinkling in disgust.

"Your destination, please?"

"Two for Pittsburgh, please. One way," Bobby said, reaching out to pull Gwillam closer, and found the boy gone.

He stood fifteen feet away, staring at a poster advertising the United States Marines. It showed the famous Iwo Jima war memorial collaged with modern marines in Iran, North Korea, and Israel. Gwillam's eyes opened wider as they moved from soldier to soldier. His lips drew back to show pink gums and white teeth and he started barking gunfire at the poster.

"You really should control your child. A kid like that can get hurt in here pretty easy."

"A kid like what?"

"He's obviously a retard."

"Actually, he's disabled," Bobby clarified.

"Oh? He sounds retarded to me. My sister has a 'tard at home, but signed that one up for the Purify America thing. Now she's just waiting. Government's slow."

"She sounds retarded to me."

"You think so? I don't know. The kid's worth more dead than alive. She's got three other kids to feed, too. Don't you believe in the Greater Good?"

"Now I know you're retarded."

The girl punched a few buttons. The tickets popped out of a machine to her right.

"That'll be a hundred and sixty-nine dollars, sir."

Bobby handed his money card over. After the financial crisis in 2008 and the market crash in 2016 (following the North Korean nuclear strike), American paranoia had peaked. The government stepped in, outlawed paper money, finding the old currency inappropriate for the new era, and had introduced the money card. All transactions were electronic, traceable, and trended. Once they realized he'd taken Gwillam, they'd run his money card first. He hoped to be out of Columbus and in Pittsburgh before then. He'd heard that resistance movements were popping up everywhere there.

They had twenty minutes before the train arrived. Bobby bought them lunch from a cart and sat Gwillam on one of the station's cast iron benches. He popped the top on Gwillam's pop can and raised his own in a toast.

"To tomorrow," Bobby said. "Let's hope you have more than just one."

~*~

Bobby sat in the window seat and when the concierge stopped next to them, he pretended not to notice. Dead crab grass and rough, broken rock lined the ground around the metal tracks and, as they rocketed past, small avalanches of dirt and debris fell away. The brakes squealed and steam erupted from under the train, fogging the window enough that Bobby had to look away and into the face of the waiting concierge.

"Can I help you?" Bobby asked.

"Sir, we have had several complaints concerning the noise your son is making."

He was a short man, with a halo of straw-colored hair, and pale cheeks. His pencil-thin mustache remained straight despite the movement of his upper lip.

Bobby couldn't blame the other passengers for complaining. Gwillam, arms wrapped around his knees, rocked back and forth hard enough to shake the entire seat assembly. The noise he made, a repeated honk, was worse than a car alarm.

"Yeah," Bobby said. "I apologize for that. He's autistic and doesn't do well in confined spaces."

He had no way of making the problem disappear and inwardly, he cursed his stupidity for not bringing something to keep Gwillam occupied. He should have known better.

Why? It's not like I'm an expert at kidnapping.

Bobby continued to smile at the concierge in an effort to be personable. He rested a gentle hand on Gwillam's shoulder, and gave it a gentle squeeze, trying to calm the boy down. The train continued to slow and Bobby glanced out the window again. Wasted land, filled with mounds of trash and debris, dominated the landscape.

"We can't be in Pitt already," one guy said. "It's usually a ninety-minute ride."

"It's an omen man," his buddy said. "The Steelers are gonna stall out halfway through the season."

"Shut up," someone else said. "The season's still months away. The Curtain will come down. Just have some faith."

Faith, Bobby thought, and smirked. I know why we're stopping. Faith isn't going to help me, or Gwillam, or anyone else. Not anymore, if it ever had at all.

He looked at the concierge. "Is there a way off the train?"

"Not while it's moving," the concierge said.

"No!" Bobby stood. "Once it stops. Is there a way off from this car that doesn't lead us back toward the front?"

"There's an exit in the rear car, sir. But it's for emergencies only. It's clearly marked."

This is an emergency.

"If you'll excuse me; I have to go see why we're stopping."

Bobby nodded his thanks and the concierge walked away. The train continued to slow and Bobby rose, dragging Gwillam with him. The car, typical of the cheap national transit system, had a single, center aisle not quite wide enough for two people and a row of double seats against each wall. Everything was stark and metallic, expect for the gray cushions that comprised the seats and their backs.

The other passengers stared at them, but said nothing, as they made their way toward the rear car. Bobby's father once told him hope was a porous shield wielded by the desperate, but right now he'd take a little hope. Anything to help shake away the despair and dry the sweat running down his face.

The train lurched to a stop and Gwillam, caught off balance, stumbled into a woman. She grimaced and pushed him back into the aisle where he fell over his own feet and landed face first on the floor. Blood blossomed from Gwillam's nose and he shrieked in a way Bobby had never heard before. The sound wasn't so much high-pitched as it was piercing, cutting through each of the passengers in turn, and they fidgeted, uncomfortable at the sound of a child in pain, but unwilling to get up and help. And when it arrived back at the lady who'd pushed him, she voiced what Bobby believed so many of them were feeling.

"Take your brat and go sit down," she snarled. "He's making a scene."

Bobby tried to smile at the woman, to come up with some kind words, something to try and turn her to his side, but couldn't. He looked around the train car and wondered if there'd be anyone that would step up and protect Gwillam with him. No one had moved to help Gwillam and, as Bobby knelt next to the boy, he knew the answer.

Bobby pressed his sleeve against Gwillam's bleeding nose and tilted his head back. Gwillam's shrieking quieted.

"Now that he's shut up, why don't you take him back to his seat?"

Bobby glanced back at the woman who'd knocked Gwillam down. He wanted to yank her out of the chair and smash her face into the floor, make her bleed, and see how much she, a normal person, squealed.

"Please, help me," Bobby pleaded. He picked Gwillam up in his arms. "I have to get him off the train."

"We all want to get off the train, pal," the man next to her said.

"You don't understand. They're going to kill him."

"Who is?" the man asked.

"The government. His parents sold him to Purify America. They're the ones who've stopped the train."

"You're not even his father?" the woman asked. "You kidnapped this child?"

"No," Sam said, and Bobby whirled to face him. "Kidnapping applies to people. This man stole item number PA-895."

"I didn't steal anything."

"The United States Government views your actions as grand larceny."

"You can't murder him. He's just a little boy."

"Murder?" scoffed Sam. "This isn't murder."

"The fuck it isn't," Bobby spat.

"Murder is illegal, Mr. McFreddy. And it doesn't apply to property."

"He's a human being!"

"No," Sam said. "He's item number PA-895, scheduled for destruction tomorrow at eight o'clock in the morning. To build a better, stronger United States."

"This is wrong and you goddamn well know it!" Bobby yelled, looking around at everyone present, including the dozen or so cops. "You all know it. Look at him!" Bobby held Gwillam up, turning him so everyone present could see the child. "Look! You're all killing him now, just because he's different, not normal, because he makes you uncomfortable—"

Pain blazed across the back of Bobby's head like fire after spilled gasoline; it started at the base of his skull and traveled up between his ears, shot over the top of his head and squatted between his eyes. Bobby dropped to his knees and Gwillam tumbled, screeching, back to the ground. Bobby shook his head, dazed, as rough hands hauled him right back up.

"Robert Alan McFreddy?"

The loud, authoritative voice, so close to his ear, chilled him. It belonged to every bully, coach, and executive he'd ever known. Someone zip tied his wrists together. Through the haze, Bobby noticed Sam standing behind Gwillam, a protective hand on each of the boy's shoulders.

"Are you Robert Alan McFreddy?" the voice repeated.

"Yes."

"Mr. McFreddy, you are under arrest for the theft of item PA-895…"

The voice read Bobby his rights, and Bobby laughed. Rights? Who had rights anymore? Bobby twisted until he met the woman's eyes. She held his gaze for only a second before turning away. Bobby smirked and faced Sam again.

"Do you understand these rights as I've explained them to you?" the voice asked.

"Will no one stand with me? Will no one stand up and save this boy's life? Purify America is voluntary today, but tomorrow it might be mandatory. They'll take your kids, or your parents, maybe your husband or wife, and they'll call them things. They'll destroy what you hold dear and make you thank them for it."

The voice's owner nudged Bobby forward, poking a baton into his lower back.

Few people returned Bobby's stare, most kept their faces blank and their eyes in their laps. One man stood up, and the nearest police officer slammed his baton into the man's face, crushing his nose and lips. The blood erupted onto the people around him and he collapsed back into his chair.

Bobby jerked away from the cop restraining him and bolted forward, head lowered to ram Sam in his perfectly dressed middle. He made it three steps before the back of his head exploded again and he found himself face down on the floor, head buzzing.

"No!" Sam shouted. "Stay in your seats! All of you!"

The vibrant noise in Bobby's head increased in volume and someone's foot landed inches from Bobby's nose. Another landed by his head, and then another. Bobby rolled, put his back against the seat. Up and down the aisle, a dozen people were out of their seats, yelling at the police, pointing and surging forward, trying to make it to Gwillam.

"Get up," Bobby bellowed. "All of you. Stand up and fight."

Bobby's urgings brought another man out of his seat, this one right next to Sam. The passenger shoved Sam into the other row of seats and reached for Gwillam. A cop smashed his baton down on the man's wrist, and then in a vicious upswing, cracked him under the chin. The second hit put the passenger back into his seat.

Bobby pushed against the chairs and rose. The train car spun in a slow rotation, and he wondered if he had a concussion. A police officer approached and rammed his baton into Bobby's solar plexus, dropping him to his knees.

"This is your fault," the officer said, and it was the voice. The cop kicked Bobby in the chest. Bobby bounced off a metal chair frame and found himself staring at the ceiling.

Always on my back. They can never let a man up.

The woman who'd bloodied Gwillam's nose rose up, pointing something small and black at the cop assaulting Bobby. A deafening boom filled the space, silencing every other sound in the train car, and as far as they were concerned, the world stopped turning at that moment. Nothing existed outside their eighty by ten foot rectangle of steel and the only thing that mattered inside was the red circle that appeared on the woman's chest, two inches above her heart. She sat, almost casually, eyes wide, jaw hanging open, as if she'd just received the biggest surprise of her life. And, Bobby figured, in a way she had. No one expects to walk on a train and be carried off in a body bag.

With that, the protest ended.

The people who'd risen sank, little more than deflated, human balloons, back into their seats. Bobby rolled until the woman came into view. She stared ahead, her eyes dimming as fast as the expanding circumference of blood brightened her shirt. She wouldn't last much longer. The man next to her pressed his hand against her chest, his mouth working, and from far away, Bobby heard him demand an ambulance. The black thing she'd been holding slipped out of slack fingers and her cell phone slid under the seat.

Bobby, hoping she'd been recording, inched toward the phone, pushing with his feet. The black screen came into view and there, running down at the bottom, the red dot indicating an active recording. Bobby lurched the final foot to the phone and knocked it completely under the seat with his head. Once found, the video would be worthless, but the audio, well that might prove priceless, especially when they learned she found Gwillam disgusting.

A cop pulled Bobby to his feet and turned him around. Sam's face swam into focus, close enough that Bobby had a difficult time not going cross-eyed. Bobby opened his mouth to talk but Sam quieted him with a hard, vanilla-scented finger to the lips.

"It's over, Mr. McFreddy," Sam murmured. "You will be remanded into federal custody and retired under section 3A.1 of the Brody Bill. You'll be in front of a televised firing squad by the end of the year. You'll make a good example for anyone thinking of impeding this great country's progress."

"This isn't progress," Bobby said. "It's genocide masquerading as patriotism.”

Sam smirked. “No, Mr. McFreddy. Patriotism, true patriotism, isn't about the individual, but the Greater Good, and the willingness to do anything to protect it, including the unsavory jobs. I'm nothing more than a garbage man, paid to take out the trash.”

Sam jerked his head and the cop knocked Bobby forward. Gwillam stood next to Sam, holding his hand. Bobby resisted, twisting until he was able to turn back to Gwillam.

“I tried, kid,” he said. “I really did.”

The boy didn't pay Bobby any attention as the cops yanked him away and led him out.

But, now, the people … well, the people took note and it'd only be a matter of time before they dove in as well.

Surrender

By
Bob Brown

My name is Vernon and I stretched as the early spring sun warmed my skin and the soft grass tickled the back of my neck. How long had it been since I'd felt grass? I pushed my palms flat onto the coolness, and dug fingers deep into the roots and squeezed. I knew I had been sleeping and it was good to wake up.

The air was wrong in a good way. No decay, no urine, just the meadowlands. I luxuriated in the sounds. The light brush of the wind in the trees and the muted songs of the birds. This was where I wanted to be.

I opened my eyes to a blue sky with sailing puff balls of light clouds. My eyes watered at the beauty, but my stomach tightened when I saw how low in the west the sun hung. The day was almost gone, where I didn't know, but little, precious little, time remained.

I climbed to my feet. Too much time wasted and I had precious little.

I stopped where a spring flowed from between a pair of boulders and slipped into an algae basin before it joined into a tiny brook.

Ahead of me, a path followed the small rivulet of water into the trees. Beyond that was home, home with its picket fence and red tile roof.

I knelt and looked at my wavering reflection the small basin. I looked as I remembered. Rich dark hair curled from my head. The hair of a Greek god, my wife had said when she would run slender fingers through it. I scooped a double handful of the cold water and washed the last vestiges of sleep away.

The blow knocked me into the water. I rolled with it and turned my head to catch a glimpse of my attacker. He stood and watched with contempt as I struggled to my feet. My back throbbed. He held a staff, one I might have leaned on in another life. I stood in the icy water and stared back at him.

He had companions,

His ilk was not the type to be found alone.

My breath returned and I stepped towards them, my feet finding purchase on the sandy soil of the path.

The men were young and sallow. Yellowed teeth protruded past misshapen lips.

"What'd ya bring us old man?" hooted the smaller one. His sharp-eyed glances shifted quickly between his fellows and the pouch tied to my waist. His hand darted and gestured as if he could bridge the distance and take my pouch by will.

My pouch. In it was all I possessed. And it was nothing. I had forgotten it. For them it was my purpose for existing, the magnet of their interest. It carried what I had and what they would take. They cast long shadows from a sun that had dipped yet lower into the sky. I would not spend my time on this. With resolve I took a step to pass them by.

"Where you going old man?" goaded my attacker. He shifted his staff until it crossed my path.

"Leave me alone." I said with a voice that we all knew told a lie.

The swelling inside my chest told me I really didn't want them to leave me alone. My muscles flexed as I rolled my shoulders in preparation for what I knew was about to happen. What I wanted to happen. As much as I hungered to step past them in the growing twilight, I couldn't deny the hunger, a lust for blood, for pain; their blood, their pain. I wanted them here so I could hurt them. They wouldn't be here if I hadn't called them.

I looked down the path to home. I could almost see the roof of the cottage. It would gleam gold in the setting sun.

"Go away," I said flatly. "Leave me alone." I meant it this time, but it was too late for that decision. They were already here.

I stepped forward boldly, the staffer made the first move. I blocked it easily, trapping his staff and pulled him into my waiting elbow. I could feel the satisfying collapse of his cheekbone.

The second youth had no time to look up from his collapsed companion as my roundhouse kick twisted his head further than the neck would allow. The lifeless body crumbled in place.

"You still hungry boy?" I growled to the third, the boy with the quick eyes and grasping hands. "I still got food," I held my pouch in my hand. My nostrils flared. I was on fire with the urge to finish this. My hands kneaded air in anticipation of squeezing the very life from him.

No. This was wasting time.

The youth looked at the pouch. His tongue darted out to wet his lips. He looked down at his companions. His ragged breath was the only sound. Finally he backed, one step at a time until, as his courage grew, he turned and ran.

I dropped the pouch on the ground. I didn't need it any more.

I let my stride stretch to a run as I closed the distance between myself and home. Between the white slats of the fence the flickers of color took on the detail of flowers, slowly fading into shadow as the setting sun expanded on the horizon.

I touched the dark cottage door, the solid wood warmed by the sun. I lifted the latch and entered.

My eyes adjusted to the cool darkness and a picture developed. Her cheeks were the color of autumn leaves under pale blue eyes. Her red golden hair, wrapped loosely in a handkerchief, fell down her back. Her lips held a half hidden smile. The simple smock, on her a gown, was crisp and clean, outlining limber curves. She was as I remembered.

"Vernon?" The sound of her voice was like music. I could feel my knees weakening in anticipation of her touch. I thanked God I had gotten here in time.

She reached for me, and I for her. Her hand was small, cool and soft. I pulled it to my lips and kissed her palm softly. She smiled as I reached my other hand around her waist to pull her closer.

She dissolved into a pixilated memory. Her soft hand hardened to the worn smoothness of poly.

Voices. Not hers. Not mine crashed into my ears. I blinked against blinding light.

Dull chipped walls materialized, a pale green meant only to cover raw concrete.

I coughed as stale dry air stretched my cracked lungs. The racking motion sent waves of pain through my body.

"Come on old-timer, outa there, your time's up." I felt the hands prying me to my feet.

My awareness returned. My name was Vernon Bancroft. I looked down at my hands. The skin was loose and spotted. I was old.

The technician ignored me as he stowed the sensor lines that fed my illusions; that gave me back my wife. He wore thin rubber gloves and was careful not to touch too much of what had touched me.

I looked at the clock on the wall. Twelve minutes had passed. I was allotted fifteen.

"I had more time," I pointed to the clock. "Please." I could hear myself. I was pleading. Begging.

"Yeah, right . . . we'll check the records," the attendant's voice softened, taking on a soothing tone. "If you do, we'll give it to you next week." Then, with a quick fluid motion, he pulled my card from the machine and placed it in my automatically extended hand. He was done with me. He turned his back and pulled the sens-pac into place as a woman took my place in the freshly wiped chair.

I stood there. My eyes glued to the clock. I had more time.

"I had more time." I said it aloud.

"Just tell them at the desk." The soothing tone was gone, I was dismissed.

I knew they wouldn't care at the desk. They didn't live here; they only worked here. They didn't have to care. Why didn't they build more chairs? I paid my taxes all my life. Was it asking too damned much for me to have my fair share?

I turned again; the attendant caught my motion.

Already the woman was settled in place. A vague yearning hung in her eyes, her tongue darted out, wetting the dried lips. I held the attendant's eyes as the client clumsily slid a packet into his waiting hands. She wasn't old yet, but she looked it. She wouldn't last long. Not here.

The attendant's visage faltered for a second, then a surly glare gained hold. The client tried to smile. She couldn't.

The vision of reddish gold hair and soft hands faded and I turned towards the exit. I pulled my oversized coat closed as I walked through the lobby. It rustled with lost lives, some people standing in silent thought, others leaned in quiet desperation with the help phones pressed to their ears waiting for the next available representative. They were like me. Old, sick, or otherwise of little use.

A pleasant looking young woman sat behind a smudged but solid panel working her screen. I suspected little of her life dealt with work. She probably got all the chair-time she wanted. Probably gave the attendants all the sack-time they wanted. I pushed the bitter thoughts out. They didn't matter.

At the exit, I slid my citi-card in the slot and passed through the opening door.

The line for the entrance lobby stretched out. Sad silent people, some clutching their citi-cards in their hands as if having it ready would make sooner the experience. The blank dismal stares mirrored my own.

Unfiltered air burned. Another fit of coughing passed as I cleared my lungs of a gray gooey mass. I had taken to noticing the red foam flecks. That told me it mattered little any more. No one else took notice.

I felt the urge to hurry again. The streets were darkening earlier as another winter came. Better to be indoors at night. Power was reserved for the streetlights and official buildings. The official buildings also included dormitories, but they were run by bureaucrats with thick rule books, and heavy guards with outstretched hands. I chose less regulated, less safe, life in the multitude of abandoned buildings. Rent was cheap, only a few food packets, maybe nothing. Few cared.

I crossed the street in the center of the block. No one feared traffic any more. I remembered when you risked your life to cross this street. Now the only cars were the rusted hulks not yet gathered for scrap. The buildings were dark.

Early on, when the power was cut back from "low-priority" services, whole blocks became rat holes where people who couldn't, or wouldn't, live in the dormitories found a place to sleep. They slept when not standing in line for food, water or Chair privileges.

The city wasn't what it used to be, there were few reasons to stay except that you couldn't leave. Exit permits were technically available, but the office that provided them opened its window for only an hour a day. The line never went away. You were shipped to the city you stayed in the city.

The trains brought in people. People from the train station usually went to the dorms. They would speak of the family on the outside. The family that was building them a room to live in, that would be sending them credits. A man I played chess with was like that. To the day he died he believed his daughter would come for him. He was so proud of her. He knew she would come. He died knowing that she would come. They hauled his body off to the crematorium. He was my last friend. There were others to play chess with but I didn't care anymore.

They were people like me. Worn out by a lifetime, shipped to "population centers" where they could be "cared" for when they couldn't care for themselves and their family wouldn't. Often times they were just criminals that didn't merit prison. Prisons were expensive. Incarceration in the city was not.

Above me the city watched from the dark faces of the buildings. The broken glass was less as you looked higher, no ground floor windows remained. Sometimes a person who didn't know any better would try and move glass windows from the upper stories down. Someone always broke it. Misery loves company; no..., misery demands it.

The food and water lines were long, but passed without effort, no one spoke. Standing in line was a learned talent I supposed, to completely pass from this existence while moving slowly in the shuffling procession. I remembered reading of mystics in the East who spent their lives learning to pass into that type of existence. It isn't that hard. You just do.

Somewhere above, the sun still shone. The diffuse yellow light lent itself well to the city. It stressed neither form nor shadow. It merely made light. Light that was strained through the thick air from the factories that ringed the city. They were almost fully automated. That meant the stacks didn't need filters, only we, the city people, lived inside their ring of death.

When my time came at the food dispenser, I inserted my card, flashed my wrist chip, and was rewarded with the sound of the food dropping down the chute. I worried at times that the chip might cease to function. If it failed, I would face a death by starvation long before it would be fixed.

When prompted, I placed my battered 5-liter bottle under the spigot and watched as 3 liters of brown water flooded it. They used to be filled full. A panel slid back and my allotment of food lay in neat packs. I took it, retrieved my card, and turned for home.

The smiling youth sat on the steps when I arrived at the building I called home. He fooled no one with the smile. It had been years since a smile from his kind had been anything more than a prelude to predation. I dreaded in my gut what I knew was to come. He stood expectantly as I climbed the steps. No hand came out to steady my step. No door was opened for me. He simply watched and then followed me inside. Once inside he pushed me forward. I shrugged off his touch.

"What the fuck, old man. Feeling froggy?" He spun me in place, his face inches from my own. The leering face was the same I had felled in the meadow. But here, there was no power in my spirit. My muscles were weak. They barely held me erect.

I felt the pain as the youth placed a hand against my chest and pushed. I fell to the floor, white hot pain driving through me as my elbow struck the step. I felt myself beginning to sob. It hurt so much. I looked up at him through teared eyes.

"Please," I begged.

"Same old shit, huh old man," he sneered as he looked distastefully through my pouch. When he was satisfied that he had taken enough of my food he dropped the remaining packets to the floor and returned to the stoop.

I picked up my food and began to climb the stairs. My elbow throbbed.

I placed one foot ahead of the other as I pulled myself up the four flights of stairs. By the second flight my chest was a mass of pain and I strained to breathe. More coughing. More blood. I sat for a time at each landing. By the time I reached my space, my breath was coming between coughing spasms.

I still had a door. That made my space rare. This was the fourth floor. It wasn't as filthy as below. I had once lived higher, but I couldn't make the climb.

I was alone on this floor except for the rats. They tended, like their human brethren, to congregate on the lower floors. My space had once been an office. It boasted little except for an executive chair and a couch where I slept. I had brought the chair from three floors up. Once a powerful man had sat in this chair, when the leather had been new. I sat and watched out of a tall window that other men had once looked out in anticipation of a better view, a better life. It was now an empty frame, broken, an open doorway to the city.

Next to the open window hung her picture. We were young when I took it. I touched it gently as I sat down. I had touched it a thousand times, each time remembering the feel of her hair, the bells in her laugh. It was only in my memory that the picture still held the golden red color of her hair. I didn't need the chair to remember the feel of her skin. My chest hurt again, but it was a pain of memory.

"Next time," I said, and leaned back into the chair and looked out the open window frame.

When she came into his dreams she was just as beautiful as ever. She stood in the open window, it was now a doorway.

"Its time," she said. He followed, stepping through the doorway into her arms. She held his hand for the brief moment until the pain passed.

In front of the window his food packs sat alone by an empty chair until the rats came.

The Hating

By
Nigel Anthony Sellars

Andrew Shaw was thankful he had a reserved parking space as he tooled his car around the parking lot outside the Petroleum Stadium in Tulsa. It was only five in the morning, and already the lot was almost ninety percent full. Most of the cars, he knew, had arrived Friday afternoon, their drivers knowing that come Saturday morning nothing could be had.

Shaw was a mostly non-descript man, which suited him fine. Average height and weight for his age, brown hair in standard manager's cut, and a business suit intended to appear bland, non-threatening. The fewer people who knew he was a producer for the Hatings the better.

Pulling in line at the checkpoint, Shaw glanced in his rear view mirror and adjusted the knot of his tie. The purple tie was his one deviation from the norm, and while it drew a few glances, it didn't reveal anything about his true profession.

He showed his identity card to a burly National Guardsman carrying a Remington-Kalashnikov automatic rifle. The Guardsman ran the card through a hand-held reader, and while clearly he saw the special symbols that came up, the man showed no reaction to the high level clearance.

He handed the card back to Shaw. "Mr. Shaw, the officials' lot is straight down this aisle to the orange pylon, then turn right. Other Guardsmen are on stand-by to keep out intruders."

The guard waved Shaw on through. As Shaw headed to his assigned, heavily fortified parking lot, he glanced in the rear view mirror to catch a glimpse of the guard arguing with the driver of the next car. This, Shaw knew, would not go well.

The security at the parking bunker signaled him on through, and he maneuvered the labyrinthine aisles until he located his assigned space. He pulled in, shut off and disabled the turbine and dynamo and put the batteries into a rest mode. He opened the glove compartment, removed his badge and handgun, and then exited the vehicle. Once out of the car, Shaw punched the button on electronic key, which secured the car. He did this out of habit and a little bit of paranoia, although he full well the bunker was riot-proof and bomb-roof, and the Guardsmen would shoot any unauthorized persons who came too close. While Guardsmen had yet to shoot anyone at any previous Hating, there was always a first time for everything,

In a typical case of poor planning, the parking bunk stood a good distance from the fortified operations center. Shaw had to walk the length of the parking lot to reach the center. While he knew that all any fans would see walking passed them was a plain-faced man, average height, dressed in a light tan Ike-jacket, black trousers, and a garrison cap, pretty much what most white-collar workers work. They might comment on his tie, but it was not something they'd dwell on for long.

As he walked toward the control bunker, he glanced at some of the more diehard enthusiasts. Shaw guessed many of the fans had arrived as early as Wednesday afternoon, if not earlier. Fans were known to camp out for days—sometimes weeks—waiting for the parking lot gates to open. Those that had were usually the first to set up camp as close to the entrance gates of the stadium proper. Many had undoubtedly had shivered their way through the cold, spring nights warmed only by thin blankets, cheap sleeping bags, or the fires of Mexican-made hibachis and braziers manufactured from old license plates. The Hating had been announced for months, so Shaw had often wondered why they bothered to come so early. Everyone who came was given that the opportunity to get into the stadium.

He had later realized why they came early. They came for the camaraderie. The parking lot fairly bulged with tailgating fans. That was a tradition older than the Hatings themselves, Shaw knew. They had started in the mid-20th century as a communal celebration of both college and professional football, and had survived the demise of the sport during the Great Deflation during the Twenty-Thirties. Only the Hatings had prevented a revolution.

The tailgaters filled the air with the aromas of their varied traditional foods. Shaw could smell the fragrance of hamburgers and hot dogs cooking on grills as it wafted across the lot. He could also detect the scent of pizza baking. Wafting through the air, the traditional fares' bouquets merged with the odor of beer and whiskey and the more exotic perfume of like lamb korma, chili rellenos, egg rolls, and falafel. Shaw could also detect another, more unique fragrance. Some folks were undoubtedly enjoying hash brownies and ganja-herbed gulab jamuns.

The pre-event tailgating festivities represented the last friendly relations before the grim proceedings of the Hating began. Shaw was aware that some sociologists argued that the pre-Hate celebrating was really the last authentic American neighborhood activity, and the "tailegations," as they were dubbed, represented a new American community.

Certainly the celebrations were the last surviving relic of the twentieth century age of sports, Shaw thought. That was back when people came to watch games rather than take part. Tailgating had originated almost a century earlier in 1960 in the Parking lot of a stadium in New York. Shaw couldn't recall if it was baseball or football, but the team was professional. Professional, Shaw thought. How odd that people were paid to play games.

The story, as far as Shaw know it, went that the wife of a sports doctor set up the "tailgate" of her station wagon (some sort of vehicle, Shaw gathered) before a game. From there she dispensed sandwiches, snacks, and beverages for her children, friends, and sports reporters. A reporter asked her about her "car picnic," but she corrected him, saying it was more of a "tailgate" party. Most people dismissed that story as bullshit, Shaw knew, despite the fact that historians had proven it was indeed true.

Most of the adults that Shaw could see were playing a number of venerable and traditional tailgate games beanbag or ball toss games like Beirut, blongo, testicle-toss, cornhole, and washoo. Others engaged in flipcup, boat-racing and other ancient drinking games.

Numerous participants staggered drunkenly about, and at first Shaw wondered why they had started drinking so early on the day of a Hating. Then he realized they hadn't started early. They'd started the evening before and simply hadn't stopped. Some were likely to be too inebriated to take part in the Hating and would regret it the next day. Maybe.

Up ahead of him Shaw spotted a fat man being interviewed for an early morning news program. The fat man wore a ridiculously small flowered Hawaiian shirt that gaped in front and strained to cover the man's protruding stomach. The stomach protruded because the man had on pants several sizes to small and had his belt buckled beneath his paunch. He wore a battered green canvas hat from under which his greasy black hair stuck out.

" When my wife and I first decided to attend a Hating, we decided we might as well make a day out of it," the man told the interviewer.

" It's a family thing. We bring the kids and let them run around, while the adults sit around, have a few laughs, drink a few beers, and eat some damn good food."

" This is our anniversary," the man's wife chimed in. She was as rotund as her spouse, and dressed in a too small pink t-shirt and purple denim over-alls. The coveralls had red bull's eye targets on the breast, roughly where the woman's nipples would be. "We attended our first Hating ten years ago. I chased him into a bathroom, and I was going to beat the crap outta him when I saw what beautiful green eyes he had."

" It was love at first sight," the man added. "We haven't missed a Hating since."

It was with the understanding that the holovision networks had established the Hatings in the first place. And Tulsa was not that large a community. However, to some people, it was a matter of personal pride to be among the first to receive their computer-coded badges.

Flashing his card to another Guardsman, Shaw entered the fenced-lined corridor that led to the armored control bunker where the rest of the officials were ensconced. Starting up the narrow concrete staircase, he ran through the plan he and Elliot had formulated and received government approval on. With luck, it would succeed.

The Hatings started life in the 1970s and 1980s as the town-competition show. In these programs, rival towns competed in athletic events designed to humiliate and embarrass the participants. Viewers seemed at first interested, but the interest soon died down. Later, under the rubric of "reality television," there emerged a more vicious type of competition. Whether trapped on desert islands in the jungle or confined in a hotel or mansion, the contestants competed to be the last one standing. Those, too, proved exceptionally popular, as did versions of Japanese game shows that put contestants through humiliating, and potentially fatal, obstacle courses.

Then, in the Twenty-Twenties, a peculiar game show premiered on one of the smaller satellite networks. It was called " Bitchin'." On this program, people aired their gripes and complaints and shouted and screamed at each other, the latter already a proven and popular technique. At the end of the show, the studio audience voted for the person with the best complaints or grievance. That contestant took home $100,000 and a houseful of products, all name brand. The show, however, folded after three months when the novelty wore off.

On the other hand, network programmers knew they were on to

something. They were just unable to isolate the missing factor. It took a junior executive named John Dexter, just up from the mailroom to hit on the solution.

" How about group participation," he cried.

" That's what we're doing," the executives admonished him.

" No," he replied, " the contestants! We make the audience the contestants!"

"What?" asked the now confused programmers.

"It's like this old show, about making deals and guessing the price of products, or something like that," he said. Seeing the blank look on their faces, Dexter decided to explain his solution in simple terms. Simple terms were, after all, the only terms that "suits" —an old pejorative term for executives that Dexter loved—could comprehend. The town shows had failed, Dexter explained, because, while group participation had an urgency to it and interested the audience; the basic concept was—to put it bluntly—"so much goat shit."

"Bitchin'," however, had failed for the opposite reasons, Dexter explained. The concept was great, he said, but no one really could identify with the persons bitching. The audience had to express and exorcise its own gripes, or the idea had no effect other than to make people angrier.

The execs puzzled for a moment, called for a computer, fed in the idea, and it came out: $$$$!!! It sent them into a tizzy. Plans were made, congressmen bought, stadiums rented, the concept given media hype (an easy thing since they were the media), and fingers piously crossed.

The first Hating, held on a Memorial Day weekend, was a rousing success. It outdrew the Indianapolis 500 and a major NASCAR race. Admittedly, motor sports were in a steep decline, but nonetheless the Hating's future was secured.

~*~

So in corporate boardrooms, the networks dallied up the profits and the airtime for the 3D broadcasts. Cries of monopoly arose, but a few well-placed dollars with the Federal Communications Commission soon killed that, and everyone was happy, especially as no one—well, almost no one—worried about the consequences.

On the other hand, Shaw had told the network execs, sometimes the 'bread & circuses' aspect could backfire badly. "Have you heard about the Nike riots?" he asked.

"Wasn't that in early 2012, something about shoes?" asked a

flushed, moon-faced network vice president named Russo.

Shaw bit his tongue and tried not to scream at the man that he was a "fucking moron and a mental midget." He knew that would be redundant.

"No," he said. "These happened in Constantinople during the reign of Emperor Justinian."

A confusing babble ran through the board members, punctuated by scattered, puzzled outbursts asking variously Who? What? When? and Where?

Shaw stared at the board members. He tried to determine if these people were as impenetrable as they appeared. Did they simply lack any doubt? Any discomfort? Any curiosity? "If you'd study some history, you might learn something," he said, wondering if they were ignorant or merely bored. Did that even matter?

"Constantinople was the capital of the Eastern half of the Roman Empire," he continued. "In the Sixth Century, the city had powerful, well-organized groups of fans, called demes, which supported the different chariot racing teams. They were sort of like twentieth century soccer hooligans or NASCAR fans, as well as being street gangs and political parties at the same time."

Shaw saw that the board members remained uncomprehending, yet confident, lacking even the smallest iota of doubt. "The city had four major chariot racing teams—the Reds, the Blues, the Greens and the Whites—all named for the uniforms they wore. Only the Blues and Greens had any real power and influence."

Shaw went on to explain that the various demes also held positions on current political and theological issues, issues that created massive rioting and violence. To maintain order in the city, Justinian's forces need the cooperation of the demes, a cooperation that was not so easily obtained. The factions, he noted, were also backed by powerful aristocratic families, many of whom believed they possessed better claims to the throne than did Justinian.

"So how does this relate to us?"

"I'm getting to that," Shaw explained.

In 531 the Imperial forces had arrested members of the Blue and Green demes for murder in connection with numerous deaths in riot that followed a recent chariot race. Most of the accused of murder were hanged, but in January 532, the executioners botched the hanging of two men, a Blue and a Green, who escaped and took refuge in a nearby church. An angry mob soon surrounded the church.

In the middle of serious peace negotiations with the Persians, and facing growing anger over high taxes, Justinian decided to announce he had commuted the death sentences of the pair to imprisonment and, hoping it would diffuse the tension he announced a chariot race on January 13.

The chariot race was held in the Hippodrome, which was next to the emperor's palace. The Emperor could watch in safety from his box in the palace. The crowd at the Hippodrome, however, was tense and angry and hurled insults at Justinian from the very start of the races. Late in the day, the demes in stopped chanting for the Blues or the Greens, and engaged in a unified chant of "Nike!" Shaw explained, "Nike meant Victory or Conquer, and all of a sudden the crowd in the Hippodrome poured from the stadium and laid siege to the palace. The riots lasted for five days, and led to widespread destruction. Some Senators saw it as a chance to overthrown Justinian."

But Justinian finally defeated the rebellion, Shaw said, first by bribing the Blues with gold and then, as the Blues suddenly left the Hippodrome en masse, the emperor turned loose his generals Mundus and Bellisarius, whose troops stormed the Hippodrome and slaughtered the remaining rebels.

"When it was over, nearly half of Constantinople lay burned or destroyed. Tens of thousands of people died violently."

One board member rose to speak, but chairman March Hastings signaled the man to be seated and to shut up. As the man obeyed his order, Hastings turned to Shaw and asked, "And your point in telling this story and providing this report?"

"If I may?" Elliot asked Shaw, who nodded his consent. Elliot turned to Hastings and said. "Mr. Chairman, as you can see from our report, there is growing concern about the long term impact of the Hatings. Instead of keeping social order, there is growing evidence that they maybe reaching a crisis point."

"And here is where my story fits in," Shaw said. "Increasingly the Hatings are taking on political and religious overtones. It has gone from being generalized attacks on specific kinds of bad behavior, and have become a means to assert political and religious agendas by committing aggression against whatever racial, ethnic, religious groups individual participants despise."

Hastings pondered the matter for a moment. Then he said, "And you fear civil unrest?"

" There will be a period of rioting afterward, perhaps a week or so," Shaw said. "Our computer models predict three days of rioting in every major and secondary urban center, but we think we' re being too conservative on this point.

"The initial loss of life will be high, unfortunately," Elliot added. "We're hoping, however, that the total fatalities will be fewer than from the Hatings themselves. At that's only because we fear that the deaths directly associated with the actual Hatings will set record highs. At least, that's what the computer models predict, and so far they seem incredibly accurate analogs of human behavior."

"The computers predict a complete breakdown of civil order if we let the Hatings go on, Mr. Chairman," Elliot said. "Our own psychiatrists and psychologists, as well as those with the Federal government, have warned us that the data proves the Hatings don't decrease violence, but instead they tend to provoke, encourage, and even condone it."

Hastings leaned back in his chair and chewed his lip. "Andrew, I know what the Hatings have done. Violent crime up by a third, murders themselves have doubled, even schoolyard violence has risen alarmingly. I've read the reports. But can't the Feds mobilize some troops or something?"

"Unlike Justinian, our government can't act in that fashion," Shaw explained. "The Feds are hamstrung by the posse comitatus laws that Congress passed in 1878 to placate the South. That prevents the military from being used as a police force, except in a crisis when the President can suspend the law. But that can't happen until the crisis has occurred, and we estimate that will be far too late."

"So, you're saying if we continue the Hatings that we run the risk of causing nation-wide rioting and rebellion," Hastings said. "And that could destroy the entire country?"

"Pretty much," Shaw said.

"But, Mr. Hastings, we can't just abandon the Hatings," Gaddis chimed in. "Our advertising revenues have tripled in the last year alone. We're bigger than the Super Bowl ever was."

Hastings was about to reply when Gaddis continued. "And may I remind everyone that the Hatings provide all the revenue we need to finance our entire operations five times over? Canceling the Hatings would be economic suicide! Our shareholders would call for our heads on spikes."

"Would it matter if I noted that the networks will take the blame?" Shaw replied. "I suspect your local affiliates will be the first things to go in flames during any the rioting. And it won't be the shareholders who'll be calling for heads on spikes."

"On the other hand," said a short, chubby, red-faced advertising executive named Orville Hitt, "if there is destruction on a massive scale, there will need to be rebuilding on an equally massive scale. Imagine the revenue we could generated from construction firms, home improvement, hardware and paint companies purchasing ad time on the networks!"

Shaw wanted to cry. He'd laid out a potentially horrifying scenario, and some self-assured ignorant jackass optimist just saw it as an opportunity to make more money. Every bloody disemboweled corpse held a silver lining for some sociopath.

Afterward, in the parking lot, Elliot turned to Shaw. "I hate to say it, but we need to get the contingency plan under way."

"We'll be hated for all time, Don."

"Small price to pay to save civilization, don't you think?" Elliot replied.

Shaw knew he had no choice. He took out his cell phone and hit the one speed dial button he had prayed he would never have to use. It rang only once and was picked up. "Negotiation failed. Implement Faubus Contingency Plan."

Loren Beauchamp, the President of the United States and the person on the other end of the call, sighed. "I had hoped it wouldn't come to this."

"Profits before people, it seems, Madame President," Shaw said.

"I know," said Beauchamp. "I'll have my staff alert all the governors." The President broke the connection.

~*~

Don Elliot was already checking things out with the rest of the crew when Shaw came into the booth. Some men were cooking an impromptu breakfast in the booth's kitchenette. A coffee maker wheezed loudly, its reservoir now emptied of water.

"You're up early, Don," Shaw said, grabbing the coffee pot and pouring himself a cup of the bitter black liquid.

" Just trying to get things in order," Elliot said with a smile." It's bad enough once or twice a year, but I hear rumors that they want to go four times a year, at the solstices and the equinoxes." Shaw sipped his coffee, yet still managed to burn the tip of his tongue." In New York and L.A., they're going under the lights for a twenty-four hour Hating. I just got the confirmation as I left the house."

"Andy," Elliot remarked, amused," they'll have to start selling concessions."

Shaw sat in his control seat and began his checklist. "Is everything deployed, Don?"

Elliot handed him a manila folder. "The Guardsmen are set out as usual, but regular troops are deployed at the strategic spots the computer models selected," Elliot whispered. "The President's order federalizing the Guard has been issued, and the order suspending the Posse Comitatus laws under a national emergency is just waiting for the critical moment. "Everything's been fitted into the timetable, but we're still pretty flexible should nothing happen."

"Sounds good," Shaw muttered. " Let's hope we can stick to the schedule and keep everything under control." He accepted a bacon-lettuce and-tomato sandwich handed to him by one of the technicians. "Aren't you eating?" he asked Elliot.

" Nah," Elliot said, "put on too much weight." He rubbed his stomach. "Bad for the heart, too, you know. I have to cut down on the coffee, as well. Doctor's orders."

" At least you haven't got ulcers."

"I would, if I had your hummingbird metabolism."

"It's because we don't participate," a technician named Russo said. "We have to deal with our problems and frustrations while everyone else gets to release theirs."

"Yeah, ain't that the truth," Shaw mumbled. He took a bite of his sandwich and then he checked his watch. Still about twenty minutes until it was time to open the gates and let the people into the stadium. He sipped some coffee from a foam cup. It was hot and acrid. Great, he thought, of course the coffee sucks. Why wouldn't it?

" Throw up what the networks are broadcasting," Shaw said, turning in his chair to face the huge banks of monitors that dominated one wall of the bunker. The monitors showed the broadcasts of all national over-the-air, cable, fiber-optic and satellite networks.

On a special grouping of two-meter tall sets the images of local television personalities came to life. Shaw hated local talent. It was the same wherever he went—idiotic perfectly coiffed and dressed meat-puppets who either spouted fact-free right-wing drivel or tried to talk "happy talk." The latter was the more annoying as it gave the local talent time to smile inanely and to show off their perfect teeth.

One screen showed the sun rising on a beautiful spring morning, with a helicopter shot view of the local crowd buzzing with excitement and anticipation laid side-by-side with a national feed from Los Angeles. A trim, blonde and well-dressed local meatpuppet with a high-pitched ditsy voice gushed about the scene in the most purple of terms. Shaw cut the sound on her transmission.

The second screen showed a news team interviewing people outside the stadium. The tall, male meatpuppet interviewer was the perfect example of a bumbling glinbek – a handsome, politically ultra-conservative, traditional values guy dressed in sartorial splendor, and without a single thought in his empty, hollow, but well coiffed, head.

" Greatest thing in the world," said the fat man whom the glinbek was interviewing.

" Where do they find these people?" Russo thought.

" They use focus groups." Elliot said. "Doesn't matter what they say, it's how they resonant with the audience."

"That explains a lot."

The fat man munched on a gyro that was as thick as a two-by-four. As he talked, he dripped mustard, mayonnaise and seemed to be olive oil onto his protruding stomach. He swallowed. " Never miss a Hating. Only time of the year I can tell the boss off and not lose my job. Love 'em, that's all I can say. Just love 'em."

Shaw checked the third monitor. It was carrying the network broadcast of the Hating that would take place in Shea Stadium, Yankee Stadium, and Madison Square Garden. But at the moment a noted sociologist was being interviewed about the background of the Hatings for the benefit of those glued to wall-size high-definition holovision sets at home.

" Actually," he said, "the Hatings can be traced back to the Pax Romana. Gladiatorial contests allowed the populace to vent their hostilities. It thereby insured domestic tranquility, which is why the Roman Empire survived so long. The Hatings go one better in that. Instead of just allowing vicarious vent of hatred, it allows direct participation. That's so much healthier for society. In fact, there are examples today in many other societies. In some isolated areas of Malaysia, if a man wishes to get out of debt and lower his place in society, he runs amok, beating trees, with large sticks and stealing bars of soap from the homes of his neighbors...."

Shaw cut the connection. " Christ, they'll stop at nothing to justify this."

Gaddis said, " Don't knock it, Mr. Shaw. The Roman Empire might never have fallen if it had let the audience fight in the Coliseum instead of the gladiators. Old grudges could be settled, friendships strengthened, rejected lovers avenged, criminals punished..."

Shaw, however, knew better.

Russo handed Shaw a sheet of paper. "Latest report, sir. They've set a new record in New York." He smiled and seemed awed.

" Imagine! Eight million people crammed into both stadiums and Madison Square Garden. Now that must be something!"

" Yeah," Shaw said, wanting to throttle Russo then and there, "Must be something."

He checked his watch and compared it with the timer set into the wall above the monitors. Counting off the last seconds to himself, he then said, "Open the gates."

The main monitor came on. It showed the Guardsmen cautiously undoing the massive padlocks and chains that held the gates closed. As soon as the chains were off, the men rushed for the safety of machine gun emplacements as the tidal wave of humanity poured through the corridors and went mindlessly into the stadium.

"They're like a bunch of mad sheep" one Guardsmen could be heard yelling.

" Well, who do you think programs this stuff?" another guardsmen said.

"Wile E. Coyote?" the first man replied before he was drowned out by the roar of the crowd.

Shaw cut the connection and picked up the transmission from the cameras inside the stadium. He picked up a camera panning its way over the stadium and locked on.

The crowd was already thick and heavy. Few seats appeared empty, and those filled even as watched. The throng had spilled out into the picnic area and the bullpen, and a few managed to get onto the field, where they were quickly hustled back into the stands by alert Guardsmen, who had taken position in the dugouts. It had all the energy and mindlessness of a fascist rally, a religious revival and the opening moments of Black Friday sales.

" Everything ready?" Shaw asked Elliot.

" Yep," Elliot said, scratching his heavy chin with a short stubby finger. "The programs are running, and we should have complete control."

" All right." Shaw turned to face Russo. "Give me a display on the first read-out."

" Yes, sir," the man replied, his brown eyes dancing behind the thick lenses of glasses.

"Enthusiastic," Elliot commented.

" An idiot, if you ask me," Shaw muttered.

The display appeared on one side of the screen, green block letters on a black background. The other side of the screen was a transmission of the emcee, an announcer for one of the local stations. The man was known in the business as a glinbek or a rimbah, both terms that dated from broadcasting personalities who preceded the Hatings historically, but who had a similar purpose in rousing irrational fears. Few people knew where the names originated, but everyone knew what they meant.

Elliot glanced at a read-out on his monitor. "Crowd enthusiasm is growing. Lots of anger and adrenalin out there."

"Nice, nothing too drastic right now; we'll just ease them into it." Shaw finished his coffee. It was going to be a long day, that he knew.

~*~

The announcer had picked up his microphone and spoke: " Welcome to the Tulsa Public Hating!" His voice carried all over the stadium, sounding harsh and tinny over the decrepit P.A. system. "And now, as all of you fine people have been waiting for, I declare this Hating open!"

The crowd released a thunderous cheer which shook the stadium and caused white powder to cascade from the roof like snow.

" What the hell's that?" Shaw said.

" Pigeon crap," Elliot said. "They haven't cleaned this stadium in years."

" And to begin this Hating, just let me explain the rules," the glinbek intoned, his voice electronically altered to sound deep, profound, and authoritative.

" The first half will be computer selected. You'll only be allowed to hate those people whom the computer selects. Got that? And how will you know who to hate? Well, their badges will turn bright yellow!"

He picked up a piece of paper." And here's the first thing. We want you to hate anybody named Jeff or Jeffrey or Geoff or Geoffrey. That's right, folks, search them out. You know who they are. They know who they are. Look for them. Find those bastards and hate them."

Guardsmen brought a group of men into the center of the playing field. They were all named Jeff or its variant, and they were all scared shitless, to put it mildly. As the crowd watched, the Guardsmen pulled back. The computer-actuated badges responded to a pre-arranged signal and changed quickly from red to yellow. The Jeffs panicked and ran. They were now fair game for Hating. The horde swarmed on them with speed. Shaw watched the bank of monitors surveying the action. One of his monitors showed a Jeff breaking free and heading for a corridor, desperately trying to escape.

The robot camera caught it perfectly as he was caught by a group of five young women in leather pants and jackets. Two of women carried old-fashioned straight razors. They quickly had him pinioned." Think you' re big stuff, hey putz!" one said. "Thought you could screw all of us and get away with it?" another said.

Shaw wondered if these women actually knew this man. Or were they simply taking their anger out on a convenient target.

Trapping his limbs, the women stripped him the Jeff and started to shave all the hair from his body, along with considerable portions of skin. They wanted him to suffer. The polished blades of the razors threw off blood in drops that glistened under the corridor lights. The man's screams were judiciously cut from the transmission.

Other monitors showed Jeffs' as they bastioned themselves in assorted places. Knife-welding kids trapped one at a concession stand. Perhaps hoping to placate him, he began to throw frankfurters and bags of potato chips at his attackers. But there was too many of them and soon he was overwhelmed. Arterial blood sprayed against the tiled walls and what appeared to be a severed head was raised aloft. Another Jeff had tried to climb the flagpole in the center field stands. Below him, a crowd was using a smuggled-in chain saw to cut the pole down.

"Referees to the flag pole! We have an illegal chainsaw in use!" the glinbek shouted, his voice anxious and high pitched. Sparks flew everywhere, the metal groaning under the stress. It at last gave way, falling into the crowd where it was lost from sight, along with the Jeff. A quartet had trapped a Geoff in the home team's locker room, stripped him naked, and were subjecting him to a scalding hot shower. To be fair the four folks holding him down were suffering the same fate. Elsewhere, Jeffs were beaten with baseball bats. There were variations of the old carnival hit-the clown game with Jeffs duct taped to the outfield walls and with baseballs replacing wet sponges.

And it was all going out in beautiful three-dimensional full-color with ambi-sonic sound. Shaw felt nauseous. Elliot brought him a fresh cup of coffee, creamed and sugared. "Not long now, just take it easy."

"Get those bastards, kill them, hate them!" another glinbek screamed. The crowd, its hunger for hatred not sated, began to search out more chosen victims as the announcer reeled them off. Screams rang out, but were drowned under the glinbeks tumults of mad rejoicings. Every time the glinbeks named a group to be hated, the crowded responded with the speed of a cheetah almost before the new victims' badges had changed color.

"There's a problem in Corridor Twelve, Andy," Elliot said.

" All right," Shaw said and punched a control on his chair. The network feed on one monitor faded and was replaced by the image of a perspiring, exhausted National Guard officer.

" What's going on, Captain?" Shaw inquired, knowing if a crimp occurred, it could destroy the schedule.

" Sorry, sir," the officer said, "but a group of yellows are trying to get out. There's quite a few, sir, and we can't do anything without authorization."

"Okay," Shaw sighed, sinking in his chair, "let me talk to them."

The captain's image dissolved and was replaced by a moon-faced man with a moustache. He squinted through wire-rim spectacles.

" Please, sir," he said, his voice shrill and desperate, "have some mercy. These people don't understand the limits on Hating. They want to kill us!"

The crowd of yellow-badged people behind the man pressed closer, like trapped rats on a sinking ship.

"I'm sorry," Shaw said, knowing exactly how the man felt and loathing every single goddamn word he'd have to say." You all signed releases before you got your tickets. You knew what you were getting into when you came to the Hating. If you didn't want to participate, you should have stayed home."

" But we didn't think it'd be us," the man shrieked, sobbing. He was on the verge of breaking.

"No one ever does," Shaw said, hurting deep within his own gut, but trying to hold it back. "No one."

Suddenly, desperately, the crowd charged the Guard position in a blind attempt to reach the relative safety of the Parking lot.

The Guard Captain barked a command and the Guardsmen fire. Shaw and the others watched helplessly. When the smoke and thunder or gunfire died away, the camera revealed thirty or forty people dead or dying on the smooth, cold concrete.

" I warned you," sobbed the Guard Captain, tears rolling down his cheeks, "but you just wouldn't listen. You just wouldn't listen!"

Shaw cut the connection from that monitor.

On a larger monitor, a glinbek happily yelled, "It's Free Hating Time folks! Hate those people you've wanted to hate all year! Yessireee! Lay it on them! Get those bosses who cut your salary or make you work for slave wages! Kill those damn liberals who want to spend your tax dollars and let people marry their horses. Get those bastards who hound you at work! Hate them! Kick them in the balls! Set fire to their toupees, and cut up their fine Brothers' Brooks suits! Stomp them! Cut them! Hate them!" In contrast, the holo station had on a smooth talking voice-over while the action was occurring.

"And remember," he said, his tone changing from frenzied to smooth, "Survivors of today's Hating will receive full medical care…and burial expenses should they fail to pull through. They'll also receive a guaranteed income should their injuries prove permanently disabling. Plus a number of dandy prizes, all of them name brands products from our many advertisers. Tell our audience about the prizes, Ed…"

Shaw went to the bathroom on that note. He grabbed a cheese sandwich from a tray and ate it in the relative quiet of his bathroom stall. Elliot was in charge for the moment, and he hoped Bill wasn't having any trouble. He ran a hand through his sparse brown hair and closed his eyes. It didn't seem to help. His hand still shook and it felt as if his bowels were going to explode. Then he heard Russo's voice, the bastard.

" Wow oh wow," a giggling Russo squealed. "Just look at this tally! Over one hundred dead, seventy-six seriously injured, and over three hundred requiring some hospitalization! That's counting the ones the Guard shot, but it's still better than last year!"

Shaw wanted to throttle the man. The thought brought him back to reality. He was tired and aching and nervous, and he was starting to think the way the crowd was thinking. The knowledge chilled him. As Shaw reentered the control room, he saw Elliot spun about in his chair to face him.

" Just fifteen minutes, Andy."

" Good."

The monitor revealed a young woman in high-heels kicking a man who apparently was her employer." That's for every dollar you cheat me out of," she said, landing a blow on a sensitive area."

A second woman joined the first and began kicking the prostate man. "And that's for every time you tried to make out with me! And that's for being a gutless wonder!" Her hair flew wildly with each frenzied movement.

The much-kicked man crawled toward the seats, hoping for sanctuary. He doubled over each time he was hit. He almost reached safety when a group, probably his employees, recognized him.

They charged him, brandishing golf clubs, umbrellas, and wooden planks. The man screamed and was overcome. Blood flew everywhere. He never had a chance.

Shaw felt a chill down his spine. These were no longer specific attacks, he realized. This was now pure mob behavior—generalized hatred, revulsion and violence—as groups sought out victims, no matter who they were.

On another screen, a group of housewives pelted the owner of a chain of grocery stores with fruits, vegetables, and table scraps. Bits of watermelon rind and eggshell clung to the man's clothes. Tomato juice stain his shirt.

Where had the women obtained the rotten produce? Shaw wondered.

The grocer found himself trapped against a chain-link fence. A fusillade of rotten tomatoes, sprouted potatoes and moldy oranges scored direct hits on his tortured and bleeding body. He tried to knock the produce aside with feeble movements of his hands, but to no avail. As the housewives—some armed with paring knives—closed in on him, a look of surrender crossed his face. His eyes rolled back in their sockets, and he collapsed to the ground.

Elliot bit his lip. "I'm just glad Maddy decided to go to Toronto this week." He wiped his sweaty palms on his jacket. " It'd be torture if I knew she were out there."

" That's why Ann took our kids to England," Shaw said.

"Thank god for countries that are still sane," Elliot said.

But for how much longer? Shaw wondered.

As if one cue, a technician said, "One minute."

One berserk glinbek jumped up and down in a frenzied dance. His toupee bounced wildly on his cadaverous skull. Droplets of his perspiration flew into the air. "That' s it! Keep it up! We got a few hours left! Hate! Hate! Hate!"

Shaw kept his eye on the timer. He punched open a panel in the arm of the chair, revealing a small black button.

"Ten seconds," Elliot said.

Shaw counted it down on the timer. When it winked off, he depressed the button and gave the command. " Commence."

The dancing glinbek was thrown backwards, then jerked forward as a high-powered rifle shell tore through his throat and exploded out the back of his head. Before he collapsed, the glinbek was hit several more times, each bullet making him dance crazily like a marionette until a round decapitated him.

Around the stadium, panels fell away to reveal machine gun emplacements. The troops manning the weapons methodically mowed down the mob in the center of the field. No one could avoid the deadly crossfire. Groups attempted to climb the fences to escape, but were picked off by snipers and infantrymen firing machine pistols. People in the stadium tried to run for the exit ramps but couldn't escape the unerring aim of the sharpshooters who picked off them as easily as plucking petals from a flower.

Those who did get into the exit corridors and ran toward the Parking lots in desperate hope of escape encountered squads of the National Guard. The Guard opened up with small arms and automatic rifle fire. Those who managed to react fast enough to turn back found the other end blocked as well. They huddled close together, which only made the Guardsmen's job that much easier. A fine spray of blood obscured the camera surveying the action. An errant bullet took out another camera. Its remote control destroyed, the camera spun wildly, giving a topsy-turvy panorama of screaming people being ripped apart followed by their tormentors and did so until it smashed into a wall and fell to the earth. Its lens caught the wide-eyed image of a dead man, before the camera itself went dead.

Shaw's head spun as well. He wanted to vomit all of his intestines, if it would stop what he had done.

" I never thought it'd be like this," Elliot said. He licked his lips, but could not take his eyes from the monitors.

Shaw noticed he had been clenching his fist. He opened his fingers and watched a trickle of blood slid from his lacerated palm.

" It had to be done," he told himself, knowing it for the lie it was. Suddenly there was a terrific pounding at the door of the booth. The armored fittings began to groan under stress." They're trying to get in," screamed Russo, no longer glib.

He was down to their level now and just as frightened.

"Andy," Elliot shouted, "that door can stop bullets, hell, even an RPG, but I don't think it's going to hold. Not against them."

" I don't want it to hold," Shaw said calmly. He then depressed the emergency switch on the chair's control board. The explosive bolts on the door sheared, the door gave way, and the mob came pouring through.

Consciousness, like a spider spinning a web of fire, blossomed in his head. Shaw opened his eyes and was greeted by a light that seemed to pulse like an amoeba. His eyes burned. Everything seemed like mounds of wet clay. There was a taste of blood in his mouth. Even moving slight produced searing pain. Even just breathing hurt. Cracked ribs, no doubt, he thought. Punctured lung? A possibility.

Shaw forced himself to sit up, banging his head on a low ceiling in the process. He realized he was under the control panels. Clenching his teeth to handle the pain, Shaw maneuvered himself, with considerable difficulty, from under the equipment.

He got to his feet, felt his legs giving way, and stumbled into his chair. It was a welcome relief. As he caught his breath, he took time out between stabs of pain to see what had happened. The booth was a wreck. Everything had been smashed, or tossed about, including the men. He wondered if they were all dead as none of them were moving.

The mob had smashed all the monitors, except one. It showed an image of the field at night. A few still forms could be discerned in the moonlight. Triage had already begun. Soldiers walked past the bodies, dispatching those who were wounded too severely to be helped. Each time a gun fired, the muzzle flash was followed by an earsplitting pop, and the form would jerk spasmodically and then be still. Collection teams driving golf carts each pulling a train of trailers soon loaded the corpses into them.

As Shaw turned the monitor off, he was struck by an odd thought. Baseball season was a week away. Could the grounds crews prepare the stadium and field in time for the Tulsa Frackers' home opener? It was stupid thought, but it was saving his sanity, he knew.

He got up and started to walk, edging himself along the control panel while using it as support. The bridge of supposed his nose hurt. He knew it was broken. His left arm was also throbbing, especially at the wrist. But he could still move it without too much difficulty, so maybe it was just a sprain. Something hooked his feet from under him, and he toppled over a bulky object. As he turned around in the half-light, he saw it was Russo's body. The man's eyes and mouth were frozen in a mask of utter terror. The man now looked like he had a third eye socket. Congealed blood ran from the corner of his mouth and ears and from the back of his now shattered skull.

Shaw suddenly felt sorry for the man, despite disliking him. Russo had suspected nothing and died in horror, his skull smashed. But there was nothing Shaw could do, so he went back to exploring

There were two other dead men in the bunker, and Shaw hoped the others had either escaped, been rescued, or died somewhere else. He stumbled into the bathroom, where he found a bloodied Elliot, sitting in the corner of the showers.

Don, he realized, was alive.

" Hey, Andy," Elliot said, smiling painfully. He was bruised and bloodied, but probably felt no worse than Shaw did. Elliot's lips were split, and he'd lost some teeth. His right eye was swollen shut. His face was scratched badly, but the pain couldn't wipe away the pleasure he felt at seeing Shaw.

" Don, you old bastard," Shaw said, tears pouring down his cheeks. "Let's get the hell out of here."

The pair, although limping badly, managed to navigate their way without much difficulty and soon reached the secured parking area. Shaw flashed his identicard to the Guardsmen on watch, and he was escorted to where Shaw's car, mostly undamaged, was parked. The vehicle had suffered only relatively slight damage. The right front quarter panel was badly dented, probably from a sledgehammer. A key scratching ran the length of the car and the windshield as cracked on the passenger's side, but otherwise it appeared whole.

He opened the passenger door and helped Elliot into the seat, securing him with the seat belt. As he came around to the driver's side, Shaw could see the lights of several fires burning in the distance. The flames flickered brightly against the horizon of night.

" The riots," he said wonderingly as he slid into the driver's seat, "they're happening just as the computers predicted."

" I wonder which ones are the holovision stations," Elliot said with a slight laugh that turned into a low groan of pain.

" The networks'll be setting fires of their own soon enough," said Shaw as he thought about the contingency plan. Congress, the President, the governors, state legislatures, and the networks—they'd all be at each other's throats with accusations after that. He wondered if President Beauchamp's administration would survive long enough to be vindicated.

" Do you think Maddy will still want this face?" Elliot asked.

" She'd be a fool not to," Shaw replied. He started the car and backed it out of its parking space. Then he turned the wheel, put the car in drive, headed for the exit. As the Guardsman waved him through, Shaw maneuvered the vehicle to begin their long journey to find the first hospital with an emergency ward that wasn't too overcrowded.

The Unbinding

By
M. P. Neal

There's going to be an unbinding in the old cathedral today. I'd hoped that they were finished after fifty years, but still she finds new victims: offerings to her one true God. The High Priestess is still cleansing the world. I can never forget the day when I saw the first unbinding.

I was ten years old and choking in a hospital basement. Only those who had sheltered underground had survived the Firestorm. A group of children had been led to the refuge by an older boy. We lay huddled together as the firestorm roared above us and buildings shuddered and collapsed. Smoke had seeped in despite the metal doors sealing the room; I think it had once been the mortuary. The air was stifling. My throat was burning. I thought that I was going to suffocate. Suddenly a man stood up and forced a door off its hinges. I staggered out after him together with a few others into a world covered in ash. Each footstep sank silently into its inches thick layers. It whirled around coating everyone and everything in a grey-white film. I stumbled over a piece of rubble and sat there for a while. I had no idea of what to do. People wandered in and out of my view, shocked and aimless. I heard a voice calling:

'There is no flesh but God's flesh,
There is no light but God's light.'

I gathered myself and stood up, drawn towards the voice. Others did the same. She appeared through the white fog, six foot six tall, black eyes blazing in a skeletal face, white hair streaming down her back. She towered over the gathering crowd as she proclaimed her commandments:

'There is no flesh but God's flesh,
There is no light but God's light.'

That was when the new religion began.

'The robots have been destroyed,' she said. There were not many left after that firestorm. 'The bionics must be unbound from God's flesh. Seize them from the place of iniquity,' she ordered, pointing at the rubble that had been the hospital.

A posse formed from the crowd as she shrieked her commands and so the hunt began. Six men ran into the basement through the shattered doorway. They emerged dragging the boy of maybe seventeen who'd helped us and threw him on the ground in front of her. He was shaking. She stretched down and drew him up upright then she raised her hands above her head. They seemed to twitch like water diving rods, but it wasn't water she was looking for, it was non-human flesh. She ran her hands over his head as he trembled before her then she ran them down his arms and legs and torso. She came back to his left hand, her fingers twitching over it. Then she raised his right hand.

'Hold,' she ordered and two men stepped forward and seizing him by his arm, holding it rigid, they pressed his hand on a blackened and fractured sandstone upright. She drew a heavy, kitchen carving knife, whittled razor sharp, from her belt and sliced his forefinger delicately. Drops of blood splashed onto the ash carpet, staining it with small, red spheres.

'Behold the true blood of God's flesh,' she cried. I found myself breathing again. The bionic parts were so realistic in those days that all that they lacked was a red blood circulatory system. Looking at a hand, holding it, you couldn't tell it wasn't human flesh. That's why some people hated bionics.

'The left hand,' she ordered. I froze as the men held the boy's left hand steady. She sliced his forefinger again. This time no fresh, red blood flowed. She chopped off his finger in a single sweep. No blood spurted as the finger sank into the ash. The boy shuddered, silent in his fear.

'Bionic plague,' she said and delicately sliced the back of his hand. No blood fell. She's going to chop his hand off, I thought. Instead she traced a thin line along the back of his arm from his wrist to his elbow until blood did seep from under his skin inches below his elbow.

'Unbind the bionic plague,' she hissed 'Cut it out of his God-given flesh.' She raised the heavy carving knife in both hands above her head. She brought it down like an axe, once, twice, more times than I could watch. The boy was screaming now, red streams of his blood clumping the ash. He fell to the floor as she held his bionic arm above her head. Rain began to fall turning the ash a dirty black as his blood was washed away.

'He's cleansed. Release him,' she ordered. A woman ran forward, wrapped a cloth around his arm and tried to help him up. I stepped forward and lifted him with her. That was the first time the High Priestess looked at me, truly looked at me, then she turned away. The crowd moved away after the Priestess, searching for other victims and we three were left alone.

I was clinging to the woman as she tried to tend to the boy.

'Hold him up,' she said to me and I helped support the boy. 'Can you hear me, Tom? I'm a nurse from your ward, Mary. Do you remember? Tom?' she kept calling him by his name. 'You have to walk. I have a place we can go.' Somehow we hauled Tom onto his feet and held him between us.

'You have to move,' Mary said. The mob had moved on looking for new victims, but the two or three people still hanging around were muttering about us. A few stones were aimed in our direction as we crept away from them.

'Keep going, Tom,' Mary repeated as we slowly moved towards the outskirts of the town. All the while blood was still seeping through the makeshift dressing Mary had tied around Tom's wound.

'I can't,' he said, falling heavily against Mary. 'Leave me. Save yourselves.'

'We'll rest awhile,' Mary said. 'This is as good a place as any.' We shuffled back behind the fire blackened remains of a wall where we were hidden from the people wandering, dazed through the ruins. Even I could see that it was hopeless. Mary was a small woman and I was only ten. Tom was a gangly teenager. We would not be able to move him any distance. Clouds of dust swirled around and settled down us. The only sound was Tom's quiet panting. The day drew on. Twice we tried to pull Tom to his feet, but each time he fell back again. We needed help and it appeared.

'Nurse Mary.' Twin boys, a year or so younger than Tom, jumped down from the wall in front of us.

'Peter and Paul, the angels must have sent you,' Mary said. Peter and Paul had been in the hospital basement with me, one of the group led there by Tom.

'We've been following you,' Peter said. 'You're not doing well.'

'Can you help us carry Tom to my place, out of town? It's a couple of miles from here.'

Paul picked Tom up in his arms. 'Which way?' he asked. I knew then that Paul was a super bionic. I knew that we could make it.

You couldn't distinguish between the twins to look at them, both rangy, blue eyed six footers. Inside it was different. Peter was just like me and only had the bionics he needed to stay alive. It turned out that Paul had bionic arms, legs, ears and eyes. He kept us alive through those first hard years and we kept him hidden. We weren't the only new family hiding a bionic.

Tom lived another thirty years with the mutilation of that day. Many did survive the unbinding if their arm or leg was removed; of those who did not it was often their blood loss that was too much for them especially when she took more than one limb. Even before the Fall, bionics had been declared androids and stripped of all human rights. They were blamed for the Fall. People thought that their false pride, their belief that they could become superhuman, had led to the destruction of the old technological civilisation.

For the first couple of years the High Priestess permitted only wooden tools. The Firestorm had left fertile soil behind it and nature replenished trees and grasses for us, but tilling the fields by hand was tough and many starved. Paul could do it. He had to be careful that no one was watching when he used his bionic strength. Paul worked first thing in the morning then Peter would take over so that they were never seen together. The rest of us weeded and harvested. All the while we lived in fear of a visit from the High Priestess.

She came the second year. Paul heard her of course. 'Horses, twenty or so, riding this way fast,' he shouted one cold spring dawn, leaping from his bed.

'You must hide,' Peter said.

Paul took himself off to a hiding place he'd made in a tunnel under the earth. 'I'll be listening,' he said as he left.

The rest of us carried on as if it were a normal morning on the farm. It wasn't difficult to look terrified when the High Priestess rode in surrounded by her guards.

They thumped on the door and yelled. 'Outside, now.'

We lined up, Mary at the front and Tom and Peter beside her. I stood behind them shivering.

'Welcome, High Priestess.' Mary bowed low and the boys copied her. The Priestess looked at me over their bent backs.

'I have come to search for the bionic plague. Step forward.' She pointed at Tom who hesitated for a moment. As two guards moved towards him he took a step in front of Mary and held up his mutilated arm.

'God's true flesh, by your mercy,' he said.

The Priestess slid from her horse and drew herself up to her full height in front of him. Her carving knife glinted from an ornate leather belt that she wore around her waist. Tom bowed his head. She raised her hands over him and leaned in, seeming to sniff his breath for an age. She's found a new way to search for internal bionics, I thought. I heard the wind rustling in the trees as time stretched out. It must have only been a few moments before she stood back.

'There is no flesh but God's flesh,' she said.

'There is no light but God's light,' Tom replied.

Peter was next in line. With him she ran her hands over his arms, legs and torso. Each time she paused I stopped breathing. I could see Tom's arm hacked off in front of me as it had been on the day of the Fall. I could see it as the Priestess raised it aloft over her head, blood dripping from it onto her face. I swayed. Tom put his stump out to help me and I leaned back onto its shelter. Finally the Priestess focused on Peter's face, peering into his eyes, forcing her hand into his mouth, gripping his ears. At the last she sucked in his breath. We waited.

'There is no flesh but God's flesh,' she said.

'There is no light but God's light,' Peter replied.

Next was Mary. She passed the examination then it was my turn. Tom gently guided me out to the front. I trembled in front of the Priestess as she looked me over from head to toe. She suspected me. I could feel her anger. Slowly her examination of my body began. She felt each of my arms in turn then she drew out her carving knife. I felt the others start behind me. What could they do against a troop of armed men? Somewhere Paul was watching and listening. Maybe it had been him I heard in the trees, but if he intervened we were all dead.

'Hold out your arm, she ordered.

I held it steady in front of her, my trembling passed now, as she inscribed a thin line from my shoulder to my wrist. A minute passed as blood seeped out all along the line. Then she pricked each of my fingers. Every time a red drop of blood fell onto the green shoots of new spring grass. She repeated the torture with my other arm and both legs.

'Turn around.'

I felt a sharp pain as she sliced through my tunic. I covered my chest in a child's shame as it fell to the floor. Then she made turn around. She sliced a line down my back from my hair to the base of my spine.

'Face forwards.' I turned slowly. 'Tilt your head back.' She sliced from my chin to my pubic bone, forcing me to drop my hands to my side and stand half naked, blushing in shame. Still my saving blood seeped out along the line where she scarred me. She slid her knife back into her belt and took hold of my face. She pulled me up towards her forcing her face down onto mine, her bloodless lips onto my mouth. She drank in my breath until I had none left to give. I must have fainted. I came too on the floor with Mary covering me while the Priestess rode off in a cloud of dust at the head of her troop. Tom carried me into the house. He sat with me for the next few days as I passed in and out of fever. It was the end of the summer before I left the house again.

'I look like I've been zipped into my body,' I said.

'She's scarred us both,' Tom said, 'but your scars are beautiful, like you.'

The High Priestess continued her cleansing, visiting every home in the town and around. I pitied the ones for whom doctors had replaced a failing part. They pleaded for mercy and she gave them hers: they kept their ailing heart. Pacemakers were destroyed with magnets…God's magnets of course. Synthetic eyes and ears were cut out. Bionics were hunted down where ever they were flushed out of cover. The ones with superhuman powers were easy to identify to spot when they fled at speeds up to at one hundred kilometres per hour. They were not easy to capture. Teams of hunters tracked them, catching them in the nets to bring them down. Paul kept well hidden. He had no future in the world of the Priestess.

All technology was banned. She drew up a list of permitted tools, wooden to begin with. As hunger bit deeper when harvests were poor, iron ploughs made the authorised list. The years moved and iron wheels joined them. Over the decades we've moved back to a mechanical world, with steam engines and boats. The basements of the libraries had held enough books so that the designs had survived. What people wanted most was light, electric light. She held out for four decades. She's losing her power, I thought, when it was permitted.

Now instruments dependent on electricity are authorised for medical uses so X-ray machines and ultrasonics are back, as a guide for treatment. Transplants of any kind are forbidden. I think they always will be. Paul was more in danger than ever then and he decided to leave.

'I don't exist,' he said. 'I can't.' I've not heard from him since.

The unbindings have died out over the decades since she could find no more victims. There's only so much she can detect when she feels a person inside and out with her long, bony fingers, pressing down on their arms and legs and torso, feeling for any resistance that's not God's flesh and bone. There's been a fresh wave of unbindings since x-ray instruments were permitted. She's found a use for them: detecting another range of implants; synthetic hearts. Those unbindings are so horrific; I've never seen one.

The Unbinding

Tom lived to become your grandfather, I think, looking at our children and grandchildren, waiting outside for me to go to with them to the cathedral for today's unbinding. Some of the unbound were babies before the Fall. They never chose to be bionic. It was a choice their parents made for them. Still the High Priestess has tracked them down and removed their bionic parts.

She still suspects me. I can feel it. She wants to complete her life's work so that no bionic escapes her. You have to be in your fifties to be suspect now so her pool is growing smaller. I passed her X-ray test that she made everyone take. Still I can feel her black eyes glowing with suspicion if she sees me.

I know what's waiting for me in the old cathedral. My grandchildren told me. It's an ultrasound arch. I saw enough when I was in hospital. She's making everyone walk under it to celebrate fifty years since the Fall. It's our turn at ten am. She says she's showing God that we have reformed and are a cleansed human race so that he will never visit his anger on us again. She's found out that plastics have a different signal from flesh so she's on the hunt again for a last wave to be unbound, those with internal plastic implants.

It's not a long walk to the old cathedral ruins. I follow my family dutifully and too soon we are there. It is one of the few buildings where the shell of the sandstone outer walls survives, punctuated by widows, bare ribs exposed to the sky. The first time I saw it was the day after the Firestorm. The stone vaults of the roof had split and smashed into piles as high as the windows. The sun had come out after the rain that followed the storm. Light shone straight and clear through the windows upon the heaped up rubble. Over the years the debris has been mostly cleared away and benches lined up inside below the altar stone.

Today the cathedral ruins are decorated in white May blossom. It's her celebration of the final cleansing of humanity from the bionic plague. The delicate blooms fill every ruined window. They flow over the stone altar and along the tops of the wooden benches. Their petals cover the sandstone aisle. Their scent cloys my throat. I feel it choking and burning as the ceremony of cleansing begins. Each row in the crowded cathedral steps forward in turn and queues down the aisle. I watch from my place at the end of the last row. One by one every person, young and old, passes through the ultrasound arch in front of the altar. When no alarm sounds she says:

'There is no flesh but God's flesh,' and each, even the youngest, replies:

'There is no light but God's light.' I suppose X-rays come from the sun like all other radiation. Bats use ultrasound. Those were her pronouncements anyway.

The row in front of us stands up. A man glances behind at me for a moment and smiles as his row queues for the final test of being human. It's Peter. He'd had his operation a few months before mine. He seems to be alone to me as he walks down that stone aisle although he is following his own children. Each of them passes safely through then his turn comes.

He hesitates for a moment before he enters the arch. The alarm sounds its long, low note. The church falls silent as she steps forwards. The screen pinpoints his throat, outlining his trachea in red. I cover my grandchild's eyes and others do the same for their little ones. The Priestess looks at me for the second time. Peter makes no resistance. He raises his neck to her as she draws the old carving knife and cuts into his trachea, holding her trophy aloft. He falls to the floor, his blood drowning him, spurting onto the white petals. How strong her arm still is, I think, and how clear her black eyes, even now when she's nearing eighty. She's always looked ageless somehow with her long white hair.

Our row moves into the aisle as Peter's body is dragged away, cleansed. Many in this cathedral have never seen a cleansing. I don't want my family to see my throat cut open. I don't want them to see my trachea ripped out. I don't want them to see my blood on the petals. I had my operation a few months after Peter. There is no escape. I walk after them down the aisle, the last person to enter under the arch. She is waiting for me, her knife by her side. I raise my eyes and for the first time I look straight into hers as I walk through, waiting for the low note that will end my life. She takes a step forward towards me.

It doesn't sound. She is next to me at the arch, her hand gripping my arm like a vice while she inspects the screen. There is no red outline showing a bionic part.

'There is no flesh but God's flesh,' I say and push her through the arch. The low note booms again and again throughout the cathedral. The screen shows bionic arms, a leg, eyes and heart. Peter's sons fall on her. I leave the cathedral with my family. I don't look behind. The last unbinding is finished.

My surgeon told me that he was using a new plastic for my trachea, with an open matrix structure, invisible to the human eye, that my own cells would colonise so that in time there would be no way of telling that I'd had a bionic transplant. He was a busy man, my surgeon.

There is no light but God's light.

COHORT 17

By
Val Muller

The room is more intimidating than Abe expected. The LED wallpaper projects the emblem of the Prince in panorama. The young sovereign rides a spotted eagle inside a wreath of laurel, arm raised in salute against the fiery red background. Even from his avian perch, the Prince seems to be watching Abe.

Abe glances up to see his uniform reflecting in one of the camera orbs on the ceiling. His identification tag reflects disproportionately on the convex surface: AL-17. The LEDs are blinding, and Abe sweats under his body scanner. He checks the command module on his arm. Sweating is a negative indicator. It is unacceptable.

He glances at the Preceptors, Pacifists of the first four cohorts. PL-3. CJ-2. FM-4. They are so far gone, Abe doubts that any of these could be his man. They stand at attention around the room. Their muscles bulge beneath synthetic bodysuits supporting small personal arsenals. Their eyes stare, unseen, from behind dark lenses. Abe watches them as he enters. Is it possible it's one of them? Could a Preceptor be the Shadow sympathizer?

At even intervals, the red wallpaper fades to black with an enlarged image of the Prince at the center with the word "Serenity" written in calm white letters beneath. The Preceptor Pacifists uniformly snap to attention and salute the image. Abe follows suit. Then the LED screens ignite back to the red emblem, and the Pacifists resume their watch over members of Cohort 17 who are arriving for their final trial as patients.

The pulsating red-black-red-black reminds Abe of a heartbeat of a patient undergoing treatment in the cryochamber: sinister and deliberate and slow. The clear lenses of Abe's glasses scan his pupils for proper dilation as he examines the empty seats. Abe chooses a seat next to a patient who looks like he'll stay composed: the effects of panic tend to spread, and Abe isn't taking any chances. Only one other member of Shadow has gotten this far, and Abe doesn't want to disappoint the organization. He sits and stills, his body poised at ready rest.

The patient next to him turns. His uniform identifies him: NN-17. NN were these man's initials before he signed his life over to Serenity.

NN-17 whispers to Abe. "Everyone says this'll be worse than the treatments." His knee jitters, and he eyes the nearest Pacifist. NN-17 is nervous. Abe has made a mistake to sit here.

"Serenity took my son to the fat camps," NN-17 whispers to Abe. "Told me they'd send him back when he achieved proper weight. But then I was reassigned to a new apartment. The parcel has only one sleeping unit. Where will my son sleep?" the man asks, raising his voice.

Abe puts a finger to his mouth, but NN-17 doesn't notice. Wires twist through NN-17's uniform like veins in a body. Each wire reports his negative indicators—pulsing temples, flickering eyelids, dilated pupils —to the Pacifists' monitors. NN-17 hasn't much time.

"I asked the new building supervisor when my son would be returned. He said he'd find out. He never did. I never asked to be relocated. I want my son back."

Abe averts his eyes. A vision of Aurora flashes in his mind, but he pushes her away. He pictures instead a gray wall at twilight. It helps to regulate his pulse. He hones in on the grayness of his imaginary wall as NN-17 continues to whisper, his voice a slow crescendo.

"So I used all my energy credits to buy fare to the fat camps. But my credits ran out. So I went the rest of the way on foot. Then my food and water credits ran out. They found me on the side of the hypertracks, and they brought me here. They said if I do good, they may send me to supervise the fat camps. And I am doing good."

The room darkens with the image of the Prince. In unison, the Pacifists and patients stand at attention and salute. While they are so engaged, Abe sneaks to the next table over.

Abe pulls out the chair, feels its weight glide over the concrete floor. He feels his muscles working over bone. He feels the way the cancer has changed the fundamental build of his bones. But after a year of treatments, there is no more pain. As he bends to sit down, he feels each vertebrae elongate, his body moving like a well-oiled machine.

Which is essentially what he is now—or what he is supposed to be —compliments of SereniCorp. He's made it through all the psychological testing. He's answered all the questions correctly. He passed his physicals. And his body reacted well to the cancer treatments: his body hasn't rejected the carcinogen like so many others. It traveled through him and worked its strange magic on his bones. He is now part of the most recent cohort and ready for promotion.

He nods to the two patients at his table: VL-17 and JK-17. They look particularly mindless. They will be good table mates.

"You have to be good," NN-17 whispers to Abe from his table. "Then maybe you can see your son, too. If you have one. Isn't there someone they took from you? Someone who got took away, away, away?"

Abe closes his eyes and finds his wall. Gray. His breathing steadies.

The LED screens change now, projecting a breaking news story. The screen shows a farmland with a small group of protesters carrying signs. "Get off my land!" one sign reads. "They took my daughter," says another.

Abe tenses his muscles. He looks down for a moment to check his indicators. He knows this is a test.

On the screen, a deep voice narrates the newscast. It is a fully-armored Pacifist standing at the edge of the screen. "These selfish farmers want more than their fair share," the Pacifist says from behind a full armor mask. "They refuse to vacate their land. This is prime farmland, and yet they have nowhere near enough water credits to keep the land irrigated. This is something best left to Serenity. These farmers would have this land remain fallow. They want to deny us all food, to squander the property that belongs to us all. Archaic sentimentality—or worse?"

"We only want to keep our land!" an elderly farmer shouts at the camera.

"So they claim," the deep voice narrates. "But we can never trust those who think they know better than Serenity."

The camera pans to follow two Pacifists riding a hovercart. They steer the cart directly at the group of protesters. The crowd scatters, leaving only the old farmer and his wife.

The Pacifists turn the hovercart towards the barn. "That's private property! This is my family's land!" the farmer screams. The camera zooms in on him.

"Look at the rage in his eyes," the deep voice narrates from off camera. "There is certainly no rationality there. He is beyond reason."

"My granddad wouldn't sell it to the developers, and I certainly ain't gonna give it up to you!"

His wife is visibly shaking now, and she eyes the camera nervously. A moment later, the camera zooms out, revealing the two Pacifists emerging from the barn, the hovercart overly burdened.

"Contraband!" a Pacifist barks. He reveals that the hovercart is laden with a pile of Pacifist armor.

"That ain't mine!" the farmer says.

"These farmers," the narrator announces, "have been hiding armor of the Pacifists. Clearly an attempt to impersonate an officer and bring down the nation the Prince has worked so hard to create. And as always, the punishment for unauthorized possession of SerniCorp equipment is death."

"This is ridiculous!" the farmer screams. "If I ever did come acrost a piece of Pacifist armor I'd burn it for sure. I'd have a big bonfire! I'd never allow that filth to desecrate my barn!"

The ground at his wife's feet darkens with urine.

Abe checks his indicators. Of course he knows what will happen. And he knows the Prime Pacifists will be watching for reactions from the patients of Cohort 17. Certain emotions are acceptable. Fear is not one of them. Neither is sympathy. Abe tries hard to create anger at the farmer.

In an instant, the Pacifists have the farmer on his knees, an electric gun pressed into the back of his neck.

"Your husband was found with contraband equipment," one of the Pacifists tells the woman. He puts his hand on the back of her neck and guides her to her husband's kneeling body. He steps back and holds an old-fashioned gun point-blank at her head.

The other Pacifist—the one with the electric gun—turns to her with a snarl. "Put your hand on this trigger."

The woman can barely stand. Her entire body is trembling.

The Pacifist helps her put her finger on the trigger of the electric gun, still pressed against her husband's neck. "You are too old to be of much use to us," he says. "However, if you acknowledge that your husband is a traitor by pulling the trigger, we will allow you your life." He presses her hand harder into the gun. "Do it," he says.

Abe knows the expected response is anger at the farmer and vindication at what the Pacifists are about to do. The monitor around his torso will confirm that he is angry at all the right moments. He digs deep to find angry memories. He's got plenty.

On screen, the Pacifist steps back from the woman. He takes out an old-fashioned gun and points it at her.

In the old woman's hand, the electric gun is shaking.

"Do it, Ellen," the farmer says, his voice shaking despite his best efforts. "Save yourself. If you don't do it, someone else will. This is my land. It's my right to die on it."

The old woman is stuck, shaking.

Her eyes shift to take in the two guns trained directly at her.

"Do it!" one of the Pacifists shouts.

"You see," the narrator says, "how cowardly these people truly are. They don't understand why they are doing the things they do. Really of no use to any of us. Not even to themselves."

The woman's hand stops shaking. The Pacifists tighten their aim on her. "It's my land, too," she says. In one smooth motion, she lifts the gun to her own neck and pulls the trigger. Her body jumps with the electricity, and the gun is thrown from her hand. It lands off-camera with a metallic clang. Instantly, she falls into a clump of smoking flesh at the ground.

The farmer has only enough time to turn toward her body before two old-fashioned bullets hit him square in the forehead. His body drops to the ground, his arm reaching toward his wife. The screen freezes on this image as the Pacifists move about the room to examine Cohort 17.

Abe tries to imagine vindication. That is what he is supposed to feel. Justice. Those farmers got what they deserved. In his mind, he pictures a day sometime in the future. A day Shadow will succeed in its mission and Serenity will fail. That will be victory. Yes, victory. It is the proper emotion to feel.

Around the room, Prime Pacifists are scanning each patient's monitor with their own. Abe's monitor beeps once. He is safe.

Three patients are taken from the room. One for sympathy and two for fear.

"Congratulations," one of the Pacifists says. "The rest of you have passed."

At the front of the room, one of the LED screens has been activated, and the rest fade to the black image of the Prince. The LED at front reads, "Pacifists for Peace." Abe tries not to shudder as a handful of new Pacifists arrive. Their heavy boots resonate on the concrete floor like drums of war. The screen changes to "Pacifists for Prosperity." They are all from the early cohorts—1, 2, a few as late as 3. They have been loyal to the cause for years. Still, Abe scans their stances for signs of sympathy or discontent. One of them could be his man.

"All Seventeens to attention!" a voice barks at the front of the room. It is JP-1, the senior Pacifist.

Like machinery, the heads of the members of Cohort 17 turn to face the front screen. The Prince's picture appears, and in unison the cohort stands, salutes, and sits. Their heads turn to JP-1.

Silence.

Behind Abe, a Prime Pacifist—WM-2—raises a hand in alarm. All is not well. Around the room, the other Pacifists raise their hands as well, two dozen gloved palms facing the members of Cohort 17. The other Pacifists turn to WM-2. A chill creeps down Abe's spine as each pair of eyes shift close to him.

Gray. Gray. Gray.

"Whispering," WM-2 announces.

It is NN-17, and he has been whispering frantically to the patient sitting next to him.

JP-1 scowls. "Return the patient for reconditioning. Place him in the next cohort. He is a disgrace to this one."

"But I'm being good, good, good!" NN-17 protests. He turns desperately to Abe. "I want to see my son! I want to work at the fat camps! You know loss," he tells Abe. "I see it in your eyes. Tell 'em how it is. Tell 'em I must see my son!"

Two Pacifists approach.

"They already took my wife. You don't understand!" NN-17 screams, now directing his pleas from Abe to the approaching Pacifists. "You took everyone! You can't take me too!"

A Pacifist grabs NN-17, drawing his arms behind his back and securing them in cuffs. Wide-eyed, NN-17 turns to his cohort. He is sweating. Rabid. "It could've happened to any of you! We tried to be good, to obey our profile. Have only one kid. The second was an accident!"

He is visibly crying now, the indicator on his torso blinking rapidly. "They took my wife away to destroy the child. I haven't seen her since. And then my son—all that extra food lying around the house! How could my son understand rations at his age? Eating was his way of coping..."

A Pacifist holds a taser to his neck, and instantly NN-17 stops. The Pacifist drags his limp prey from the room.

The room falls silent. "Now," JP-1 says. "Any of you with negative indicators will end up like him, so I suggest you focus. He's lucky we've invested so much in his body. Otherwise he'd become fertilizer for farmland." JP-1 surveys the room. The threat of a smile teases the corner of his lips. "Now, when I raise my hand, I want silence."

The members of Cohort 17 nod like drones. Even Abe forces his head to bob up and down. He thinks back to kindergarten. He remembers his teacher using a similar strategy on toddlers. Still, Abe feels his hand rise with the leader's.

"You've all survived the cancer. It's made you stronger. Your bones will not break. Your wounds will heal. Your metabolisms are slowed and your lives thus extended. You are super-human, superior to everyone that will soon be in your charge. Even the earth's gravity pales compared to your strength!"

At first, the room is silent. Slowly, one of the patients rises to salute. Abe follows suit with the others.

"You should all be grateful," JP-1 says, dismissing the cohort to their seats. "And you are all still endeared to me. You know it. Your lives are in my hands. The cancer has done wonders for your bodies. But it will continue to reach out. It will try to harden your organs along with your bone. It will try to heal parts of your body that don't need to be healed. It will try to clot the very blood in your veins. To prevent all this you are endeared to me. Indentured. Only I can provide you with the serum to keep your cancer in check. Let me hear you say it."

"We are endeared to you," the cohort echoes. "We obey you in mind and body, for your serum keeps our lives." It is something they'd been taught to memorize even before the cancer treatments were completed. Some of the cohort died repeating those words, for not all bodies accepted the carcinogen so readily.

"We have found a position for each of you, but we must complete some final scans to ensure loyalty. Our ears tell us that Shadow is active again—or trying to be. One would think they would have learned after the last incident. I trust that none of you would be so stupid."

He storms up to a random patient and slams his fist onto the table, which cracks under the force. IL-17 trembles. "Feeeeear-ful!" the leader declares. At that, a Pacifist drags IL-17 out of the room. "Back for reconditioning," the leader shouts to the cohort. "Could be a spy! Could be a Shadowalker!"

Abe focuses his breathing and tries to find his mental picture. His wall. Where is his gray wall? He sees a wall, but not a gray one. No, his mind shows him a brick wall.

A crumbling one.

An abandoned school building scheduled to be demolished. A sign declares that it will be the site of the newest Youth Education Center. Abe—a younger, healthier, more fragile Abe—climbs over the rubble into the vestige of the building's lobby. His memories of the place, his alma mater, are nauseating in light of present circumstances—memories of the time he dyed his hair blue for the state basketball tournament. The time, on a dare, when he wore a dress to school. Learning to drive in the parking lot.

Now, he creeps through the rubble, keeping soft feet as he makes his way to the basement. He doesn't even know what to expect. All he's seen is a hand-written flyer:

DISCONTENT?
J. CLYDE HARKER HIGH SCHOOL
BASEMENT
7 P.M.

As Abe descends the stairs, he sees a group in shadows. They huddle in the darkness, away from the evening light that shines in from the dilapidated ceiling above. Abe can feel the group's collective anger even before he hears them speak. As he creeps closer, he hears the muffled echoes of a woman crying.

"…a summons," she sobs. "…exceeded my allotted number of children…clinic," she manages before her voice degenerates into sobs. Abe can't help but think of Aurora.

A shadowy figure collapses on the ground in sobs, and another sits to comfort her. Abe hears bits of familiar complaints as more join in:

…the water rations…

…out of business…

…What they're doing with our land, I'll never know…

…was a cattle farmer…honest living…footprint rations…took our farm…

…Relocated us here…one-room parcel…push paper…

…wife bikes to fulfill her exercise debt…

…could never afford the energy credits to ever go back…

Abe steps forward.

"Who's that?" they ask.

"A friend," says Abe. "They confiscated my car. Poor gas mileage. Took the bus. That's why I'm late…"

The group parts for him, and he descends the last few steps and enters the darkness among them. The angry, passionate darkness. Shadow.

Abe shakes off the memory. He must focus. There it is: his gray wall. His breathing steadies. He looks at his torso. No indicators. Good.

Up front, JP-1 is still speaking.

"And with the rights you've signed away come great privileges and great responsibility. That patient they've just taken: you will face many like him. You are above people like him now. You have been given elevated status, and this you must use for the Greater Good."

"For the Greater Good," Cohort 17 mutters in unison. It is the first thing Abe can agree with. He is doing all this for the greater good.

"And now," the Pacifist continues, "an inspirational video before we assign you to your new duties."

On every LED screen around the room, the Prince's face smiles. The Pacifists make a flourishing salute. The cohort does likewise. The temperature in the room seems to soar as the video begins.

A calm voice narrates the Prince's biography, from humble birth through rise to power. Video footage shows his selfless humility at an early age. In kindergarten, the young Prince takes a smaller portion of his lunch and gives his extra food to a hungry peer. All so willingly. The teacher applauds his efforts, and the class makes him a gold medal out of construction paper.

During college, the prince gives up his three-bedroom apartment for a one-bedroom parcel with three bunk beds, smiling at how easy his new home is to care for. He even convinces a hesitant and angry roommate that this is a good idea.

Abe fights nausea. How many times has he seen this video? The narrator's voice is deafening; the heat, unbearable. Abe loses his gray wall. Instead, he remembers things that bring the anger, and it is so hard to fight these feelings. They bring negative indicators, and Abe can't let down Shadow now.

Still, the memories come.

It is the week the rations came. He has been camping with college friends during fall break. Aurora is with him, of course. Swimming in the lake, fishing, sitting around the camp fire. Aurora. It is perfect.

Returning to campus, they find scanners have been placed on all the shower stalls, the faucets, the toilets. These would track each student's use of water. Some applaud the effort. Others grow fearful, siphoning off the remains of their daily rations, which they store in jugs in campus refrigerators.

Aurora accepts it like a puppy fearful of its master. She even tries to calm Abe.

Abe tries to push the violent imagery out of his mind. He scans the room, trying to determine whether any of these Prime Pacifists could possibly be his man. But he is inundated with flashes of memories: The protests as rationing travelled like outbreaks of the plague. The water being expelled from fire hydrants by angry demonstrators. The subsequent population being allowed to dehydrate to death or else pay penance at the work camps. The mass shooting as the Sacramento Protestors charged the Pacifists. The pain of his identity chip being inserted into his thumb: the red blood growing in two bulbous dots around the site of the implant…

Abe shakes off the memories and checks his body scanners. Levels are elevated but still within limits. He has to calm down.

He looks at the LED screens, hoping the video might numb his mind. The Prince is all grown up. He and his wife are seated on their bed, a happy toddler playing on the floor of their two-room parcel.

"Let's have another baby," his wife suggests.

The screen shifts to a close-up of the Prince. His friendly eyes water and twinkle as he contemplates his wife's request.

"I hesitate," the Prince says.

She protests. "You're a paragon! The people worship you. Look at your lovely daughter. Wouldn't you like another? And another? People will pine for our genes. And wouldn't you like to try for a son?"

Abe looks for his wall, but each time he finds it, Aurora's eyes project themselves through the grayness. Those green, penetrating eyes.

"Surely," the Prince says, "if every man succumbed to such a temptation, our world would perish. Where would we get the resources to feed such children? No, we shall be content with our one child."

As the Pacifists watch the screen, Abe allows his eyes to wander. The two members of Cohort 17 who sit at his table watch the screen with passion. VL-17's eyes water. JK-17's head nods vehemently. All around the room, the cohort is transfixed.

"We must learn to do without," the Prince tells his wife. "For the Greater Good."

Abe allows himself to blink. Slowly. Slowly enough to afford a memory.

College.

Senior year.

Abe is the king of doing without. All the girls know him, but he has eyes only for Aurora. They've been together for years now. Always together—walking in the park, stargazing, reading, skating around the parking lot at midnight. Anything that doesn't consume rations. Aurora loves Abe's resourcefulness. Abe loves her smile.

They are lying on the lawn in the quad. It is 2 a.m., damp and cool. He's had the ring in his pocket for weeks now, but the moment never seemed right. They heard about the meteor shower last week, when the weather was supposed to be clear. But now they lay together on her flannel blanket, gazing up at the dull gray sky.

"You would have thought…" she says. "But all this cloud cover…"

"I know," Abe responds. "For something that only comes around twice in a lifetime, you would have thought the weather would clear for us."

"Just one shooting star…" Aurora pleads. Her voice soothes him. Even on the coldest of nights it is like the whisper of a warm summer wind.

The thought appears capriciously in Abe's mind, and he knows it's cheesy as soon as he thinks it. But he can't help himself.

"Mother Nature couldn't get you a star tonight," he says quietly, rolling onto his side to face her.

Aurora looks at him with a queer smile.

Abe's voice gains strength. "So I caught you one…" He pulls the velvety box out of his pocket the way he'd practiced so many times. He is so nervous and excited that he doesn't see her smile fade as he opens the box. "Will you do me the honor of mar—"

But before he can finish, she pushes his hand down.

"Abe, I've wanted to talk to you about this."

Abe closes his hand on the ring and stares at her. Her green eyes glow against the gray sky. Her blonde curls spill out from the hat he lent her, framing her face. She looks like an angel.

"I had my senior counseling a few weeks ago."

"You didn't tell me that," he says.

"Just let me say this," she whispers. Abe can tell she is trying not to cry. "I had my senior-year counseling, and my DNA is in high demand, it turns out. Abe, I've been allowed to have two children!"

"That's great," Abe says.

"No, you're not understanding. During your counseling, they said you could only have one."

"But…"

"Abe, you know how it works. If I marry you, you still get only one."

"Well then we'll only have one child, Aur."

"I was talking to my mom. It's not often someone's told they can have two children. I can't pass up this opportunity."

"Then don't. If kids are so important to you, we'll find a way to make it work."

"With all the rationing, Abe? Not likely." She sits up and crosses her legs. "My mother found someone—the son of a friend—who is also allowed to have two kids. I've only met him once, but he seems nice enough…"

Abe shakes his head. "You and me together—we can do anything. That's how it's always been."

"No, Abe," she mutters and stands. "It's not like that anymore. I can't—live without."

Abe watches her leave. She never looks back. Not even in his memories. Abe sinks back into the flannel blanket and stares up at the sky. The gray, gray sky.

Gray like his wall.

"It is agreed," the Prince's wife says on the screen. "We will live with what we have. As for another child, we shall learn to do without."

The room fills with inspirational music as the narrator resumes his role.

"…and so did our Prince choose to live his life, and…"

"…so shall we all. For the Greater Good!" the room echoes, Pacifists and the cohort alike finishing the mantra along with the video. The room salutes the image on the LED screen.

"If there are no indicators," JP-1 announces as the LED screens turn again to the Prince's red logo, "you will be promoted from patient to Level 1 Pacifist. Proceed to the door, patients, for your final screening and work assignment."

Abe stands from his chair, feeling muscles working over hardened bone. He thinks only of a gray wall as he slides his heavy chair underneath the table without any effort at all, as if it is made out of thin air.

~*~

"Relocation escort, huh?" Abe's partner asks as they sit on the transport. His tag identifies him as EA-14, a recent cohort, but still Abe's superior. EA-14's uniform, a dark red synthetic, is wired to communicate with his command. Weapons and tools adorn his belt, his back, and his legs. He is sitting on the hypertrain's bench, sheathing and unsheathing his black hunting knife from his ankle holster. Dark lenses obscure his eyes. "Is that the kind of job you expected when you signed up?"

"That's what they assigned me, Sir," Abe mutters.

"You should feel honored," EA-14 says. Abe detects jealousy. "My first job was far less glorious."

"What job was that?" Abe asks as grayly as possible.

"What job was that, Sir!" EA-14 corrects.

"Sir, sorry, sir!" Abe ejects. "What job was that, Sir?"

EA-14 smirks. "Trash collector."

Abe nods.

"It's an important job. You'd be surprised what people throw out. Or try to. The waste that went on!"

"I can only imagine, Sir," Abe says.

"Of course you can," EA-14 says. "Because if you were one of those offenders, they would have scraped that little discretion out of your memory by now, wouldn't they?"

"I guess they would have, Sir," Abe says. "I'm here only to serve Serenity."

"Serenity," EA-14 grumbles, making the obligatory salute. "I had to work my way up. Took me two years to become a Relocation Escort. And you're here day one. You must've impressed someone."

"My body took well to the treatments, Sir."

EA-14 dismisses the conversation by thrusting his knife into its holster. "Ever see a real farm?"

"As a kid, Sir," Abe answers. He sees visions of pumpkin picking and tractor riding with his parents, and he tries to hide his smile.

"With cows? And goats? And old Farmer Brown with a pitchfork?" EA-14 asks.

"Yes, Sir."

EA-14 points to an equipment bag in the corner of the train. "Yours," he says.

Abe opens the pack. Body armor. Helmet. Dark lenses.

"Ever see a real farmer fighting with everything he's got, to hold onto his land? Land he's been born on? Land he'd rather die on than leave? Old Farmer Brown with that pitchfork… he isn't afraid to use it."

Abe is glad for the dark lenses. He puts them on right away. He's sure EA-14 isn't his man.

"Suit up, Rookie!" EA-14 insists. "Think you have what it takes to force him to a one-room apartment parcel in the city?"

Abe flexes his muscles under the body armor. It moves well with his body and feels lighter than he'd expected.

"Do you have what it takes up here?" EA-14 taps his head.

"I serve the Greater Good, Sir," Abe answers.

Three high-pitched alarms sound, and the hypertrain starts moving. Abe's body convulses with the force, and he stumbles into his seat. EA-14 cracks a smile.

Abe stares straight ahead, his body jostling as the hypertrain hits magnetic interference.

"You'd better hope you're as good as they think you are. Screw up, Rookie, and it's a one-way ticket back for reconditioning. If you're lucky. And don't think I won't report you." EA-14 plays with his knife again. "Imagine—starting out as a relocation specialist!"

They ride in silence. The landscape flies by too fast for Abe to observe much of anything. Like the landscape, Abe's command module has been scrolling information faster than he can process it.

Abe allows himself another memory.

Shadow.

They have been meeting for years now. A different location each time. Invitations now only by word of mouth. They had a Shadowalker for two years. A Cohort 9. A sleeper agent within Serenity. For months he'd been sending coded messages back to Shadow, but the messages stopped. In their guts they knew: their Shadowalker was dead. But he had a man on the inside—a high-ranking member of Serenity sympathetic to Shadow's cause. But the sleeper died before revealing the sympathizer's identity or location.

At the meeting, one of the members has acquired a DNA test kit. The same kit Pacifists from SereniCorp use to determine likely candidates for the cancer treatments. Shadow needs a new sleeper. They need to find the insider and continue building support against Serenity. The DNA test will help them choose. Everyone's test comes out negative. Everyone's except Abe's.

"Focus, Rookie!" he snaps. Abe nods but stares ahead. EA-14's eyes scrutinize him from behind those dark lenses.

"And if you think I'm tough, wait 'til you meet the boss. She's a real hard-ass."

"She, Sir?"

"Yea, she. A real piece of work. Boy, did they do a number on her. She was damaged goods, you can tell. Probably more damaged than you were. Rumor is they took her kids. Do you remember how bad you were —before the treatments, I mean?"

Abe considers this. The treatments were supposed to wipe out most of the memories from before. Abe has fought to keep his.

"Aren't we all damaged goods?" Abe asks. "Isn't that how Serenity gets new patients?"

"Not me," EA-14 says proudly. "I signed up on my own accord. I wanted to serve the Greater Good. My sister stole a birthday cake once. It was my twentieth birthday, and she wanted to do something special. She didn't have the rations saved up, so she stole it. When I got home, everyone was in on it—mom, dad, sis… I had them all arrested that very evening."

Abe shudders.

"That's when I was officially invited to serve Serenity," EA-14 concludes.

"For the Greater Good, Sir," Abe says half-heartedly.

"The Greater Good!" EA-14 shouts back.

Simultaneously, Abe's and EA-14's control panels beep.

"Incident at the next station."

"Incident, Sir?" Abe squints at his screen.

"This isn't our district," EA-14 explains. "But a hypertrain supervisor noticed some strange movement across the tracks. An escapee. When the train arrives in thirty seconds, we'll be the closest Pacifists to the incident. We'll have to hold the escapee until the local Pacifists arrive."

"Hold him?"

"A female," EA-14 reads off his screen. "A cakewalk. In fact… I'm going to let you handle this. A field test. An initiation."

A moment later, the hypertrain halts at the station. EA-14 smirks as Abe's body slams into the plush seat.

"That way," EA-14 directs him, pushing him off the train.

Abe follows the GPS map on his command module. It moves with him. He jumps the tracks in a single bound and lands at the edge of a wooded area. The implants in his ears help him perceive stifled breathing to the north. Abe bounds through the woods effortlessly, clearing a kilometer in no time. His muscles feel good to be free, to do real work rather than exercise on machinery.

There, ahead, he sees the source of the breathing. It is two females and a baby.

The older woman hands the younger woman the baby and approaches Abe. She wields a branch from the ground, swinging viciously at him.

"Leave us alone!" she screams.

Abe grabs the stick from her. The woman ducks and rises with a fist-sized rock, which she hurls at Abe. Abe catches it in mid-air.

"It's pointless," Abe tells her. Still, he recognizes the anger in her eyes.

The woman drops to the ground. "Please, you can take me. But please, let my daughters go. My daughter," she adds as an afterthought.

The woman is dressed in rags. Her daughter, who appears to be barely fourteen, carries a backpack and cradles an infant.

"It's my daughter's baby," the woman whispers. "Please, let them both go."

"Your daughter," Abe whispers, "looks a little young to have a child. I'm supposed to scan them both."

The woman stills, but her eyes seem to nod. Abe reaches for the girl, but there is nothing to scan. Her hand is lightly bandaged, a bloody mess where the thumb should be.

Abe's command module beeps as two local Pacifists appear at the edge of Abe's map. They are a kilometer away. Abe dismisses the girl with a wave of his gloved hand. He grabs the woman roughly, dragging her up toward the tracks. He lifts her weight effortlessly, bounding out of the woods and landing in front of the two Pacifists. He places the woman on the ground. He is barely out of breath.

"I caught her," Abe tells the Pacifists.

"Was anyone with her?" one of the Pacifists asks, rereading his screen.

"I doubt it. If there were, the other is long gone. This one was traveling alone."

The Pacifist nods and binds the woman's hands.

The second Pacifist scans her thumb. "A grape farmer assigned for relocation. She's been missing for months now. Her husband was killed during an escape. Their daughter is still missing."

"She's dead," the woman cries. "We ran out of rations trying to escape, and my daughter fell."

The two Pacifists look at Abe.

"It's probably true," Abe says. "This one barely had the will to fight me."

The Pacifists make a note of it on their command modules and march the woman into the train station. Abe follows.

Before Abe boards the train, the woman looks back at him. Her hands are bound tightly, and her captors are treating her harshly. But in her eyes there is a twinkle, and on her lips, a smile.

~*~

"The boss will appreciate that," EA-14 says back on the train. "Taking initiative on your very first day. You should thank me for letting you have the opportunity. I could have easily done it myself." EA-14 has already read the report. "Of course, if it were me… I'd have found the daughter's body, too. But I can't expect that of you on day one."

Abe stares straight ahead, thankful for his dark lenses.

"How does it feel, having a catch under your belt?"

"I serve as I can, Sir." Abe pictures his gray wall.

"Serenity!" EA-14 says.

Abe salutes.

When the train pulls into the station, Abe is nervous. He tries to hold onto his wall, but he can't push the eyes of that woman from his mind. And her daughters; they seemed so helpless back there. Besides, Abe is not looking forward to meeting his new boss. Males have been easier for Abe to fool. Females have always been more perceptive. Would she see right through Abe's façade?

They enter an office building guarded by two Pacifists. The office building reminds Abe of old-fashioned skyscrapers. Spacious vestibules, flashy architecture. They weren't designed for efficiency. Not the sort of efficiency the Pacifists enforce.

EA-14 escorts Abe onto the elevator, something that should have been converted during the first Energy Sweep. This one has been left intact. It's lined with mirrors, and Abe watches a million versions of himself, each one standing at parade rest. With his body armor and weaponry, his dark lenses and helmet, he looks like a model Pacifist. His reflection even scares him.

The elevator opens on the top floor. The room is full of glowing monitors and equipment. A single Pacifist sits at a desk. She is dragging data from one monitor to the next, inputting commands into a master module.

Abe holds his head high as he approaches her. Her uniform, laden with weapons, shows off her svelte figure. Her hair is pulled back in a tight bun. Her eyes hide behind dark lenses. Her name tag showcases her experience: AC-7.

Abe's mind flashes. AC. Aurora Cameron. Why does everything have to remind him of her? He pushes her image away and focuses on his gray wall.

"AL-17, reporting for duty, Ma'am," Abe says, snapping off a salute.

"Welcome," she says gruffly. She barely looks at him. It is all business. "We're relocating a small but resistant farming community. They've been… difficult. Our orders are to save as many as we can, but this is easier said than done."

"Are they that bad, Ma'am?"

"Ever heard the expression live free or die?"

Abe nods.

"It's their mantra—in their blood. One of them took out a Pacifist a few days ago."

"Ma'am, was the Pacifist… armored?" Abe asked.

"Fully," AC-7 says. "So you know who we're dealing with here. They've booby-trapped the perimeter and approaches, and they have a minor arsenal there, too. No one goes in alone."

Her voice reminds Abe of his gray wall. There is something dead about it. And yet…

"I see you've captured one already. Day one, one capture. Good work." She reads over a report on her wrist module. "You feel comfortable with EA-14?" She finally stops to inspect him. "Can the two of you work together?"

"Yes, Ma'am," Abe lies. He knows better than to offer his true opinion.

"Here's a map of the area," AC-7 tells him. He follows her to an LED map on the wall. She touches the farm community to enlarge the map and transfer it to Abe's wrist module. "Have the map committed to memory by morning," she orders. AC-7 steps back to assess his appearance. "Who gave you that armor?"

"EA-14, Ma'am."

"Figures."

"Pardon, Ma'am?"

"EA-14 has worked hard to earn this position. You have not. He wants you to be at a disadvantage. This is not standard-issue armor. It's light-duty. For training. The agent recently killed was wearing the heavy-duty armor. You don't want this tissue paper."

At her command, Abe removes the body armor.

"EA-14 knew what he was doing. He will be disciplined."

Abe breathes heavily. This one is perceptive.

"That's not your worry, though," she continues. "All you need to know is not to cross me."

As she bends down to find some equipment in a locked cabinet, a lock of hair falls loose from her bun. It is curly and blonde.

Like an angel.

She hands him a large bag of equipment. She lifts it effortlessly, though it weighs a great deal.

"This is standard issue," she says. "Put it on."

Abe takes the equipment. It is at least twice as heavy as what he wore. He tries to concentrate as he places each piece of armor on his body, but his wall is nowhere to be found. She stares at him as he dresses.

"Ma'am, you… remind me of someone." He cannot believe the words are his. He could blow this for Shadow. All this work. All this pain. For what?

"Residual memories are common," she says as she scans his armor's serial numbers into her command module.

Still, Abe cannot let it go. The curls. The initials. "Her name was Aurora…"

Abe cannot read his officer's expression from behind her dark lenses, but she stops what she is doing, just for a moment, and the tiniest muscle in her face twitches.

"We move in the morning," AC-7 says mechanically after a moment. "Family farm. Four generations refusing to leave. Blood will be shed." She punches a button, and Abe's command module beeps with new information. "Study these profiles tonight. Our priority is to save the younger generations, as usual. Now, return below. Send EA-14 to me. He must be dealt with."

Abe adjusts his armor and salutes.

"I've been looking through the files of the Seventeens," she says as Abe makes his way to the elevator. "I requested you specifically. I like your stats."

Abe half-salutes, awkwardly, unsure what to say. This officer is violating protocol by continuing such a personal discussion.

"I'm glad to have you aboard." The last words she whispers so that they're barely audible. Like the whisper of a soft summer wind. "You and me together—we can do anything. That's how it's always been." She removes her dark lenses just as the elevator door starts to close, and Abe gets a glimpse of her eyes. Penetrating green eyes. Eyes he hasn't seen since college.

As the elevator descends, Abe watches a million versions of himself, and each one is smiling. He has found his sympathizer. It wasn't a man after all. This time he is sure of it.

Data Crabs

By
Deborah Walker

I hadn't mentioned my approaching birthday to my children. I guess I was in denial. So it must have been a shock when the police turned up at our home. They both tuned out of the data stream immediately.

"Mum, what's happening?" asked Dinah. Dinah . . . I wonder if she misses me.

I didn't know what to say. So I just said it, "I'm fifty today."

"No!" Dinah collapsed onto the settee.

Pete's reaction was slower. He's already showing signs of the brain deterioration that took his father. Pete would not embarrass his children by living too long.

"No . . . Ma . . ."

I patted him on the cheek. "It's okay, Pete. Don't you worry about it. You go back to your show."

"Come along ma'am," said one of the officers. They both looked embarrassed. It was an unpleasant duty for them.

I reached for my handbag. I looked at Dinah and Pete. They'd be okay without me. The house would run smoothly, the food would arrive, the machines would keep the rooms nice and clean. A thought occurred to me, "Will there be data streams under the sea?"

"Of course, ma'am."

That was a relief. I'd been watching Sunrise Palace for fifty years. I wouldn't want to miss an episode.

~*~

We bathe in artificial light in the Aqua Institution. The walls are thick, made of dense, strange metal. Trevor Bimble says the machines mine the metal from asteroids. No Earth-found compound could withstand the enormous pressure down here. The underwater currents knock against the walls of our home. I worried at first that it wasn't safe, but after a month I got used to it. You get used to everything, eventually.

I'm expected to work down here. Work! Me! It's all very strange.

We're allowed four hours a day of data stream, so I can still watch Sunrise Palace, but only in the attenuated version. A punishment, I guess, for growing old or for being mad.

I work in the factory. The people who are like me, the old ones, cluster together. This is a facility for the insane and for the old. I never expected to be here. I never expected to pass my fiftieth birthday. Who does? Maybe only one person in a hundred thousand, certainly nobody in my family had ever done such a careless thing.

Mickey, who's fifty-five, works beside me. He's been certified sane, but I'm not so sure. There's something about the light here, working constantly under fluorescent lighting that might drive a person mad.

Mickey keeps up a monologue while we work, "I shouldn't be here. Out of sight out of mind. The other people don't want to see us. We're a waste of space. We make everyone uncomfortable. So, they send us out here, under the sea. Make us live in these metallic snow globes. Like we don't deserve to feel the sunshine. Natural light is not a right it's a privilege, and it's slipped out of our fingers. We're the fluorescent people. We deserve it, but every now and again the machines make a mistake. I'm not mad, you know, Hester."

"No," I say patiently. "You're not mad, Mickey. You're just old, like me."

I wonder what my children are doing. Are they working for my release? Are they petitioning the government for an exception? I don't know what grounds they'd give. I was never exceptional. I just did what everyone else did: had children and enjoyed myself watching Sunrise Palace. I think that Dinah will be trying. Poor Pete wouldn't be able to manage anything like that.

A stream of data activates my computer screen. I work on input analysis. There's so much data to be collated. It's surprising how much actual human input is needed to refine and interpret the data. I'd always assumed that the machines did everything. I didn't realise that data was refined by the mad and the old here under the sea. Live and learn, eh?

~*~

After my morning work session, I eat a sandwich at the canteen.

Then I am at a loss what to do. Usually I would catch up on the events of Sunrise Palace. But the data streams are down – again. I decide to take a walk. The Aqua Institution is a mile square.

As I run my hands over the cool metal surface, feeling for leaks, I hear a jangling sound. I turn to see Bertha. She wears a necklace made of pound coins threaded together like beads, they make a jingle-jangle noise as she walks. The pound coins sway as she ambles towards me. They're a symbol of her status as Queen Bee of the Institution.

I have no decorations. Some of these people have been here a very long time. They've had more time than me to collect their relics. Until six months ago I used retinal credit like every other normal person. If found a coin, I wouldn't have even picked it up. It would have no value to me. But here I long for even a penny to show that I'm not a loser. Symbols change with circumstance. Down here the abandoned monetary system has reclaimed its status.

Bertha appears to be coming over to me. I look around. There's no one else here. I straighten my resolve.

"I hear that you're not mad." Bertha's breath stinks of sea water.

I shrug modestly, trying to indicate that although I was fully sane it wasn't something that I wanted to brag about.

"You don't look fifty."

I shrug again

"I'm mad you know."

I don't know what to say. Should I congratulate or commiserate?

"I'm mad like a fox."

"Crazy." It just slipped out.

"'Beg pardon."

"You're crazy like a fox."

Bertha punches me on the shoulder. "I like you. Even though you're scared stiff, you still correct me." She looks at me thoughtfully. "Are you sure you're sane?"

"I'm sane alright. I'm here because I'm old, not crazy, or mad, or whatever else you want to call it." I don't care what she thinks of me. I wish she'd just clear off, and leave me be.

"You'll do," she announces. I've apparently passed some type of test. Or maybe it was because I was sane, not many of us down here.

"Damn salt gets into everything here," says Bertha shaking her head. "Most of all it gets into your head. And the data crabs get free. They scurry here and there. Nipping a little bit, having a taste of whatever they fancy."

I smile, while out of the corner of my eye I look for a distraction to get me out of this conversation.

Bertha seems to be expecting some sort of response, so I venture, "Very nice."

She stares at me. The fluorescent light bounces off her eyes.

"Very nice?" She frowns. "Never mind that. Come to my laboratory at six tonight."

"Oh right. Okay then."

She leaves me. I hear her mutter, "Don't know what he sees in her." I listen to her clanking jangles receding into the distance.

~*~

I work in the factory again in the afternoon. I'm only a simple data processor. Some of the mad have more demanding roles. The machines aren't very inventive. They can only follow the outlines set up for them. They can't create anything new. So if any alterations are needed to, say, the food distribution centres, it needs to be done here. I just process the steady stream of data collected from the electronics in people's heads. The machines collate it, and I use my human mind to look for odd patterns. If I find anything, I pass it onto the laboratories and they sort it out.

Trevor comes up to me. He's the leader of us oldies. He's been here a long time. Rumour has it that he's seventy. I never fail to marvel when I see him. The patterns of his skin are marvellous to me. I never knew that the human skin could enfold upon itself like that.

He touches my shoulder in a friendly gesture.

"Hello, Hester. How are you holding up?"

"I miss Sunrise Palace," I say. For the past two weeks, we haven't received any entertainment. Apparently there's something wrong with the reception down here. It makes me angry. To deny us our basic human rights to entertainment is callous.

"Ah, well. I'm sorry that you're upset," said Trevor. He's still got his hand on my shoulder.

"I miss the story so much. I think I'm going to die if I don't find out what's happening on Sunrise Palace." But even as I say the words they sound a bit pathetic. Is that really the worst of my troubles? I'm in an institution under the sea, for goodness sake.

"I'm sorry for you." His sympathy makes me feel a bit better. I look forward to his visits. Even though he's old, he's still interesting. "Bertha came to talk to me today. She really is mad, isn't she?"

Trevor smiled. "It's just her way. Her way of coping down here.

She's got a fine mind."

I don't want Trevor to talk about Bertha like that, like he cares about her. I feel a stab of regret when Trevor moves on to Mickey. I wish I could have been more interesting so that he would have stayed with me a little longer.

"Hey, Mickey."

"I shouldn't be here you know, Trevor."

"I know, my friend. None of us should be here." Trevor turns and looks at me as he says that.

~*~

When the factory shift finishes, I make my way over to Bertha's laboratory. I'm thinking about Sunrise Palace. It's a strange thing to be committed to a show for forty years and then to have it ripped away from you. But then I thought it was a strange thing to watch a show for forty years. It seemed to me as if my real life outside the Institution was more about Sunrise Palace than anything else. Eight hours a day of quality programming issued directly into my mind. I'd lived in Sunrise Palace all of my life. It was only during the intervals that I conducted the other business of my life.

I missed it dreadfully.

~*~

Bertha's the leader of the mad in the Aqua Institution. They outnumbered us oldies four to one. She's rumoured to have invented hundreds of strange and wonderful items in her laboratory, but I doubt that is really true. There isn't too much time in life to do stuff like that. You have to be committed to your program. Still, if the data streams were patchy down here, I imagine you could get some inventing done when they were offline.

I wonder what I might have done in my real life if the data streams had ever gone offline. But of course they never did. Could you imagine that? There'd have been riots.

~*~

Bertha wears a white lab coat and thick glasses. They make her look intelligent.

And Trevor's here too.

"Come over here, Hester." He waves me over to a machine. "This is an electron microscope."

"I know," I say. Does he think I'm some sort of idiot? I remember seeing one on the data stream once.

There are some teenagers here, wearing lab coats, doing experiments. It doesn't seem fair, really. What kind of life will they have down here?

I walk over to the microscope and look down through the eye pieces. Through the lens I see some shapes, circular bodies with elongated legs. "What are they?"

"Data crabs. I invented them," said Trevor. He's standing very close behind me.

"Very nice."

"Very nice! Is that all she can say," Bertha pushes me aside and puts her eyes to the microscope.

I try something else, "What do they do?"

"They burrow into peoples' minds," says Bertha. "They'll break down the electronics wired into people's brains."

That didn't sound good. That sounded a bit mad. "Why would you want to do that?"

"Are you sure she's the right one?" asks Bertha looking up from the microscope.

"She'll do just fine," says Trevor. I don't know what he's talking about, but I feel proud that he trusts me.

Bertha sighs. "I'm not so sure, Trevor."

"Bertha, we've already discussed this. They're my invention. I get to choose the carrier."

I look at the way Bertha's looking at Trevor. I've seen that look many times before on Sunrise Palace. Bertha's in love with him. And I think she's jealous of Trevor's interest in me. I feel like this situation is getting away from me. I ought to say something. "I don't understand," I say. "What will the data crabs do? Why would you want to mess with peoples' heads?"

Bertha sighs again. But, Trevor smiles at me, "The data crabs will make everyone free. They'll destroy the data stream network. They'll make everyone human."

I can't believe it! "Why would you do that? Everyone loves the data streams." My voice is loud and harsh. How dare they? How dare they try to destroy Sunrise Palace?

Bertha smiles sarcastically. "Oh yes, the data streams are just great. Every wondered why people died at fifty, Hester?" Most people anyway?

Every wonder why everyone dies of brain damage?"

Because of the data streams? Was that what she was implying? People died because of the data streams? My son, Pete, was he ill because of Sunrise Palace?

"Ever wondered why we're all mad down here?" asked Bertha.

What kind of question was that? "You were born mad, I guess."

"We're not compatible with data stream technology. The machines don't want us around, reminding everyone that you can live without a head full of wires. Just like they don't want you around, reminding everyone that people can live beyond fifty. People might start asking questions."

"The data crabs will dissolve the connections," says Trevor. "People will people again."

"But what will be the consequences?" I ask.

"There will be an adjustment period, certainly," says Bertha.

More like anarchy I thought.

"But the thing is . . ." I say.

Bertha interrupts me, "The thing is people ain't human anymore. There are too many wires for people to make any real decision for themselves."

Trevor puts his hand on my shoulder. "We've arranged for you to be released. I want you to be the one who releases the data crabs, Hester. I want you to be the one to free everyone. "

"Why not Bertha?"

Bertha smiles at me, "You know that I said I was mad. Well, I reckon I am. I like it here. We've enough food to last us a couple of lifetimes. I don't want to go outside."

I don't think she's mad anymore. I think she's like no one I ever met. But I'm afraid of what she and Trevor are planning. "You shouldn't do it," I say.

"We've done it already," says Trevor.

"What?"

"We released the data crabs two weeks ago into the Aqua Institution air vents."

No more Sunrise Palace – ever?

Trevor nods. "Think about it, Hester. You've been off the data stream for two weeks. Don't you feel better? Aren't you starting to think again? To feel things that you've never done before?"

I can see that Trevor wants me to do it. He looks at me in such a way that I want to make him proud of me.

"What about my children?" I ask. "I don't want to do anything to hurt them."

Trevor takes my hand and says quietly, "What do you think they're doing right now. Are they living their lives? Or are they wired into Sunrise Palace?"

~*~

I'm released from the Aqua Institution. Bertha has somehow managed to alter the records. Bertha has arranged to have me released at sunrise. And I laugh when sunlight touches my face. In my exhaled breath a stream of data crabs emerge, invisible and silent they will change everything. With every breath I take I will change everything. I stare at the sunrise for a few moments, before continuing my journey.

The First Price

By
Benjamin Sperduto

"You seem a little more comfortable today. Have you been getting out of your apartment a bit more?"

The words were distant echoes, each one bouncing from one end of his skull to the other until they merged into an indeterminable murmur.

By the time the noise receded, she was already dumping more of it onto him.

"Well, you look like you've been getting some sun, at least."

A sharp, staccato ripple broke through the droning.

She might have laughed.

"Do you feel like talking today?"

The pitch of her voice shifted half a step upwards as she spoke.

Another question.

He shrugged.

"No? How about looking up, then? Do you feel like we could start there?"

Questions, questions, questions.

Less than a minute in and he was already getting tired of her and her damn questions.

"Lyndon?"

He raised his head slowly, letting his gaze pass over his cheap khaki pants and then creep gradually across the laminate surface of the coffee table until it reached the splayed out cables feeding into her diagnostic machine. They were a tangled mess, but the console wasn't in much better shape. Its thin, metal casing was dented and cracked in several places; the spindly sensors and instruments sticking out of it were so rickety that they might as well have been held together with tape. The thing probably hadn't been serviced in years. Firmware was probably more out of date.

An articulated arm uncoiled itself from the center of the console like a scorpion's tail rising up to strike. He almost would have preferred a venomous stinger to the sensor suite that was packed into the appendage's bulbous tip.

A quick scan would reveal everything that his silence sought to conceal: metabolic rate, toxicology, brain activity, blood pressure, electrical impulse levels, the works.

She didn't like secrets.

"Trouble sleeping again, I see."

Lyndon looked past the device to see her sifting through the data that its sensors were relaying to her tablet. She must have caught his movement, her eyes snapping upward before he could look away.

For a painful fraction of a second, she made eye contact.

She might have smiled before Lyndon looked down.

"I sleep fine," he said.

"I'm glad to hear that, but how many hours of sleep would you say you're getting?"

Her voice was piercingly clear, always tuned to just the right frequency, one that couldn't be ignored.

He shrugged, his head sagging towards his left shoulder.

"Three hours, maybe four?"

There was no sense in lying about it. Not with that damned machine frisking him all the time. He managed to confuse it once with a combination of contradictory answers and forced emotional reactions, but lying to a machine wasn't the same as lying to a human There was no way to do both at the same time. When it gave her a false reading, she just smiled that practiced smile of hers and kindly asked him to cut the bullshit.

"I think we've talked about this before, Lyndon," she said. "There are more and more studies coming out that show the effects of sleep deprivation on emotional well-being and productivity."

There would be at least three such studies waiting in his inbox by the time their session was through. They were probably already en route.

She had a study for everything.

Lyndon nodded slightly.

"Still having trouble letting go of the day?"

"I guess."

"How many hours are you working on an average day?"

Lyndon tried to do the math quickly. He glanced at his hands to tick numbers off with a flex of each digit.

"I don't know. Fourteen? Sixteen? Depends."

"Any days off?"

He let out a faint grunt; it was the closest he could get to a chuckle. "Not really."

"Can you remember the last time you had a day off?"

He sighed. There had been that day he went to get his transit pass renewed. He'd been due for a full assessment diagnostic this year; insurance liability, they said. Stood in line all day for a med-droid to tell him to cut back on his caffeine. The rest of the day was a blur, though. He might have gotten something to eat afterwards, but maybe not. Didn't much matter; he was back in his chair next thing he knew.

When had that been? A week ago? Two? Surely not three, was it?

"Week and a half or so, I guess," he said.

The answer did not provoke a reply.

Lyndon fell into the trap, glancing up and meeting her concerned gaze.

The machine on the table hissed softly.

She smiled. It was the softer one, the one that didn't look quite so rehearsed. She saved it for moments like this when she wanted to convince him that she gave a shit.

"Have you thought about taking some time away, Lyndon? You must have bit of vacation time, don't you?"

He shook his head, but couldn't quite break eye contact.

"I can't," he said. "Not this time of year."

Her gaze was magnetic. Every detail of her blue eyes leapt out at him, held him with a firm, dispassionate insistence.

"You're entitled to that time, Lyndon," she said. "The enclave's bylaws are-"

"Yeah, yeah, I know!"

The machine buzzed excitedly, harmonizing perfectly with his raised voice.

She blinked.

The smile was gone now.

"I just can't do it right now, okay?"

She stared at him. Her eyes seemed a little less vivid.

"All right," she said, nodding. "I understand that you feel that way."

Lyndon sighed and looked back to the floor.

"We're almost out of time for today, Lyndon."

The voice was distant again, practiced and measured.

"I have you down for next month on the same date and time. You'll get a reminder, as usual."

He shrugged.

"Fine. Whatever."

Their sessions always ended the same way. She would tell him now about the terms of his counseling rights and the therapy requirements spelled out in a subheading of his employment contract. Something else about his benefits package and leave eligibility.

But the familiar drone of her voice rattling off procedural protocol did not begin.

He looked up to find her still staring at him, her eyebrows slightly furrowed and her lower lip clenched between her teeth.

This face was new.

"Can I ask you to do something for me, Lyndon?"

He didn't know how to answer. She didn't usually ask permission before telling him to do something.

"Sure," he said.

"I want you to think about what you would do if you did take that vacation. Think about where you would go, where you would stay, how you would spend your time there."

He blinked and rubbed the back of his neck as he tried to process the request.

Something rattled inside the machine.

"If you like," she said, "imagine you could take someone with you. Who would it be? What would you do together?"

The machine rasped as Lyndon stood up.

"See you next month," he said.

He reached across the table and pressed the sensor on the upper left hand corner of the monitor. The screen went blank, taking her image away and leaving him alone with the diagnostic machine.

It wagged its rickety appendages at him.

"Fuck you, too."

The thing clicked as he left the room.

There were three people sitting in the waiting area outside. He recognized two of them, but didn't know their names. The other one must have been new.

He didn't say anything, turning instead down the long corridor that led back to his workstation.

His shift wasn't even half over yet.

~*~

The chair had been specially designed for ergonomic comfort by dozens of engineers pouring decades of cumulative experience into producing the ideal centerpiece of the 22nd century workstation. Test studies had shown that it all but eliminated lower and upper back strain, completely prevented or arrested wrist ligament deterioration, and helped to stimulate circulation during prolonged periods of use. Once incorporated into the workplace, research indicated that medical claims associated with degenerative physical strain declined by as much as 90%. Healthcare savings in the first year alone were usually enough to cover the steep implementation costs, but the elevated productivity of a healthier workforce often helped to recoup the investment even faster.

Lyndon hated the damned thing.

His workstation consisted of little more than the chair and the array of keypads and monitors that were connected to it by dozens of articulated armatures. It was merely one of several dozen similar setups, each one occupying no more than a few square feet of space on the giant office floor. A small canopy covered each station, shielding it from the harsh fluorescent light bulbs burning just a few feet overhead. Although nearly every seat was filled, the room was silent save for his own breathing and the steady footsteps of the floor supervisor as he stalked from chair to chair monitoring the productivity of his subordinates. Sophisticated sonic dampeners prevented any sound from escaping each workstation, which helped to reduce potential distractions and unnecessary interactions between employees.

The supervisor stopped when he noticed Lyndon. He made a big show of glancing at his watch as if he didn't already know the time from the retinal display on his contacts.

"Get a lot out of your session today?" he asked.

Lyndon wanted to tell him to fuck off, but that would only prolong their interaction.

"Went a bit over. Shrink's busy today."

"No different than the rest of us, then. You'd best get back to your station; we're far enough behind as it is."

"We're always behind," Lyndon said.

The supervisor laughed.

"It just feels that way because we've added new clients recently."

Lyndon didn't see what was so funny about his explanation. Adding new clients was precisely the reason that they were always behind. By the time the department got around to hiring more people to deal with the workload, they would be shorthanded again.

"Make sure to check your messages," the supervisor said as he resumed his rounds. "Looks like it's going to be another long night for you guys."

Lyndon climbed into the chair's harness and slowly strapped himself in. Hundreds of tiny sensors embedded in the seat padding detected his presence, each one sending a different signal to the many processors that helped to regulate the occupant's comfort. Sheets of nano-motors woven into the fabric activated to massage his muscles while thermal regulators worked to keep the temperature of his skin constant. The leg clamps disengaged as the mag-lev field kicked on, leaving the chair floating tranquilly in the air.

Keypads, touchscreens, and display monitors swung into position all around him as the chair's armatures contracted like long, skeletal fingers over the seat. A few quick keystrokes brought the system online and the monitors glowed to life. The narrow screen floating to his left displayed his current task load; it had more than doubled since he left his station.

He reached up and tapped the first item on the screen.

Topic: 2034 Metro Phoenix Riots.

Client: Suncast Media.

The client's information unfolded across several screens. News reports, blog entries, video clips, text messages.

A single request loomed above the jumble of raw, unfiltered data.

Query: Sources point to military cover-up and clandestine plot to destabilize problem city; please verify.

Lyndon sighed.

Sifting was a thankless task. The pile of information thrust upon him by the client would only scratch the surface of the hoard of available data spread across the antiquated databanks of the old Internet. There would be gaps, of course; virtual records lost for all time owing to equipment failure and memory corruption from the widespread system crashes some fifty or sixty years ago, back when the old network started to crumble under its own weight. What remained was a disorganized heap of virtual trash, an archeological relic of the nascent information age. Facts mingled with fictions, knowledge with pseudo-knowledge, truths with half-truths. It was a minefield of consciousness; stumbling upon an unseen fallacy could shred reputations as surely as hot shrapnel tore through flesh.

Lyndon didn't bother looking at most of the client's information. There was no point in trying to verify the accuracy of data that lacked anything that might pass for research. He fed the unsourced info into a collator program and let it filter through the nonsense in search of firm consistencies while he went to work sifting through the harder data. As he skimmed over several screens of text, he flagged inaccuracies and assumptions that betrayed a lack of methodological rigor and dumped the offending files into the collator.

The data he was left with painted a clear picture of the event in question. There were statistics on unemployment rates, water shortages, and housing prices throughout Metro Phoenix. A few studies on political paralysis at the state and local level drew connections between the statistics and the simmering social tensions that led to the outbreak of violence in the summer of '34. There were records chronicling the eventual military response, imposition of martial law, and subsequent federal administration of the metro.

Nearly all of the more scintillating stories surrounding the riots were gone. The collator traced the allegations of clandestine conspiracies to hundreds of stories connected to similar events. Some of the results even went back to fictional sources like television shows or spy novels. Most claims had been repeated so often in so many different forms that they were taken uncritically as articles of faith, situating themselves deep within prevailing narratives of "reality" that ran through the old Internet like swirling currents of a powerful river waiting to pull down unwary swimmers.

Lyndon was already typing his response when the when the collator finished its exhaustive search cycle.

Sources unreliable; no verifiable evidence of plot or cover-up beyond organizational incompetence; see attachment for filtered results. Thank you for turning to Veri-Finder Systems for your research data needs.

He paused for a moment before continuing.

Not that you really give a damn anyway. I don't expect you to ignore all the shit that I just told you isn't true. Now that all the data is nice and organized, go ahead and make whatever truth you want out of it. It's not like anybody will fucking know the difference, is it?

Although he derived an impish glee from seeing his sentiments in text form, he quickly deleted them before transmitting the response.

The client request blinked twice and then vanished from the workload screen after he sent his reply. He glanced at another screen to verify his performance.

Time: 10 minutes 24 seconds. Files Sifted: 16. Files Collated: 151.

"Shit."

He was halfway through his second client request when a message icon appeared on one of the touchscreens. After answering the query, he tapped the icon to view the message.

A review of your recent workload has indicated that your average performance time has exceeded the contractually mandated threshold of eight minutes and fourteen seconds per client. In order to refine techniques for conducting optimal reviews, please complete the Veri-Finder Systems Performance Efficiency program at the conclusion of your shift. Also, to remind you of the importance of our obligations to the clients who depend upon our swift and accurate services, please review Chapter 1, Section XI, Pages 16-19 of your Veri-Finder Systems employee handbook and complete the attached assessment. Thank you for your diligent work and for taking these measures to improve your performance.

There was a small box below the message. He tapped it to send an automated reply that informed his superiors that he had both received the message and would comply with its dictates.

The Performance Efficiency program was anything but efficient. Lyndon had taken the interactive tutorial several times before and hadn't managed to complete it in less than two hours. The policy assessment was hardly difficult, but it would take at least an hour to review the materials and answer the adaptive prompts accurately.

There were still more than five hours left on his shift.

Before turning back to the workload screen, Lyndon noticed four unread messages in his inbox. They all bore the same subject heading.

FWD: New Sleep Deprivation Studies.

He let out a single, mirthless laugh as he pushed the message screen aside and opened the next client request.

~*~

The monorail car was as tightly packed in the late evening as it was at midday. Half of its occupants were staggering homeward, scarcely aware of the other half that were mindlessly shuffling towards the impending workday. The scene would be repeated throughout the day, the rail system facilitating the constant cycling of the enclave's perpetually productive labor force.

Lyndon felt lightheaded. Jammed in the car's crowded walkway, the bodies pressed against his own were unfamiliar. The usual faces and odors of his commute had reached their respective destinations hours ago when the Performance Efficiency program was bashing him over the skull with its insufferable obtusity.

Not that he knew any more about the passengers from three hours ago than he did about the current batch. He couldn't associate a name with any of them and had never engaged one in a conversation that went beyond "Excuse me" or "Sorry," but there was a familiarity to their presence that he found mildly comforting. Together, they formed a predictable, closed eco-system, each inhabitant of their artificially established confines mindlessly co-existing like single-celled microbes clustered together upon a Petri dish.

He did not belong here. The people around him started when they bumped against him and their normally sightless gazes regarded him with extra scrutiny. Removed from his native environs, Lyndon was noticed and he did not like the attention.

As the monorail car pulled clear of the office building and the firewalls that kept its occupants cut off from the outside, his contacts' retinal displays were bombarded with messages. Most of them were meaningless, advertisements from various corporate affiliated retailers, political groups, and utility service providers or status updates and comments from strangers in his various networks. The rest were scarcely more important. A few friends going to the bar in their residential block or planning some work related event.

After spending a day sifting through antiquated data files, sorting out his personal messages seemed like an even more thankless chore. He fished his phone out of his pocket to access the information sprawled across the outskirts of his vision.

With a few quick swipes upon the touchscreen, he deleted everything and shut off the retinal display.

The ride to his flat was mercifully short, lasting only about ten minutes. He pushed his way through the mass of unfamiliar bodies as the car slowed, each one of them moving away at his touch as if remaining in contact with him might pass along some virulent contagion. The doors hissed open just as he reached them and he lurched out onto the station's loading platform so quickly that he nearly crashed into the woman standing at the head of the throng waiting to board the car.

He took an awkward sideways step to avoid her and almost fell over.

A lilting, delicate sound rippled through the air around him and Lyndon felt the blood rushing back to his head.

The woman was laughing.

"Watch your step, there," she said.

He turned to face her, but she was already moving towards the car. Her curly brown hair bounced with each step, the tips brushing against her shoulders. The hair obscured her features now, forcing Lyndon to reconstruct an image from the brief glimpse he got as he exited the car. He quickly lost sight of her as the mass of commuters on the platform shuffled through the exiting crowd to fill the spaces left behind.

The door slid shut and the monorail car slipped away quietly along the magnetic track.

Lyndon stood alone on the platform watching the train shrink into the distance. By the time it vanished, he had forgotten her face.

His solitude lasted for nearly a minute before someone walked up alongside him. Another person joined them before another minute passed. The flow of commuters increased steadily until a small crowd formed on the edge of the platform. Most of them kept a pronounced distance from Lyndon. Although some probably lived in his building, he was not a familiar aspect of their daily routine.

Lyndon turned and moved through the gathering crowd. The strange faces gave way before him without any resistance.

He felt lightheaded again.

~*~

Lyndon dreamed about the woman on the platform all night.

Although he couldn't remember the details of her face, his lucid subconscious was quick to fill in the blanks. Sometimes her features were long and sharpened; a cold, statuesque beauty chiseled out of the most precious stone. But just as often her face was round and warm, her smile and plump cheeks happily driving away his worries. She ranged from inhumanly gorgeous to endearingly homely without warning, but Lyndon cherished her company in all its forms.

No experience escaped his slumbering mind's hallucinatory attention. They hiked along wilderness trails, drank coffee in streetside cafes, made love in their wedding bed, and shared their deepest secrets with one another beneath the glimmering stars. But the joy of her company was marred by pain as well. She mocked him with his mother's words and struck him for forgetting something important to her. He caught her in his bed with another man. She overdosed in his bathroom. He killed her when she threatened to leave him.

The images and events flashed through his consciousness without any semblance of structure. She was everything to him in those moments: friend, tormentor, lover, victim, mother, and prisoner. He could feel her at all times, sometimes warm, sometimes cold. It was a dream more vivid than any reality he had ever experienced.

When he woke up, he cried.

~*~

"I see here that you've been having some difficulties with your job."

Lyndon didn't look up.

"That what my file says?"

The diagnostic machine let out a wheezing huff of air.

"You've been falling short of your benchmarks since we last met. Is there something going on that you'd like to talk about?"

"Why?"

"So we can help you feel better about yourself and your work."

Lyndon leaned back in the chair and crossed his arms. He glared at the woman on the viewscreen.

The machine snorted.

"No."

"I'm sorry?"

"All you care about is getting me back up to my benchmarks."

"Lyndon, I'm your therapist, I don't-"

"Bullshit. The company pays you to keep us productive. Isn't that why we have these little sessions?"

The machine was rasping heavily now.

She pursed her lips slightly, her blue eyes trying desperately to hold his attention.

"I think you need to take some time off, Lyndon. You just need a little space right now. Did you think about the vacation like I asked you?"

Lyndon felt the soft tips of curled, brown hair brushing against the back of his neck.

A sharp clicking noise sounded from somewhere inside the diagnostic machine.

"What's the point? I'll just have to come back when it's over."

~*~

The client's request flashed in the center of his screen.

Topic: 2019 federal abortion legislation.

Client: Yale University of Atlantic Technologies Enclave.

Query: Rider stipulations provided doctors financial incentive to perform abortions; please verify.

Lyndon had sifted through the same data for a client last month. It would be a simple matter to recover the results and use them again.

Such recycling could drastically improve his productivity.

He looked at the time counter tracking his progress.

Time: 15 minutes 03 seconds. Files Sifted: 0. Files Collated: 0.

There were several messages calling for his attention on another screen. All of the subject headings had something to do with efficiency.

He closed his eyes.

She was wearing the black dress that he liked so much. The sunlight filtered through the curls of her brown hair, leaving her face obscured in shadow.

She said something. A warm breeze swept over him as she approached. She touched his face. Her skin was soft and cool.

Lyndon opened his eyes.

Time: 20 minutes 48 seconds. Files Sifted: 0. Files Collated. 0.

"Shit."

~*~

He didn't go to the office the next day. A hasty message to his supervisor mentioned something about a headache, but he felt fine.

After the first few hours went by, he regretted the decision.

He got out of bed and paced around the flat for a while before settling on the couch in the living room.

None of the messages on his retinal displays caught his interest. Only a few even seemed to be addressed directly to him, but he wasn't sure if he actually knew the people that sent them. He caught himself sifting through the backlog of messages and quickly shut the display off.

The rest of the day felt long and empty.

He was already dreading returning to work tomorrow.

~*~

The monitor was off when Lyndon walked into the room, but the diagnostic machine sniffed at him as he eased himself into the chair.

"Yeah, yeah. Good to see you too."

He stared at the screen for some time while the machine hissed quietly.

The door opened behind him.

Lyndon turned to see a slender, dark-skinned man in a cheap, but well-fitted suit enter the room. He strode over to the monitor stand, rolled it out of the way, and pulled up a nearby chair to sit on the opposite side of the table.

"Good morning, Lyndon," he said, leaning forward to adjust one of the dials on the diagnostic machine. It sputtered briefly as something inside it recalibrated.

"Who are you?"

"Oh, I'm sorry. I guess you wouldn't know that, would you? My name is Isaac Vemel. I'm the coordinator of psychiatric treatment for Veri-Finder."

Lyndon nodded his head in the direction of the monitor.

"Where's Jenica?"

"I'm afraid that Ms. Ware's employer is no longer under contract with us. We're in the process of negotiating with a new counseling provider and there's going to be a bit of a gap in coverage until we get everything in place."

"Oh," Lyndon said.

The diagnostic machine rattled coarsely. Lyndon had never heard it make that sound before. Vemel glanced down at it briefly; he seemed as surprised as Lyndon by the noise.

"I've been looking over your file and reviewing your sessions with Ms. Ware. I do wish that she had reported your state of mind to me earlier; it would have made your treatment much easier."

"Treatment?"

"Yes, for Type 3 Social-Operational Displacement. Your case is quite advanced at this point."

"Jenica never said anything about-"

"I know she didn't. That's one of the reasons why we parted ways with her employer. Too many serious cases were not being called to our attention."

Lyndon felt lightheaded again.

"Given the circumstances," Vemel said, "I'd like to commence with your treatment right away."

"Wait, shouldn't you be going over this with me or something? I don't understand what's-"

"You don't have to understand, Lyndon. You've already consented to treatment as part of your employment contract. Once a diagnosis has been made, we can get on with resolving the issue. We'll have you back on track in no time."

The machine clattered hoarsely as Lyndon leaned forward in his seat.

"What if I say no?"

Vemel raised his eyebrows.

"On what grounds? Your contract clearly states that-"

"What if I quit?"

Vemel shook his head as the machine twittered. Something inside it sounded broken.

"Lyndon, you can't voluntarily terminate your contract without company approval."

Lyndon slumped back into his chair.

"You may not feel like it right now, but you're still a valuable asset to the company."

The machine wheezed like a dying cat.

~*~

A message icon appeared on one of the touchscreen monitors as Lyndon finished his report on a client's request regarding a 20th century musician.

Sources unreliable; no verifiable evidence of subject's association with human sacrifice cults or devil worship; see attachment for filtered results. Thank you for turning to Veri-Finder Systems for your research data needs.

The time counter blinked onto the screen after his reply was transmitted.

Time: 6 minutes 11 seconds. Files Sifted: 18. Files Collated: 204.

He clicked the message.

A review of your recent workload has indicated that your average performance time falls well below the contractually mandated threshold of eight minutes and seven seconds per client. This is a significant improvement on the results of your previous two evaluations. Thank you for understanding the importance of upholding our obligations to the clients who depend upon our swift and accurate services. Keep up the good work!

Lyndon closed the message and looked back to the client list. If he maintained his pace, he might be able to clear out the entire queue for the day.

~*~

The man standing next to the monorail car's door seemed to move according to a carefully delineated script of predetermined behaviors. He read something on the datapad screen, looked up to the ceiling of the car, sighed, looked out the window, and then turned back to the screen. Every third time he looked up, he scratched his nose. After completing the cycle five times in the course of two minutes, he craned his neck around to scan the interior of the car before repeating the entire process.

Lyndon watched the man's mechanistic habits closely. Such attention to minute details was, he had been told, a side effect of the treatment. It had proven useful to his job, of course, but it created difficulties in other parts of his life. He would often stare out his window for hours. Twice he had been so absorbed by the buildings passing by the monorail car's window that he missed his platform stop.

It took a great deal of effort to look away from the man, but he managed to divert his attention by sorting through the piles of messages flooding across his retinal display. He wasn't entirely sure why he kept responding to some of them. Although a part of his mind told him that doing so was a waste of time, he felt some compulsion to interact with these people that he was only vaguely acquainted with. They contacted him and he replied, an exchange that appeared to please everyone even though it seemed relatively meaningless.

A gentle tone sounded as the monorail car slid to a stop at the platform. The sound helped Lyndon to focus and pull his attention away from the myriad distractions surrounding him. He was vaguely aware that he was tired. His newfound single-mindedness made it easy for him to forget when his workday ended and he regularly found himself working several hours longer than he should.

No one seemed too concerned about it.

He fell in with the small crowd of commuters exiting the car. A comparably sized group waited on the platform to replace them. They exchanged places smoothly, their bodies scarcely brushing against one another as they moved towards their respective destinations.

A woman's large purse bumped against Lyndon's arm.

"Sorry," she said.

He looked back and stared at her. She was about his age and height. Her curly brown hair dangled just above her narrow shoulders, framing a friendly but forgettably ordinary face.

She smiled and shrugged.

"It's a bit of a wide load."

Lyndon said nothing. Her smile quickly faded, replaced by an uncomfortable, confused expression.

She turned around and boarded the car.

~*~

Lyndon ate a small-portioned dinner and took a quick shower after returning to his flat. He watched a news report on the state of the enclave's market performance and then got dressed for bed.

His alarm was set to wake him up early enough to exercise before going to work. Vemel said that physical activity was an important part of his treatment. Lyndon was not sure if it had any real effect, but he was being more productive at work, so it seemed worthwhile to keep up the regimen.

As he settled into bed, his mind turned back to the work that would be waiting for him in the morning. There would be a new list of client requests and he had resolved to get his average time under five minutes.

It did not take Lyndon long to fall asleep once he set his mind to the task.

He did not dream.

Jötnar

By
Colonel D. R. Acula

Her hands were cold and aching from the deep chill of winter's snarl as she fastened the buckle on her satchel. It was only in the darkest of nights that she would open it and peer inside at its contents. The kind of night that pierced deep into the bone and enshrouded the soul in ice. Those moments when fire or fur would not shake the howl of the wind. Those times when the only deliverance from the wrath of winter was found within...

She draped the stiff leather strap of the satchel across her shoulder and reached her hand behind her, adjusting it so it rested comfortably on her back. The night was middle aged and hours would pass before dawn's bleak light would fall upon the horizon. She looked forward into the darkness and heavy snow. She was sure of the way. Although she had never trekked this way in the past, months of preparation and mapping gave her the confidence to venture forth.

One foot in front of the other, yard by yard, carefully and slowly she made her way across the snow fields. It wasn't the cold she feared, nor was it encountering animals or others who may harm her. No, it was what the snow may have consumed, covering and obscuring. What may lay under her feet? This question daunted her mind. Many who traversed atop these ruins were never seen or heard from again. If one of the structures collapsed from the weight of the heavy snow, it may suck her down into the depths, trapping her in a frigid tomb.

The eye could not see the wreckage of what was once a sprawling city. The ice and snow denied any prying eye. As she walked, she distracted herself from the cold by recalling the stories from her Grandfather. The children of the village that she called home would gather around him as he recited grand tales of his younger days in the big city. He told them of life before The Change, before it got cold. But it wasn't the words of the shimmering, warm light of the sun that held her interest. Most who gathered around him begged for one more description of the beach, or of the park on a hot summer's day. But not her. She yearned to hear of and see the tall buildings that now lay beneath her feet.

He described them as great hands that reached up and up as if reaching out to caress the sky. He talked of places to make purchases, and of towers to live in and work in. There was nothing like this now, and her mind would run wild with imagery of stone and metal stretching up into the stars.

In her mind's eye, the shades of the thousands upon thousands of people that journeyed through the streets of the great city sped by her. The roaring sound of the prosperity of a bustling metropolis filled her ears. The lights that burst forth into the heavens, which could be seen for miles and miles, illuminated her smile as she drifted into thought. Her eyes ran from the street to the top of the behemoth buildings. "If I could stand on top of those buildings today, I surely could hold the stars in my hands." She thought, as she dreamed of an age before her time.

Then she would catch her over active mind, and remind herself that she did in fact stand above the buildings by several hundred feet or more, and yet, in her hands were no stars. This far North, the stars slept behind the clouds that spat out slivers of ice and snow. She had only seen the stars on rare occasions. The clouds above her village, which lay over a thousand miles away in the Southlands, refused to bear the light of the heavens above to those below. It was only in the trips to trade and barter along the gulf with her father that the sky above had granted her the privilege of seeing the stars.

Over fifty years ago the earth shook, and the oceans surged out of their beds to consume the land. After The Change, the snows began to continuously fall. Those who survived The Change waited until the waters receded, then moved as far south as they could to escape the monstrosities of the growing cold and the subsequent war that it initiated. The government established a new capital North of New Orleans, and the people began to build a new way of life. Her family was lucky. They had moved to Kentucky only a year before The Great Change. Her Grandfather, who enthralled children and adults alike with his tales of the great city of New York, was much younger then, around the age of thirty, when he moved the family to a small town in the Eastern region of the state. His uncle had fallen ill and he sought to take care of the man who raised him.

While the winds and weather of Kentucky were cruel and wintering, they were nothing like the arctic wasteland of the North, especially the New England region. Unlike where she was now, at least in Kentucky they got to enjoy two seasons. Winter, and Brutal Winter. Summer, Spring and Fall were things of yore. But life and a way of living in Kentucky was possible, as long as one was willing to fend for it. And unlike those who lived along the Gulf under the eye of the ever watchful New American Union, at least in the tundra of Kentucky there was a level of comfort and peace away from the police and military that patrolled the far South.

The New American Union had formed from the death throes of the old world, disbanding democracy, and suspending elections and all forms of government except for the Executive Branch. Their actions were justified due to the widespread scattering of the American populace, and the need to establish order in the midst of the conflicts that resulted. The new politicians declared that this was for the best, and that it was in the best interest of the people. There was nothing anyone could do. The Change had plunged the world into chaos, and it had come quickly with no warning. In one night all that was, was suddenly no more. The only option left to those who survived was to cope with the world around them and the oppressive grip of those in charge.

She looked over her right shoulder as she walked, catching a glimpse of the beading ember of the sun as it began to brighten the clouds far, far off. The night would shortly give way to a weakly luminescent day. She was certain that by now she had made it half way across the great city below her feet, and had made it that much closer to her destination without incident. If her instincts and mapping skills were correct, her feet now rested high in the snow and ice above what was once the lush and green Central Park of New York City. She was tired and exhausted from the long journey to this place, having not stopped to rest very much in the past two days. She almost gasped a sigh of relief, but stopped herself short. Taking in too much arctic air would hurt her lungs, even with the protection of the mask on her face.

She kept pressing on, each step seeming harder than the last. She was cold, and the longer she walked the colder it would become. Though her gear was carefully selected for its endurance in keeping the cold out, at this point even a fire wouldn't help much, and its light would only betray her position to those of ill intent. Most who made this trek died long before they reached their destination. The cold had claimed many a poor soul, and if the cold didn't overcome you, there was a good chance that the raiders who preyed upon those making this pilgrimage would.

Every year the raiders camped out, plundering what valuables the pilgrims carried from their homelands. She had already come across the corpses of those who had headed out before her. It was fairly easy to tell what fate had occurred. Raiders would leave nothing when they made the kill. They would only leave a bare corpse behind. The flesh was still warm when they robbed from the dead. If a body was still dressed, then whoever came across it only took what wasn't frozen stiff to the body.

It seemed insane for one to set out on such a journey, traveling to the Northern ruins under constant threat of frigid temperatures and heartless scavengers, ever marching toward certain death.

But it was a necessary journey. After The Change occurred, giant beings of frost and ice had emerged. Their breath had driven the winds and ushered in the snows. Some said they came from the depths of the planet, from a place in which they were imprisoned long ago, now released by the great quake that had shaken the planet. Others claimed they had ridden in on an asteroid, or on a moon sized chunk of ice that had slammed into the planet. No one truly knew and the true source mattered not. All that mattered was that they existed.

For the first ten years after The Change, a war raged across the planet. Human against Ice Giant. The already shattered human resistance waged failed attack after failed attack, until they grew desperate and launched an all out nuclear assault against the Ice Giant controlled North. The result was a truce. The Ice Giants and the leaders of mankind met, and terms of ending the war were reached. The Ice Giants agreed that they would not proceed any further into the South, if the humans would send one female from their lands each year to deliver a tribute, an offering.

Each year, one female was chosen at random by their local council to carry out these demands. And this year, she was chosen. While most went through bouts of fear and terror, screaming fits and vain attempts at running away, she didn't act out. She didn't scream or cry, nor did she try to flee. She knew it had to be done. She knew a great responsibility had been placed upon her shoulders. A great honor.

As always, the pilgrim was chosen months before the journey began, and a rigorous training regiment had to be undertaken. Nearly all the inhabitants of this new world had to fend for themselves, and this lifestyle had led them to be in above average physical condition, but the journey North was an especially grueling one, and only the strongest had even the slightest chance of success.

She had always known deep down that one day she would be chosen. It was as though destiny had descended from the sky and whispered deep in her ear. She had trained for much of her life to hunt, to weather the cold, and to draw strength from the very core of her soul. She was determined that if she was in fact chosen, she would not let her people down. Most importantly, she would not let her family down.

Her family had been instrumental in the rebuilding and institution of their village. While the outside world descended into the madness of The Change and all the horrors that followed, her family had stepped up and established the community she called home. She knew that she owed them and the future generations of her bloodline something more, something to look back and marvel upon when they spoke her name.

Ten more miles and she could rest. In ten more miles she would be on the frozen Long Island Sound, where she could carve out a niche in the ice and snow and finally get some rest. A tent was a death trap, a clear beacon to raiders. The only way to rest was to hide. A hole in the Ice wouldn't be very warm, but at least she would be away from the wind and the snow, and she would blend in.

The once wide body of water was now Ice Giant territory. Raiders surely wouldn't risk venturing that close to them. As she counted down the miles to the Long Island Sound, she grew more exhausted, yet at the same time more energized by the adrenaline surging through her veins. She felt as if sweat would burst forth from her skin at any moment, but she knew notions of such were silly at best. After all, she was almost numb from the extreme cold.

Five miles to go. She found a will inside her that lifted her heavy legs faster and harder than she ever thought possible. Four miles to go. "Steadfast. Continue on." Her thoughts encouraged her. Three miles. "Come on, just a little more." Two miles. "Almost, almost." One mile. "Yes! I can see it." She proclaimed in her mind. The glacier that had formed over the continent began tapering off ahead, and for miles all she could see was a declining landscape.

She finally made it to an area she felt was safe for rest, behind a snow drift which would provide some semblance of cover for her. She unsheathed her pick and quickly began chipping away at the ice. She didn't need to make too big of a hole. Two feet deep, and a little under six feet long. Strategic hits into the ice gave way to breaking points that made the process easier on her, and soon she finally reached the desired dimension and depth. She unpacked the sleeping bag and laid it in the hole. She removed her satchel, and joined the sleeping bag that would enshroud her body and cover her like the Ancient Egyptian corpse she had once seen in a history book. The falling snow would soon cover her and the hole, removing all traces that anyone had been there. This provided both ease and concern. Sleep too long and you will never escape from under the crushing weight of the snow.

She looked down at her wrist computer, taking note of the time as she lay ready to give in to sweet slumber. She held the satchel close to her heart. It contained the item of tribute. The Ice Giants demanded the thing that held the most value to the pilgrim. She smiled, her mind venturing to the contents of the bag. A moment of peace fell upon her as she vanished into the realm of dreams. She dreamed of home, and her Grandfather's stories of the old world. She dreamed...

BOOM-BOOM-BOOM

The sound shook her awake. Her eyes squinted as she looked at her wrist. She had slept for seven hours. She quickly slid out of her sleeping bag, breaking through the snow above.

BOOM-BOOM-BOOM

The thundering sound grew louder and closer, shaking her even more as she frantically rolled up the sleeping bag and stowed it away.

BOOM-BOOM-BOOM

She went to wipe her face, but the mask that kept the cold at bay prevented any actual facial contact. Her eyes still blurry from sleep, she tried looking around to access the source of the sound. She could barely make out a hazy, silvery shape in the distance, growing closer and closer. The ground began shaking violently, the sound growing more and more deafening as the figure moved closer. She dodged into a near by snow drift to hide.

BOOM-BOOM-BOOM

Faster and faster, louder and louder the sound became. It didn't take a clear sight to figure out the blurry image she had seen. It was an Ice Giant. It must have seen her, for now it was running right at her. She started digging through the snow drift, trying to clear her way to the other side. Her heart was beating faster than the thunder of the giant's foot steps pounding toward her. She rammed her hand through to the outside of the embankment of snow, pulling herself through with all her might. She hoped to run... She hoped to escape...

An awful pressure felt as if it would crush her torso. She looked down and realized she was flying through the air. Then, turning her head to the side, she saw it. The Ice Giant. It had grabbed her just as she was about to make her way out of the mound of snow. She was clenched tight in its fist, being carried away. She soared back and forth in the behemoth's hand, its arms moving forward and backward as it ran. But her fear began to dissolve as she gazed at the world flying by. From this height, she imagined this was what birds saw. What people before The Change saw. Her grandfather's stories of planes and helicopters trickled through her mind. She was certain this didn't have a good outcome, but for the moment, it was almost a dream come true.

After what felt like an eternity and more miles than she could have ever walked on her own, they came to a giant hole carved into the ice beneath them. The hole was circular, and brimmed all the way down by some sort of metal that seemed to hold the ice of the Long Island Sound back. From this height she could peer down, deep toward the bottom of the hole. Flashing lights and the sound of activity shot forth from its depths. It was evident that it had been constructed and maintained by beings of superior capabilities.

Since The Change, human projects were reduced to a much simpler level. This was a gaping abyss of no less than two miles across, and from what her best guess determined, much larger than anything humans were capable of, especially this far North. Indeed this was not the glory of human endeavor, but Ice Giant ingenuity. Rumors concerning the Ice Giants and their activities were in no short order among the towns and villages to the South. Yet, no one had ever mumbled or whispered tales quite like the one that unfolded before her now. But such lack of tales didn't much surprise her, considering...

The Ice Giant bent over, opened its hand, and rested her body on the ground. She hadn't gotten quite a good enough look at its face until this moment. The earlier swaying and motions that cast her about as the giant ran with her had only produced a blur in her eyes when she tried to look at the creature. But now it stood still, peering down at her with its cyaneous, glowing, opalescent eyes.

"Beautiful." The phrase fell from her lips before she realized the uttering of the word. In awe, she was mesmerized by the sparkling warm glow of its gemstone like eyes. The Ice Giant seemed to entertain, or perhaps incite her state of enthrallment, prolonging her episode of awe. Then a high pitched noise, similar to the squelching of speakers, burst forth out of the pit. It was a comparison she accessed from memories of traveling with her father to Louisiana. The government routinely made announcements in the coastal cities, and the sound was frequently heard before such imperial dictations. The Giant before her stopped looking at her at the moment the sound became audible, turning and dipping down into the pit. Other Ice Giants came from all around the perimeter and started to climb down. She stood on the edge, watching them descend. Although far away, she could see the bottom. The distance was hard to determine. More than a mile, perhaps two.

The Ice Giants were large in their own right. If not for their gigantic towering size, no doubt she couldn't make them out as clearly as she did. They gathered around in a massive circle, at the floor of the pit. "What ever are they doing?" She thought to herself as they joined hands, completing and locking the circle formation. The illumination of their blue hued eyes grew in intensity, until it was almost too bright to look at. She reached up to her mask and flipped a small switch, dimming the visor, making it much easier for her to spy on the glowing spectacle below.

The squelching noise she heard before was starting to sound once again. This time though, as it continued it varied in frequency, taking on a deeper, more bass like tone. The prior occurrence had lasted only a short time, unlike this second round. Before the sound was clearly emitted from the pit, the direction of this noise couldn't be comprehended. It seemed to come from all directions. Left, right, up, down. It began pulsating inside her head. She could feel it moving down her spine, through her arms, her torso, invading the pit of her stomach, creeping down into her legs. Greater and greater the intrusion became. She grabbed her head, trying to secure it, applying a little pressure to negate the feeling that it would explode. Painful, the sensation of the vibrations of the sound had become.

She staggered back a few feet and fell to her knees, struggling for breath, her hands pressing even harder against the mask that adorned her head. The bright white snow below now took on a dark reddish orange tint, and suddenly her face felt wet. She looked down. The tinted colors came from the blood pouring forth from her nose and filling her mask. Her muscles began jerking violently as the world grew darker and darker.

She awoke, her body unresponsive and numb. She tried lifting her arms, to no avail. Delirious. Confused. She coughed, sending a burst of phlegm and blood into the air. Through the blur that imprisoned her half opened eyes, she watched the substance glide through the air. Combating the daze that inflicted her mind, she noticed a strange room around her. She wasn't alone.

Her eyes began adjusting, revealing a clearer vision. She could see other females lining the walls. Her body started tingling, and sensation started to return. She slowly became more and more aware of her surroundings. She could wiggle her fingers now. Warmth. The unmistakable grace of warmth. She felt it on her fingers, and on her face. It had been so long since she had felt warmth. The morning that she had opened the door of her home to take the first step of this pilgrimage was the last time she had felt warmth that caressed her entire body.

She deferred her mind, shaking the thoughts that focused on the sensation of the room temperature. Her cognition became clearer and clearer. Her head was lighter, recalling the blood propelled by the cough that had careened across the room. Her mask! The mask that protected her face was gone. Someone... Some thing had removed it. Almost absent of thought to the Ice Giants, she shook her head, regaining more clarity of the situation. "The giants must have removed it." She concluded in her mind.

Her thoughts began focusing on the other females in the room as she regained more sense of perception. Her eyes scanned them for answers. Some females were alert, quietly watching her, while others were struggling to awaken, most of them still limp from being in a state of unconsciousness. Each was dressed much in the same fashion that she was, in gear that appeared to be appropriate for extreme cold weather survival. There were no more than a couple dozen of them. Her eyes ran up and down the walls, sizing up the small room. Trying to lunge forward was useless, as she fought to break free from an invisible force that kept her pressed against the wall. She turned to the girl that was next to her, and opened her mouth to speak. Mute. It was even more useless to try and speak than it was to break free from her invisible chains. She could think and process the words in her mind, but any attempt to give them sound was frivolous. This explained the lack of cries, and the lapse of desperate murmurings throughout the occupants of the room.

Suddenly, the floor of the room gave out a high creaking noise, the same sound an un-oiled hinge makes when force is applied to it. In the middle of the floor, a red beaming light burst through and shot up to the ceiling, as the floor itself retracted slowly back into the walls. As the floor opened further and further, the red light filled the room until eventually everyone was bathed in the crimson. It was blindingly bright, shielding whatever lay in the chamber below from sight, but the intensity was minute and unlike the previous blinding light she had seen before she passed out. Soon the ceiling started to retract, taking its turn to open and yield to a chamber above them. As it finished the process of sliding back to the walls, the red light below ceased, and she looked up. Far above her stood one of the Ice Giants, accompanied by a group of smaller, more human sized figures.

Now the walls themselves began to move away from each other, each side separating. As they cleared each other by some distance, they started rotating to all face the same direction. Each segment faced the beings above and continued moving, forming a single line. By now it was clear, this was part of the pilgrimage. Part of the offering. The walls, now locked together, raised up until they were level with the human sized beings. Although, their size was where the similarity ended. They were not human.

The wall drifted closer and closer to the figures, until they were a little over an arms reach away. She looked to the girl on her left, unable to speak but vividly displaying a look of sheer terror. The same reaction was found with the girl on her right. But she wasn't like the rest. She wasn't afraid. She was ready. She had prepared for this moment her entire life, expecting to encounter the mystery of the inhabitants of the North and face it, face them with courage.

One of the beings stepped forward from the group and looked each of the females over. As it made its second pass over the group, its eyes rested on her. Unlike the beautifully illuminated eyes of the Ice Giants, this creature had cold, dark eyes. It leaned in close to her, appearing to examine her before turning to its peers and shrieking some verbal ferocities that she could not understand. Some of the others returned the same manner of sounds. They were conversing. The creature turned back to her, placed its long scaly hand under her chin, and lifted her body up. Somehow, the force that kept her bound to the wall was no longer trapping her. She rose through the air as the being applied pressure under her chin. As she floated upward, the wall that contained the other females flew back. It appeared they had made their choice. The creature removed its hand from under her chin, and somehow, her body floated on its own.

The being slightly cocked its head to the side, pointing to her chest, and then pointing to its own chest. Confused by this gesture, her eyes and mouth fluttered, expressing her inability to understand the creature's expression. The being repeated the action once more, but she still didn't understand. Her voice still suppressed, she was unable to speak and ask for clarification on the meaning of the gesture. The creature stuck out its hand, motioning its fingers back toward its palm. A moment of realization occurred then. The offering. It wanted the offering. Whatever was in her satchel, the one she had cherished so much, the creature demanded its tribute. Her arms heavy and sluggish, she fumbled around and removed the pack. As the strap floated into the air, the being grabbed onto it and pulled it closer. Resting its dark toned claws on the buckle that secured the contents, its big dark eyes glared at her before jerking the satchel open.

A paper came floating out, and the being let go of the satchel to grab the paper. It examined the paper closely and turned around to show the others, handing it to one of them. They turned it over, held it up close and held it out far, then handed it to the one next to them. They bent it, folded it, wrinkled it, tried to study it, and did their best to examine it. After a thorough inspection of the paper, one of the beings stepped out of the group and walked to the being that had interacted with her. A shrill string of verbal snarls came from its mouth. It held up the paper and they all made the same horrible noise. It was hard for her to determine if they were pleased or displeased by her offering. She studied their movements, trying to gauge their actions as they emitted their nauseating voices, but their inhuman forms made her assessment impossible.

The being that had taken the satchel from her suddenly grabbed her by the leg and pulled her back down to its level, as she had now floated up too high. Then it wrapped its long fingers around her head.

"Thank you for your offering. It has been most appreciated." As it made contact, she heard a calm voice in her head. It was the being in front of her. It let go as soon as it made its point. The beings turned and exited the chamber, and the Ice Giant that stood with them grabbed her and followed the group through a massive set of doors. They ascended a long set of stairs. Beautiful and intricate geometric designs were carved into every surface the eye could see, and statues in the likeness of the strange beings adorned the sides. As they neared the top of the stairs, a gigantic throne came into view. Sitting on the throne was the biggest Ice Giant she had seen thus far. The giant that carried her brought her closer to the apparent King of the Ice Giants and set her down.

The massive being in front of her pointed, and the domed walls surrounding them opened up. She looked in the direction it was pointing and peered out the windows. A bright blue light reflected upon her face.

"Beautiful." Her lips formed the words, but no sound escaped. One of the beings put one of its cold hands on her shoulder, the other hand on the small of her back. Another being held up her pony tail and supported her head. Another stepped in front of her. Her eyes looked up and beyond the being, fixated on the blue light.

She felt a sudden sharp pain and a great pressure. Her legs gave out and she would have fallen, but the beings were holding her up. Her body shook as she fought hard to breathe, unable to take in air. The pain was becoming worse and worse, and she was becoming weaker and weaker as the blood poured from her neck and drained down to the floor, seeping into the crevices of the intricate geometric designs. As the throes of agonized breathing became unbearable, she looked out the window at the beautiful blue glow one last time, studying the clouds, seas and continents of the planet before her as she drifted into death.

Fudgesickles

By
Brick Marlin

The scratching in the ceiling returned, then quit.

Fudgesickles shuddered. He had been trying to shut out the spine-scraping sound without any luck. As unacceptable as hearing fingernails clawing down a chalkboard.

He sighed. He knew he would have to find out the mystery of the sound whether he wanted to or not.

But, his stomach growled. Hunger poked him.

The investigation would have to wait a few minutes.

Eating too many cans of Barbequed Beanie Weenies had finally run its course. Frequent visits to the bathroom more than twice daily acquired a sore rear-end. Other than a few boxes of stale Saltines, a can of red beets, and a can of creamed corn, poor Fudgesickles had nothing else to choose to eat for dinner, unless he wanted to make a trip to the grocery.

Not a good idea.

The moon already showed its face and the possibility of the mutant kids lurking in the dark, hunting fresh meat, steered him away from the idea. He preferred his flesh hiding his bones just fine, thank you very much, and had no desire to share it with anyone or anything. Earth had taken a slight left when it should have taken a hard right in this post-Shift world. To Fudgesickles' knowledge an evil entity had caused the fall of the world, shifting it into an apocalyptic realm by infecting each and every child.

He had heard this from his closest neighbor, old man Crannet. The guy had pushed the ripe age of eighty before being dragged out of his window in the middle of the night by those creatures. Fudgesickles figured this to be so after witness to the black birds fighting over the leftovers of old man Crannet in the street.

So much for an early morning visit to ask for a cup of milk.

Hobbling over to the kitchen window and sneaking a peek outside, Fudgesickles watched the current of the river carry the cadavers along, pre-fed from the automated, hands-free Neutralization Center up north; a very calm, very peaceful place where one could commit suicide if he or she did not want to live out their miserable days suffering from the disease called the Scourge, an illness which attacks the nervous system rendering the victim to live inside a motionless husk with only their brain as an active receiver. Some were immune to it. Fudgesickles being one.

Or who had chosen the path of cannibalism.

At any rate, Fudgesickles had never made the decision to pack up shop and trek north and commit the horrible act of ending his apocalyptic life.

He thought to himself: "What would the little ones think of their favorite clown killing himself? Why, it would be monstrous! Even if I did make it to Heaven the kids would turn their backs on me while I perform my act and make balloon animals and tell jokes and dance jigs (careful not to do this part on my prosthetic foot I should add) and stand on one hand with both feet in the air and hop around on a purple pogo stick and honk my blood red nose and squirt water from my carnation that I wear on the breast of my jacket and drive around in my very small car using its very small steering wheel while sitting in the very small seat built to specs just for me."

Nope, the Neutralization Center would be fine and dandy without belching out his body.

Living a normal, Fudgesickles life equaled a dedication to the children.

He held his chin up at the thought, breathed deeply, feeling the honor of being a clown – even if living in a dome beside the river eating stale crackers dipped in a can of cream corn. As well as a few more, er, cans of Beanie Weenies…

The scratching above started again, stealing Fudgesickles' honorable moment.

He ran a hand over his clown face and shuddered. He wished he did not have to solve the mystery. Not a fan of the dark, climbing up into the attic to investigate, did not exactly sit well with him. The enclosed, dark, claustrophobic-space scared him.

Wait.

He smacked the side of his head and said: "Cotton candy stuffed up an elephant's poop-shooter!"

He did have a flashlight!

So, still harboring the decision to feed his stomach first he grabbed the box of stale Saltines out of the cabinet and, sitting down in his favorite recliner, took a minute to clean the wax out of his left ear with his pinky finger, using the same finger to pick his nose, finding a small green treasure, rolling the ball of yuck using the accommodations of his thumb and flicking it away, he opened the box and began to eat.

Carefully inserted between the time he crunched and the time he did not crunch, he heard the scratching.

This action lasted for a whole two minutes, long enough to see something out of the corner of his eye, brown in color with a long tail, scurry across the floor with its six tiny legs and feet, grab a cracker crumb close to his right foot, and rocket away before the scratching above quit.

Fudgesickles sniffed, frowned.

He licked his red lips, noticing for the fiftieth time he did not taste lipstick, which he found pretty cool. His makeup had been tattooed into his flesh. He could still grasp the memory two days before the end of the world and his boss summoning him into his cube on the fifteenth floor, his boss' face a mask of crimson, asking him what the hell he thought he was doing, coming to work with a face painted like a clown?

Fudgesickles' defense began with a shrug and: "Boss, it's for the children."

His boss countered: "Children do not work here, Mr. Harnell. Humans and automatons do. There is no room for clowns in this workplace."

"Jenny Hineser down in accounting loves clowns and balloons." Fudgesickles smiled.

"She also has a very mild case of schizophrenia and sometimes think bugs are crawling across her keyboard whispering to her what the vendor on the corner of Main and Liberty cooks his hot dogs in. Good thing she can keystroke blindfolded while listening to her headphones, programmed to tell her what to type."

"Oh. Well, I could wear makeup or a mask, boss. How about one that looks like a hippopotamus winking at you, sticking out its tongue?"

His boss glared. "Harnell, do you see that chart on the wall, the one rating your level of sanity?"

Fudgesickles took a look.

"Your sanity is below the red line. In fact, four notches below the minimum threshold, labeling you insane. Adding this determination to the fact children are involved with your work, this company frowns on any association or frolicking with minors."

"I frolic because it is for the children. They love me!"

"So they do, and they should probably love you more now that you will be able to do your clown act fulltime. Get out of my office. Clean out your desk and leave the premises immediately. There is no room for you here anymore. After next Friday your last paycheck will be delivered electronically. I will see to it to have the computer wipe out your personal information. Good day. "

Fudgesickles never received the money in his banking account. Two days prior the Scourge escaped the government labs, caused by a careless scientist who dropped the glass vial, shattering it, shattering the prospering future of humanity.

A large group of religious people from a large dome out west and many of the church-goers dabbling in hypocritical thoughts claiming they were "saved and wore the shroud of love from the gods on their backs" said the world ended as the Good Book said it would.

The rest of the population said the end had just begun.

Fudgesickles agreed with the second statement. Killer mutant kids and Neutralization Centers weren't around before the world shifted on its axis, spun out of control, sputtered and fell into the toilet.

~*~

Above, the scratching pulled him from his thoughts.

Feeling courageous, he grabbed the flashlight in the kitchen cabinet over the sink and pulled the cord to the attic stairs. The hinges creaked when it opened, a reminder of an old coffin lid, adding an extra scrape to his spine.

Out of the corner of his eye, he saw the brown thing with the tail and the sextuplet feet dart across the floor, grab another crumb, and run off.

Fudgesickles paid it no attention and climbed the wooden steps.

The scratching quit.

Inside, he took a moment to gaze into the darkness. Too bad he did not have an outlet nearby where he could stick a battery-operated nightlight in the shape of a gnome's face in the slots, similar to the one at his bedside. The fear of never being able to find another battery had crossed his mind more than a hundred times.

Anyways, fumbling for the button, he turned on the flashlight — well, he tried to, having to shake it four times for the light to flicker once, twice, three times to work. He settled the beam on wet insulation caused by rain slipping in the many holes in the curved roof. Soiled cardboard boxes stuffed with Fudgesickles property of the past – board games, puppets, unopened clear plastic bags filled with multicolored balloons, a Jack-In-The-Box with a Mohawk and a very sad expression, handkerchiefs of various colors, each tied together in the exact length of a hangman's noose – as well as a large, white garbage bag nestled in the corner under the louvered attic window. An old furnace sat silently, long but died since the gas company decided to shut utilities down for good.

Just couldn't keep good help on the payroll to fight off mutant kiddos.

Below, the cuckoo clock on the wall cuckooed eight times.

Fudgesickles scanned the attic a little longer with his flashlight, not seeing a sign or hint of anything causing the scratching. He sighed, shook his head, closed the attic door, soon returning to his favorite recliner to sit and ponder this unnerving situation out again.

His stomach warbled and growled; evidently, the crackers did nothing to calm it.

He gazed at the front door and shook his head. Nope. Not going outside at night, he thought. Not on the agenda.

A minute later the scratching returned.

It really started to bother him. What would be up there, he wondered, scratching and such? Could it be mice?

He rose, returned to the kitchen, and snatched a peek out the window.

He wished he hadn't.

Aside from the fact of other cadavers, the body of a child face-down in the water floated along, one small hand grasped tightly to a pink teddy bear.

Fudgesickles shuddered. He supposed when rigor mortis set in, it froze your entire body, making this young girl grip her teddy bear for dear life. His imagination brought up the picture of the child walking through the doors of the Neutralization Center, breathing in the poisonous gas, slumping to the floor, grasping her only friend, a pink-colored stuffed animal which would accompany her dead body as it drifted into the afterlife, and the steel floor sliding open allowing the small corpse to drop into the water, enabling it to join the festivities of every other floating individual taken by the river's current.

Now very disturbed, he had the shakes. He cursed his imagination for giving him such a terrible scene.

More scratching.

He gazed up at the ceiling. This had to stop! Using his trusty flashlight, giving it a few shakes again so the beam would work, he peeked inside the attic again.

The scratching quit.

Huh.

He could have sworn the garbage bag had been further away, rather than before, closer to the attic window. And why a small rip in it?

Strange…

He stood on the steps for a little longer scratching his head, imitating Stan Laurel – hand over the top of the head, palm slightly bent, fingertips doing the job.

His stomach growled.

Fudgesickles returned to the kitchen and sorted through the cabinets over the sink, locating another box of stale Saltines, the can of creamed corn, and the can of red beets. He stopped. Wait a minute. He forgot the cabinet over the washing machine and dryer. Ha! He opened its doors, revealing garlic salt, sage, cumin, cinnamon, black pepper, toothpicks, napkins, an out of date packet of oatmeal, and an out of date plastic bottle of parmesan cheese with something squirming inside. Stepping on his tip-toes and using his hand he dug deeper, feeling around inside for anything else.

He nearly stumbled and fell backward.

Small automaton roaches had skittered over his hand, startling him, and squeaked and beeped and dashed across his arm and shoulder and took a leap, landing on the floor, hurrying into crevices and cracks.

Darn it! Forgot about those things! Should have kept them in the box when the mailman delivered them! Years ago he found an ad in a magazine for small robot roaches and thought it'd be really cool to have such a thing. Problem was, he didn't know they were fully functional when he opened the box, and since then have kept them hidden in the shadows until now.

Fudgesickles' black eyes gazed at the refrigerator nestled in the corner. Off limits. The fruits and vegetables he never ate were still in there, as well as the piece of chocolate pie, each possibly taking on a mutated growth spurt, wearing decayed organic flesh, harboring tiny razor-sharp filled maws ready to eat him.

He grumbled. Nothing good to chow on.

The scratching made yet another appearance.

Trying to shove away the sound and the hunger, Fudgesickles sat back down and picked up an old science-fiction novel and began to read. He wondered if the author had died by the Scourge or had made the trek north to end his life or turned cannibal or had been eaten by a cannibal.

At any rate, not even his reading or his thoughts could shut out the scratching. He slammed the book down on the end table by his rubber chicken-shaped lamp and climbed up into the attic, shining his trusty flashlight beam, not seeing the perpetrator of the scratch.

He did notice the garbage bag had moved further from the window, into a dark corner.

Fudgesickles decided to crawl further into the attic and see if he could see the culprit responsible for the bone-scraping noise. This. Had. To. Stop.

A rustling came from within the garbage bag.

He directed the beam, noticing another rip and something shifting around under the plastic.

Fudgesickles tried to sift through his brain, attempting to locate a memory. Too many doors were either locked or jammed. What the heck did he keep in the bag? Too many doors were locked or jammed.

Huh.

Careful not to step in between the wooden beams and fall through the ceiling, using his knees, he ventured closer to the bag, almost losing his balance, falling into a wet, cardboard box.

"Well, cotton-candy dipped in toilet water!" he spat.

He regained his balance and closed his distance to the bag. The beam allowed him to see another rip being slowly torn and another rustle of something shifting inside. A scratch came from within. A fourth rip made another wound in the plastic.

"What the darn?"

Outside, a scream and a shout. Seconds later somebody tried opening his front door.

He twisted around and moved across the wooden beams slow, cautiously, and as his foot hovered over the first step of the attic ladder to descend the plastic rustled louder.

He redirected the beam and horror drape over him, noticing how many small faces pressed against the plastic, their mouths wide open, their screaming unheard – except for the scratching.

Someone pounded on his front door, shouting.

The sound of a crowd drew close outside. Giggles, laughing.

Fudgesickles froze. The plastic ripped open, revealing six different children's faces set atop six different metal appendages connected to a beach ball-sized object with a kaleidoscope of shifting colors. Two large claws snapped at the air, sticking out on each side.

Fudgesickles gasped and his flashlight winked out.

The sound of boots hit the front porch and the one pounding on the door shrieked the same time Fudgesickles was bit on the cheek. Small teeth sunk into the front of Fudgesickles' throat and chewed out a wet chunk, causing him to drop the flashlight, and causing this lone, clown-faced man who wanted to scream but could not, gasping for oxygen through a torn windpipe.

Screaming boomed in the night air. Fudgesickles wished he could have matched it as his body began to lose consciousness, step by step, fading out:

"Come play with us, Mr. Fudgesickle," five different voices said at once; the sixth one had its mouth full of Fudgesickle meat, but managed to say: "Come 'ay w' ush, Misher Fushickle."

"We are so very afraid of the dark," the five said, "our faces being so cold…so decayed…so not buried properly."

The sixth child swallowed and said:

"Show us how to make balloon animals!"

The others added:

"Show us how to pull a rabbit out of your hat... If it doesn't move no more, that's okay, they taste better dead anyway...''

"Show us how to do that cool card trick!"

"Show us how to do summersaults!"

"Please show us, Mr. Fudgesickles, and we'll show you how to die!"

"You sure showed us, did 'n ya?"

Giggling from the kids fluttered throughout the attic while a scream gurgled outside, fighting to be heard.

The attic door slammed shut.

Something brown with six legs and a long tail scurried across the floor, snatching another Saltine crumb, while four small metal objects chased it and the cuckoo clock on the wall cuckooed nine times.

Scarecrow, Scarecrow on the Hill

By
Tracy Fahey

The wind is high this morning. The wet grass flips sharply against my legs as I start my automatic ritual. I count them first – one, two, three, four, five, six. I walk around them, checking, wrapping a scarf tighter here, pulling a jumper down there, stuffing straw in, tight and snug under the tattered clothes. My eyes hurt with the low, queer light of dawn, a dirty white glare that touches the hills with a sallow glow. I tip the scarecrow hats back, one after the other, to reveal blank faces of ratty brown, with rough black marks for eyes. My body is clumsy with tiredness, my feet stumble, heavy-footed, over each other. I take out the jam-jar from my pocket, and unscrew it. The contents are a dark, gelid red. I close my eyes and dip a finger in, then trace two daubs of red on the brown sacking that mimic where the eyes should be. His red glare follows me as I move on to the next. One, two, three…I stop after the third one, and let my arm fall to my side. What am I doing? What am I doing? I screw the lid back on with chilly, reddened hands and throw it convulsively into the long grass. My legs fold up like a deckchair and I sit flat on the damp grass, crying in great, draining gulps, tearing, hoarse cries that rise up into the still, ghastly air of dawn.

~*~

I remember Mrs. MacDonnell coming into our shop. It was first thing in the morning and I was sleepily filling a mop-bucket when I heard three things happen in a row like ticks of a clock - the ping of the bell, the creaking backswing of the door, and the excited suck-in of breath. Her apron was dirty and tied on wrong. Mrs. MacDonnell never left home unless she was immaculate.

'Mary?' From that one word I can tell my mother's surprise at her appearance.

'Oh Jane! I have to tell – I came over straightaway – You'll never guess-' Mrs MacDonnell's lips work over each other like purple maggots.

'Hush now.' My mother holds up a hand. 'Come through, won't you. We'll have tea.' She turns around and notices me. 'Keep cleaning the floor, there, good girl' she says, distracted. I see Mrs. Mac Donnell pass through the door to the kitchen, her hands patting down and untying her apron as she scuttles in. Of course I don't keep washing the floor. I lower the bucket, slop out a noisy mop full of grey water, and then slip my feet out of my heavy shoes and pad closer to the kitchen door. The old door leaks sound through its network of cracks and draughts. That's how I heard about our money troubles and the big fight that led to my father leaving. That's how I've heard my mother crying, day after day, in a dull, useless sort of way. I press an ear to the mottled, chipped paint.

'…I tell you, it's him. Oh yes!' Mrs. MacDonnell.

'Mary, now, you can't be sure'. My mother's voice, softer, more hesitant.

A large sigh. "I must say, I thought you'd be more excited. You know it's the only way.' My mother mumbles something inaudible. I feel a sudden, sharp desire to pee. I squash my thighs together and concentrate. Behind the door, the voices drop into a murmur. I jig up and down noiselessly in my socks and try to focus on picking out a word here and there.

'I'll be off then.' I hear the squeal of chair-legs scraping back on the worn lino. I step back into my shoes and lift the mop, churning it round the edge of the floor in a thick, wet tangle of fronds. There is a low-voiced goodbye, and then the bell pings again.

My mother takes the mop gently out of my hands. 'Go on, then, I'll finish that. You need to go and do the rounds on the hill.'

'But it's morning! You know I go there in the evening!' I am reluctant to go. I am curious. The ping of the door still hangs in the air, ominous, interesting, even the air here holds bubbles of possibility, barely touched.

Her face is sad. 'I think you need to.' She looks around the familiar terrain of the shop, the stacked shelves, the little fridge, the counter. 'I think everything is about to change.'

~*~

In the village we all have our jobs. Village-jobs as opposed to family-jobs. You'd call them chores, I suppose. Mr. Kelly from the village hall allots them. He's the nearest thing we have to a mayor. Some of us fix fences. Some check the locks on the barns. Others put flowers at the church door. The old men stand at the perimeter points of the village, at the crossroads, the church-gate, the new estate. No-one really knows why this is important, but it fills their days. They suck their pipes and watch the traffic, with every sign of enjoyment. My chores are different. I look after the scarecrows on the hill. It's nice up there, you know. I spend a lot of time on the hill, especially now, in high summer, when the coconutty smell of the gorse hangs warm and thick in the air, and the grass interweaves to form a springy carpet under bare feet. I secretly think that it's the best chore of all. These are my favourite times, sitting on the hill in high summer, overlooking the village, the late evening sun in my face, the silent ring of scarecrows at my back.

I've counted all six, checked them all and they are pristine, every straw in place, nothing that needs adjusting. From here the village looks so small. I can trace its perimeters easily, from the dark hedges around the church down the dusty road that ribbons past the school, the line of old estate cottages winding past the two pubs, the post office and the shop, down further down the road to the new estate at the end. From here it looks like any other place.

Nearer to hand, it feels like nowhere else. It is the place I was born in, the place I have always lived in and the place I will probably always live in. As I climb down the hill, the air becomes heavier, stranger; it smells of old dust and unopened windows. There is a feeling in the air here in the village, a feeling of inevitable endings, of rain about to fall, of shops getting ready to close, of gates swinging slowly shut. The fields stretch out like a neverland of wet mud-ruts. Down the road, the eternally identical view of the street and houses, the stomach-sink of sameness. It is a village forever trapped in a listless Sunday afternoon where the main street is dead, and clouds tremble on the edge of rain. Time is drawn out here, like old, stringy chewing gum. There is a dull rhythm to life here, a sense of seasons demarcated by matches, the steam threshing, the pattern and church holidays. Cars hum to life in the mornings and evenings. Apart from that there is the dead silence of overheated stale air in summertime, replaced by a cold, frozen stillness in the winter. We're different here. Ask anyone. Ask anyone from the neighbouring villages about us and they'll look at you sideways, trying to gauge how their answer might offend. If they're being tactful they'll say we're different. If pressed they'll say strange. If honest they'll give a more forceful answer – quare strange, I've heard them call us. It fits. But it hasn't always been that way.

~*~

I hear the children chanting as I scramble down over the slippery grass towards the village, thin voices rising high in the still air. They are singing the scarecrow song, the one that begins with the chant- *Scarecrow, scarecrow on the hill/ Watching over all until.* Their twig-legs skittering over and back, across the rope that thwacks solid against the road. I see a group clustered outside the pub, heads together, voices lowered. A pulse of unease clenches in my stomach, low and insistent. Something is different. I walk down the road. The trees along the street shade it dark green, I feel the heat of my arms turn to a welcome coolness as I walk. Everything is neatly ordered, the houses all in a row, the cars parked tidily outside, even the tombstones in the cemetery are ordered and precise. The village, although lifeless, is polished, except of course, for the new estate. A never-finished jumble of half-finished houses, it stands raw and awkward against the mellow stone and green lawns of the village. Seen from the hill it's all knees and elbows, half-finished walls and piles of building material. I wander past and kick at the dirty 'For Sale' sign that leans against the verge. I hear again the muffled sound of weeping behind the shop door, my father's angry, low voice, my mother's words twisting out between sobs —'You knew it wouldn't work. You knew!'

We all knew, in our hearts that the estate wouldn't work. Why we knew is one story. But the more important one is what we knew.

The oldest story told is our village is the story of St. Finn. According to the stories, Finn (or Fionn) was an early disciple of St. Patrick, spreading the new doctrines of Christianity. He came here, to our great-great-our-many-times-great-grandfathers and grandmothers. He stood on the hill and told them about a holy, dark-skinned man who could make magic, turn water to wine, return sick men to whole states. And when he finished they picked up stones and threw them. Threw them until there was nothing left on the hill but a melted red flesh-blur, heaped with splashed stones. He cursed us before he died, they say. He said 'Never prosper. Never leave.' In the centuries that came after, the legend changed, adapted. He cursed us, they started to say. They say it still, knowledgably, as the sun goes down, and men talk of dark things. He cursed us until we can make restitution. That's what the children sing about, a time that the curse will be lifted. That's why we have the perimeters, the scarecrows watching us, the locked barns, the fresh flowers at the church, a maze of ceremonies, generations of apologies, and endless, vigilant, anxious rituals of protection. It needs to be so, we say. It needs to be so until the curse lifts.

In the meantime, we are careful. Careful not to brag. Careful not to leave. There are generations of us here now; layered on each other, aligned through a series of increasingly close unions. We don't try to leave. Not anymore. Not since the last lot tried, not since the subsequent rash of accidents, the big car-crash, the drowning, the disappearance of the hitch-hiker. Now we hug the village close, close as the hill that wraps around it. But the caution doesn't banish the fear. This fear touches on the fringes of living here. You feel it in the evening when the cattle stop lowing abruptly, for no reason. You feel it when a branch snaps behind you on a dark night. You feel it when a dog starts barking, insistently, louder, hysterically at an empty yard.

I scuff my shoe against the old breeze block that rests on the road verge. Time to go back, I suppose.

'You'll kick holes in those shoes.' It's a friendly voice, but unfamiliar and close behind. I turn, startled. The stranger smiles at me, eyes creased in a sociable grin. His hair is long and the bright sun behind it creates a hazy copper halo. He is, I guess, in his late twenties, ten years or so older than me.

'What happened here?' he asks. The sweep of his arm encompasses the estate.

I squint against the sun. 'Well, the village came together to buy the land and hired a developer. He ran out of money before he finished and left. No-one knows where he is now. But the houses were never finished.'

He suck-whistles through his teeth. 'All of it gone? All that investment?'

I shrug. 'Curse of St. Finn', I say nonchalantly.

He laughs. 'I heard that story when I was a kid. My aunt is from the village. You know Jinny Kelly?

Mr. Kelly's wife. 'I do' I say, looking at him with frank interest. 'Her husband's the one that gives out the village jobs. I do the scarecrows.' We fall into step beside each other as we walk away from the estate down the dusty road towards the main strip of houses and shops. Dust puffs around our feet as we walk. His name is Ryan. He tells me that he is writing a book about the local legends in the area, and the St. Finn one was one that he was particularly drawn to. I tell him about the people who tried to leave. I make it dramatic, my voice low and meaningful as I describe their unfortunate histories. He is rapt, fascinated.

'So the scarecrows protect the village?'

I shrug, 'Maybe. That's what they say. The children sing a song about it.'

'I've haven't heard it yet. Look forward to that.' He pauses. 'So everyone still believes in the curse, right?'

'Of course. Isn't that' – I turn and point at the estate – 'Isn't that proof of it? Nothing goes right here.' He nods absent-mindedly. This is good. I walk proudly alongside him and feel vital, important. I know he is storing all this information I can give him. With an effort, I resist the urge to skip. 'And here is one of the barns. We keep them locked, you know. I can't really remember why, it's something to do with keeping the village valuables safe.' He nods, we walk on in silence.

'Well, I'm going here' I say, stopping at the door of the shop. 'See you around.'

'That you will.' He smiles again, that warm, creased grin. I stare at him. A watery, desperate fear fills me. My legs feel disconnected to my body, and my voice when I find it, comes from a long way away. 'Your eyes' I finally manage to say. His eyes are wonderful, strange, one blue, one brown.

He laughs. 'In another century I would have been burned as a witch!'

I watch him go, a heavy, hopeless feeling deep in my stomach.

~*~

I don't see him again. I don't see him at all till later the next night.

It had been a strange, thundery restless kind of day, the air rippling with hot, sharp gusts of wind, like an oven opening and shutting abruptly. Late in the evening it started to rain, a long, monotonous downpour that slapped the window panes with a splattering rhythm. I had a headache and went to bed early, burying my hot face in the cool underside of the pillow. Sometime later, I woke, tense. A noise? There is was again, a shout. I switch on the lamp and stumble towards the window, eyes blurred with sleep. There is a knot of men outside in the rain, with torches, arguing. I open the window, and the rain hits cold and hard on my face. There is a struggle outside, some shouts, the sound of a blow. Then I hear grunts, the noise of something dragging. Footsteps squelch by. I strain to see. They are carrying something heavy between them. As they pass by, I see them for a second, outlined in the warm spill of lamplight from my window. The familiar faces from the shop, the houses, the barns, the hills, all pass by. Between them they are carrying the heavy body. His eyes have rolled upwards, but I would recognise that long copper hair anywhere.

I shake, frozen in the window-frame, my throat works, my lips move uselessly. Ryan, I think in a sharp agony. In an instant, unheard, soft, my mother's hand is over my mouth, her warm body pressed to my back.

'Hush there, quiet now, she breathes in my ear. Her breath smells of milk.

I twist away from her. 'What's happening?' I scream. 'What are they doing?'

'It's what always happens.' Her face is in shadow, but I feel the sadness roll off her in waves. 'It's what happens every time. They think it will reverse the curse, you know.'

'It's happened before?'

She sighs. 'Twice that I remember. More times your grandmother would remember.' I start to cry helplessly, hot tears rolling down my face. She holds me tight to her in the darkness. Outside, a voice pipes up, a child's voice singing, thin and true;

Scarecrow, scarecrow on the hill
Watching over all until
Blue and brown eyes!
Brown and blue eyes!
How many red men must I kill? – one – two – three – four

~*~

I don't follow them. I am ashamed that I don't follow them. But I hear what happens, every bit. His cries tear the night air. At dawn the men take him away up the hill. Soon the village is silent again. All the time I don't sleep. I lie in bed, electric with horror, then give up, and simply sit at the window, waiting. Later, just as the sky is starting to lighten, I see Mr. Kelly knock on the door of the shop. My mother opens it cautiously, a crack. I can see his coat is splashed with mud and something darker, stickier.

'For the scarecrows' he says, passing my mother the jar. He nods slowly. 'You'll tell her what to do.'

~*~

I'm on the hill. I've finally stop crying, cold and exhausted, face stiff with salt tears. The sun is starting to streak a livid yellow across the bottom of the skyline. My head hurts with the horror of it all. I drop the jar. It falls, unheeded in the long grass. There is only one thing I can do. I get up and walk towards the perimeter, by the scarecrows, and on, through the wet stalks of corn, down the rutted path. The scarecrows stare blindly, after me. And as I walk, I feel a sudden marvellous sense of lightness. I shed it all like snakeskin as I walk; the shop bell dinging, the thick silences, my mother's low crying, the elaborate rituals, the pervasive unease.

It is only on the border of the village that I pause, and look back. I can feel it dull and low and insistent, low in my gut, the pull of the village, the steady drag of the familiar and the sour, repetitive rituals of life there. I hesitate for a moment before I start to walk again, slowly, and then with increasing rapidity, away from the village and into the woods beyond. Even the air seems to smell better, sweet and wet, with the green scent of flattened grass. I walk, surely and steadily, away from the darkness of my yesterday and towards the uncertainty of my tomorrow.

The Unnaturals

by
Michael J. Epstein

The cold, silent night teetered on the threshold, gently spitting Serug 99 off the street and into the once holy confines of St. Raphael the Archangel. Serug had first been assigned to report to Raphael, the patron saint of his September birthday, almost half a century ago.

"Father, I am here for confession." Serug had made this statement every Tuesday evening since before he could remember. Those same words meant something else when he first recited them. Things were different back then.

The Priest released the broom with one hand, dropping his arm to his side. His frock rustled, sending pulses through the thin, still silence and he sighed, "You are late my child. Confession ended seven minutes ago." He paused as Serug's eyes fell. As much as he felt a duty to adhere to The Code, Father Pilgrim knew that he could not leave Serug to face the inevitable consequences of missing confession. "I'll tell you what," he spoke with a reluctant pause, "I am still wrapping up some work here, so I'll let you complete your confession requirements late this one time, but you know this cannot become a habit. The Great Caretaker does not tolerate tardiness."

"Thank you father," Serug whispered as he followed Father Pilgrim to the confessional.

"Step onto the scale," Father Pilgrim said in a voice marred by the reluctant tedium of the state-mandated confession process. It hadn't always been like this. "BMI 18. That's good. Now please sit and plug into the purifier."

Serug bent down to grab the interface wire for the purifier, fumbling nervously to grasp the line. Each movement rippled down through the cord from his hand to the machine, lazily cresting and nearly inaudibly cracking like the sort of training whip used on a young boy who hadn't made his mandatory diary entry on time. Father Pilgrim knew that Serug was always nervous about confession, but he seemed particularly troubled this week. Serug 99 lifted his hair from the side of his head and, opening the clasp on the end of the cable, hooked the wired fangs into his interface.

Father Pilgrim turned on the monitor, which after flickering for a few seconds, settled in to display Serug's memories, starting at the moment immediately after his last purification. Pilgrim held the speed-change button until Serug's week flipped by at a rate of about an hour per second. Serug was never sure if Father Pilgrim could really even keep up with the display rate, but like clockwork, something would get extracted from his week by the machine that did require penance and purification. A few words and a promise to try harder was all it took to go on his way.

"Good, good Serug! Very pure this week," Pilgrim said with enthusiastic approval.

Maybe he was just tired and wouldn't bother to make Serug repent. Maybe that was an advantage of being last in line for the week's reset. The percentage readout on the screen was showing that the confession was nearly complete. According to protocol, Serug wasn't supposed to look directly at the screen, but he always did.

Pilgrim had always figured that Serug, a man who was clearly uncomfortable in his own body, was just peeking nervously, hoping that none of his minor transgressions would reach the threshold to trigger purification. Many of his congregants peeked. That made him all the more perplexed when the image cycling halted and the screen flashed bright red. For just an instant, as both Pilgrim and Serug saw the color shift, the church fell as silent as it ever had. Raphael's perpetually sad stained-glass portrayal suddenly appeared sadder than it ever had previously. The hovering presence of the almighty, The Great Caretaker, vanished.

The air was so thin that neither man could make a sound that would carry to the other. In that moment, not even Raphael's majestic wings could be imagined sufficient to lift them up to the heavens. Their eyes locked, sharing the basest feeling of fear, a fight-or-flight response they had inherited from the simplest creatures. Logic and reason yielded to lizard brain. The emptiness was not to last, however, as the entire block that cradled the church shook with thunderous alarm. The lights both inside and outside flashed with great urgency.

Although, as mandated, he was a non-believer, Serug locked eyes with St. Raphael and whispered a prayer. He turned away from Father Pilgrim, who reached silently toward him, and ran as fast as he could.

The fangs of the purifier remained locked and the serpentine projections of the device held to Serug's head as it detached from its own body. Many venomous snakes will conserve poison by dry-biting in self-defense if they believe their target is of no real threat to their wellbeing, and Serug 99 was no threat to the purifier, or the State that issued it, but he was undoubtedly a symptom of the growing illness.

The non-biological memory implants themselves weren't a real concern, but the idea that someone, somewhere in Capital City had the technology to create devices to deliver false memories to the purifiers meant that the panopticon would no longer be enough. The Great Caretaker could no longer be sure to help protect the citizens from their own destructive thoughts and ideas. This did not sit well with anyone.

In a matter of seconds, the streets flooded with uniformed protectors. The good citizens were told by pole-mounted bullhorns that a very dangerous man was on the loose and that they would need to take cover to protect themselves, and more importantly, their children. Still, they need not fear if they follow protocol, as the protectors would be certain to have the situation resolved in mere minutes. The record length for a pursuit since The Great Caretaker came to protect the citizens was ten minutes, eight seconds. While Serug 99 had a slight head start on the squad of protectors, he was not a runner trained nor destined to break records.

The head regional protector barked orders for the unit to move toward the perpetrator and then announced into his communications watch, "Deviance Squad Unit 108 in pursuit. Active pursuit time, 18 seconds. Cost: 36 credits." Serug was by no means a fast man, and the few hundred feet he had were unlikely to last him long... "Active pursuit time: 1 minute. Cost: 72 credits." "Active Pursuit time: 1 minute 26 seconds. Cost: 142 credits."

Pursuit costs were determined by a dynamic economic model that could account for market fluctuations down to the millisecond. It was actually quite a brilliant and efficient system and it led to very reliable estimates of budget surpluses and deficits in each region.

Serug 99 had nowhere to go. He knew it, and he didn't want everyone he cared about to be charged for his mistake, so he turned into the darkness, hoping the low light might at least partially obscure what was about to happen. The possibility of escape faded from his thoughts, but one troubling issue remained. Serug really didn't want to make The Week's Best Pursuits on television. The alleyway was his last hope, as low light often relegated even the most exciting chases to unpopular late-night-pursuit recaps. People just wanted something cleaner and more true at prime time.

Three protectors closed in on Serug 99. He was grabbed on each side by two of them, and did not resist as he was spun around and thrown face down to the ground. The third protector triggered the punch blade on his safety glove, and bent down to slice through Serug's shirt, revealing a two-inch scar on his lower spine. The head regional strolled casually toward them, reporting to his watch, "Deviance Squad Unit 108 pursuit termination. Total pursuit time, 3 minutes 7 seconds. Cost 5,832 credits."

A disembodied voice replied from somewhere inside the watch, announcing the outcome, "324 credits withdrawn from the personal account of Serug 99. Insufficient credits available to cover pursuit costs. Additional withdrawal of 5,508 credits required. Commencing withdrawal from family accounts. Insufficient credits available. Commencing withdrawal from neighbors' accounts. Tertiary financial sources secured, 5,508 credits withdrawn. Pursuit costs covered."

The protector who had cut open Serug's shirt now flipped him over. "Looks like no one on your street will be eating this week. I don't feel bad for them though. That scar must be months old. They had plenty of opportunity to report you. Now read us our rights." The protector shined a light into Serug's eyes, holding up a small camera.

As practiced by rote since before he could remember, Serug recited, "I have no right to remain silent. You have right to arrest me and to use as much force as necessary to restrain me…" Serug was blinded by the protector's light as he recalled himself as a child, parroting these words he never imagined he would say directly into a real protector's camera. The training protectors that came to visit school twice a year to test the children were quite enough for him already.

Things were different back then. For one thing, cameras weren't as good in low light. There was no way a chase like this would make The Week's Best Pursuits—not if the climax was in a dark alley like this one. But things were different now.

Fit to Rule

By
Stephanie Neilan

The king was dead. Blood drizzled down his wrist and dripped to the dust beneath him. Roc hit him one more time in the head to be sure. Except for a small spasm that jerked down his leg, the king didn't move.

Smiling, Roc tossed the stone to the side and sat down on the king's chair to wait. Soon they would discover the body and crown their new leader.

This was the day he had been dreaming about for years. Every boy does at some point, but most die before they ever get the chance. Those that survive the wilds and make it back have a chance at being king. They just have to defeat him.

If they fail, then they swear loyalty to him or die. That's what made his conquest so great. He had not been the first one to strike. He was just the last in a long line that spanned over a decade.

The former king had made many allies. Each one was bigger and stronger than the last. Brute force would never have won the day. That's why he had to wait. He watched. He learned. He found out when the king would be alone and then struck.

It had gone perfectly. Less than 5 minutes, and the deed was done.

Soon the women would be his.

All of them.

That was the rule.

The king was the best of the best. The next generation would be the best as well.

The first man to enter the tent grasped his sword as soon as he saw Roc. His eyes darted around the tent until he saw the body, then looked back. Roc nodded. The guard released his grip, bowed, then bent over to carry the body out of the tent.

Noise rose exponentially as the body was discovered. Women wailed and a few of the men joined in. Roc frowned.

After a few minutes, he lifted the flap and went out. Everyone was staring at the body. Some were draped over it. Mara, a short woman he remembered from his childhood, was measuring his body. He yanked the rod out of her hand. "What are you doing?"

Mara grabbed the rod. "What does it look like I'm doing? I'm getting him ready for burial."

"No. He will be cremated."

"But he was king."

"Was. I am the ruler now."

"This isn't right. He was a good man, a great leader. He fathered many strong sons and daughters. He deserves recognition."

Roc took the rod and broke it. "I said, no."

Someone gasped.

He scanned the crowd. Several people refused to meet his eyes. Roc raised his voice and addressed the men. "Your leader was strong, but I am stronger. Your leader was smart, but I am smarter. You failed to beat him, do you think you can beat me? When the great democratic experiments fell, our fathers agreed on one simple principle: Survival of the fittest. I am the fittest.

"Swear loyalty tonight or meet me in the valley of flight tomorrow. One at a time or all at once. I am not afraid." He pointed to two men who held his gaze while he spoke. "You two, prepare the pyre."

He turned his back on the crowd and walked back to the tent. He smiled as he thought about what he didn't tell them. If they didn't swear loyalty, then they wouldn't get the antidote to the poison he had placed in their water supply. It would kill them by tomorrow afternoon.

The next morning several men had sworn allegiance to him. The rest were dead. They never even made it to the valley.

After fortifying his personal defenses, he re-familiarized himself with the village and its inhabitants, especially the women. Several girls had turned into real beauties. Every night, he called a new one into his tent.

The only ones he overlooked were already pregnant. It was time to start his own legacy. The number of young children living in the village confirmed how fertile this group of women was.

Several months passed. He survived two assassination attempts without much difficulty, but they should never have gotten so close. The men weren't holding their oaths as faithfully as they should. He called them into the square.

"You all swore loyalty to me. A man's word is his vow. It's more than just farming my crops and helping me hunt. It is guarding the borders as well. Do you understand?"

The men shifted in their places.

"I said, 'Do you understand?'"

The men finally nodded.

"There is a saying in the wilds, 'A life for a life.' You fail to protect my life so I will take one of yours."

"You can't do that," Mara yelled from the back where several of the women had gathered. "If you are too weak or stupid to protect yourself then you shouldn't be our king."

"Shut up, woman. This is man's business."

She stomped away, a splinter he couldn't remove. If it wasn't forbidden to kill females, then he would have done away with her that first day. He was king!

He turned back to his men. "I repeat what I said the first day, 'Reaffirm your oaths or die.' I am king for a reason. Swear a loyalty that you will hold with more firmness this time or meet me in the valley to die." His lips curled into a smile as eyes widened in recognition. Discovering that tasteless poison had made his sojourn into the wastelands worth it.

Everyone gave their oath this time.

Assassins still came, but now he wasn't the one stopping them. He refused to grow complacent, however, and swept his quarters every time he entered before relaxing his grip on the knife he kept by his side at all times.

That was why he noticed the man hiding under his covers. He had tried to disguise his bulk, but Roc had hidden that way himself and knew what to look for. He didn't even bother pulling the sheets back before placing his knife through the layers.

He stabbed again and again, letting the red color stain his blankets. He could order the women to make him a new one.

Blood finally stopped coming out of the wounds. He placed it to the side of his tent and brought it to the square the following day. He lined up all the men and pointed to the blood soaked rags. "One slipped through. You know the penalty."

He walked back and forth along the line, choosing his victim. Women watched, like always.

From the side, Mara said, "Please, don't do this. It's not their fault. They stopped dozens of killers. So one got through. One will always get through. That's the way of things. You can't take it out on them."

Roc's grip tightened on the knife. He let out a yell as he slit the throat of the man who looked the most like Mara.

"No!"

He wiped the knife on the side of his leg as she rushed forward and flung herself at the body. He turned to the men. "You are dismissed. Don't let it happen again."

Everyone dispersed until it was just Roc, Mara, and the boy. Tears ran down her face as she looked at him. "He was my son."

Roc scoffed. "I might have known. You should have taught him loyalty."

She shook her head. "I taught him too well. He should have killed you. That death would have been noble. At least your line ends with you."

He grabbed her by the shirt collar and lifted her up. "What do you mean?"

"Haven't you noticed the number of pregnant women around here?"

Roc's grip loosened as he mentally sorted through the girls. None of them were expecting. His face paled.

"Your year is almost up, and then your days of being king are through."

"You're wrong. It can still happen."

Mara shook her head. "No, it won't. We women have our ways. You do not deserve to be king so we will take it away from you."

He smacked her, but that didn't quiet the echo in his mind. *We will take it away from you.* Word of his infertility would spread like a clap of thunder throughout the land. He could never maintain his position now. There were too few people left to let some women go childless.

He had thought of everything that might bring him down.

Except that.

When the Wind Blows

by
Pam Farley

My son Daniel howls from within the forest. The noise is dreadful and his outrage is bone chilling. He is paying the price for the careless people of this planet.

I am old now and ready to join the earth in the next month or two. The sputum I cough up is blood tinged and foul, a legacy to the self-destruction my kind was once so adept at creating. We were smokers, we were polluters, and we almost killed the earth. My time has almost come and with my departure the world's population of humans will be but a few thousand.

Although Daniel and the rest of the forest sadden me, I am not bitter. I understand that the earth had to fight back. The human species had tainted every part of the planet. From water to sky, plants, and soil, we had plundered and caused ruin.

It was many years ago now when humanity discovered that it was not as clever as it thought, and that mother-nature had a few fail-safe mechanisms of her own. A strange smell tainted the air in all continents. It lasted for almost a week and then a stinking fog rose up from the ground and clung to the earth. It was meters deep, but as quickly as it came, it disappeared again.

My wife and I were returning from a European trip. We were young professionals contemplating the start of a family life. The holiday was our reward for hard work before the nest was begun and we became housebound. Two months after the fog had cleared we sat in Munich airport looking at an odd photo on the cover of a German newspaper. Neither of us could read the language, but the picture was disturbing. At first Jan and I thought it was some kind of stunt, maybe a morphed picture from the hands of a computer whiz. I cannot forget the horror on my wife's face.

Soon television broadcasts were full of wailing mothers who stood beside their young offspring, firmly rooted in the earth. Only the children's soft pink faces and torsos differentiated them from the saplings they otherwise resembled.

Daniel was born almost a year after it started and we fretted constantly while Jan was pregnant. By then every newborn child was affected and the changes were being seen in children as old as three. Desperate parents had tried to move their young, but once an infant had taken root there was no way of severing the connection without causing death. Specialists, of both medical and botanical types, were called in to help but it was useless.

When Daniel was born doctors were trying all kinds of new preventative therapies. Our son was six months old when the strange buds began to develop on his back, shoulders, and within the arches of his feet. We applied lotions and weed-killers. His bottles were laced with different courses of antibiotics, autoimmune therapies and growth-retardants, but all to no avail. Even surgery was a failure; the new growths kept swelling and ripening.

Many parents tried to halt the grounding process by keeping their children shod with sturdy shoes, but when the time came, the roots would blast their way free. The change was inevitable.

The first forests were established in China, India and America. With such high populations their highways had become lined with the sprouted young. It was disheartening, as well as distracting, for drivers to see and hear so many wailing young faces self-planted along the roadsides.

The governments, in their wisdom, started the forests within national parks. Before long the land was gobbled up. The deformities of these children had not affected their fertility, on the contrary, the population was booming. The plant-children went into procreation over-drive, shedding their spores on the ever-freshening breezes. Soon parks had to be ripped up to make way for the crops of young. Over time the suburbs went too.

When Daniel's feet began to swell we decided to move to the country. Jan and I had wanted him to set down roots somewhere nice where we could be with him. Although we knew it was inescapable, it still broke out hearts the day it happened.

Our boy had just begun walking, two weeks before his first birthday. It was a difficult enough feat for a normal child. For Daniel it was made harder still by having misshapen limbs. The buds above his shoulders had grown unevenly and this made balancing difficult. We knew it was futile, but we still persevered with protective leather boots, and he was confined to the house.

The morning it happened I had been transferring our dwindling funds on the home computer when I heard Jan scream. She had gone to the toilet, leaving Daniel alone for only a few minutes, but in that time the little lad had made it outside.

He must have crawled down the paved pathway to the bottom of the garden. Jan clutched my hand. With her long hair blowing in the wind, and her crazy, desperate eyes she resembled a wild woman. There was nothing I could do or say. For a moment we just stood and drank in each other's agony.

Then we raced to our son's side. In the few seconds we stood by him, he seemed to be straightening and stabilizing within the earth. Jan shook him and he wailed.

'Pick him up,' she begged me. 'Don't let him stay in the ground.'

She knew what she was asking me, but I couldn't do it. I couldn't kill my own son.

Day by day he lost the features that had made him human. His eyes became filled with sap, blind, and rock hard. A membrane covered his ears and nostrils, flattening out his features and taking away his senses. Only his mouth remained functional, although it would never utter comprehensible words, it still communicated his indignity and misery.

We watched our son grow over the years. Somehow, he remained a source of pride to his loving parents. He is still a healthy specimen, tall and strong. Even now he towers above many of the others. His long limbs and green leaves reach up to the sun and happily greet the falling rain.

Jan has long since died, and soon I will join her. Our planet is green again and the air is sweet. The earth will remain in healthy existence thanks to these drastic changes. This is a good thing, I know, but some days, when the forests moan and wail; I have to clamp my weary hands over my ears while the tears stream from my eyes.

Invisible People

By
James Dorr

Manuel Peterson got the notice with his paycheck. Termination. He had lost his job.

It happens, he thought, still not quite believing the next Monday morning when he came in to clean out his desk. The people who worked in the office with him -- all middle management just as he was -- refused to look up as he walked to his cubicle. Refused to speak until he was finished.

Even then, only one touched his hand.

"Tough luck, Manny," Dick Anton said. Peterson nodded and clapped his shoulder, trying to smile. Anton had been with the company eight years, almost as long as Peterson had. Possibly he felt vulnerable too.

After Peterson left the building, he took a five dollar coin out of his pocket, scarcely thinking. He almost dropped it into the hand that suddenly thrust at him out of the air. He squinted. Stared. Began to make out a shadowy figure.

He snatched the coin back. He turned and ran. The air tasted good today -- not so thick that it might impair vision. And yet, he thought, he had never seen the beggar before. Only dropped a coin out of habit, every day when he left the office, as if into nothingness.

Anyway, he told himself, he could no longer afford to give his money away. Not even fivers. Not until he had found a new job

He hefted his briefcase, amazed at the lightness of the few items he'd had to pack in it. He turned toward the monorail station -- again out of habit -- then changed his mind. The day was a pleasant one for the city. The temperature just right. Perhaps he would walk to his apartment and use the fare money on fax credits.

Start sending out application forms for new employment right away.

~*~

Manny Peterson was a businessman. Yet, after eight years with the same company, going on nine, the job he was doing had reached a dead end. His work had never caused any problems but, at the same time, he had not risen into the ten or twenty percent who might have progressed further. And so he had been given terminal notice.

The word was out that he was a loser. For all the forms he had circulated, he received only two interviews in more than a week, and, in both of them, personnel officers only went through lists of set questions as if scarcely caring what talents he might have that set him apart.

Then, ten days after his termination, his wife gave notice.

"Manny, this can't go on," she said one night when she returned from her own job. She sidestepped, avoiding his waiting arms as if she did not recognize him, then sat on the couch while he prepared dinner. "I mean," she said, speaking more toward the TV wall than to him, "it's like we no longer do things together. As if you weren't here. I can't go on like this."

"Honey," he said, "you know the reason we don't go out is that we can't afford it right now." He put two plates down on the living room table. "But I have some feelers -- a couple of jobs that should open real soon. Things'll get better."

She ate her food as if she had not heard him. Stood up when she finished.

"Manny," she said, "I'm going to the bedroom to pack a few things. I've already arranged to stay with friends tonight, then move into my own apartment first thing in the morning. I'll send for the rest then."

"Darling?" he started, then realized she had already walked past him into the next room. He raised his voice, going through the motions of trying to talk her into staying, but understood even as he did so that she was right -- that it wasn't so much their not going out as their no longer really knowing each other the way they once had when they had first married. When she came out again, suitcase in hand, she sidestepped in the funny way she had when she had first come in, again avoiding his outstretched arms. But even funnier to Manny was that he was not sure he even still cared.

~*~

He watched TV every night after that, after another day's searching for jobs. But then one night the TV flickered. He leaned forward to adjust it, got the picture back for a moment. Then it flickered again and went out.

He tried to think about what he'd been watching. He could not remember.

He went to bed early and, when he got up the following morning, the first thing he did was turn on the TV, the same as he had every morning before. There still was no picture, in spite of the fact that full-wall TV was a guaranteed right. He tried to think what he might have done to have had it cut off. He could think of nothing.

All his life he had never caused trouble. His mind went back to when he'd been a child, how he'd always done well enough in his schoolwork -- but not too well -- and how he had always obeyed the rules.

He remembered, in particular, one schoolyard incident when the class bully had gotten him cornered. An older boy, somewhat overweight, but muscled like iron underneath the fatness. He'd tried to smile and blend into the circle of other kids who gathered around them.

He'd let the bully strike him twice before he had gotten his smile just right.

The third blow never came. The larger child's fist seemed to stop in mid air, as if its owner had simply lost interest. The other kids started to drift away and Manny shuffled right along with them. The next few months he practiced his smile -- a sort of bland, open mouthed grin. And he was never bothered again.

The following winter the bully was sent to a different school, but it no longer mattered. Manny had already learned to survive.

A lot of kids, he remembered now, had survived the same way.

~*~

He had never caused any trouble at college either. Or at his job. And yet he had been fired.

His wife had left him -- he tried, but could not remember her name.

His TV service had been turned off.

And now, in his mailbox, he found a letter telling him he had been evicted.

Apartments, too, were a guaranteed right and, this time, he *would* make some trouble. He put on his topcoat and left his apartment, hearing an odd, grating noise as he shoved through the outer door to the street.

The air smelled acrid.

He hunched his shoulders -- the air was too cold and, even though it was nearly mid morning, the sidewalk seemed a jumble of shadows.

He strode to the corner, then stopped, short, when he felt a hand grab at his coat sleeve.

"Manny?" a voice said. He turned and scowled -- the beggar that used to stand outside his office smiled and faded into the dimness. He blinked and saw, for a flickering instant, an alley he could not remember ever having noticed before.

He thought about the beggar's face.

About something -- in the voice or the smile -- that seemed almost familiar.

~*~

Forty minutes later he arrived at the Corporate Housing Bureau. He pushed through the heavy double doors, to be confronted with a line. He took his place at the end, noting the drabness of his surroundings with some surprise. The last time he had been here he recalled that the walls had been bright, the furniture cheerful -- it still looked cheerful, in a way, when he glanced aside, catching it only out of the corner of his eye. The last time he had come here was to transfer to married quarters.

He *was* married, wasn't he? His wife had left, but not yet divorced him. And yet he had trouble recalling the marriage, recalling her name.

Or -- the memory seemed to slip from him the farther he got toward the head of the line -- recalling that he even *had* been married.

He wondered if his wife had looked like the woman whose desk he finally arrived at. Blonde, expensively dressed, wearing pearls, her hair drawn back into a single short braid.

She shoved a form at him before he could speak, then went back to the papers that littered her desk.

"Missus?" he said. He cleared his throat. "Excuse me, Missus. I'm not just here for an application. I've been evicted."

The woman looked up, checked a box on another form, and pushed it toward him.

"That'll be Form 47," she said. "Fill it out, along with the 48-A I gave you, at one of the tables."

He glanced at the paper -- it seemed to have nothing to do with housing. "Missus?" he said.

"Form 56-B, then." She marked an identical piece of paper and shoved it toward him.

"Please, missus. . . ."

"Form 39-D or 17-F, then." Two more marks, two more pieces of paper thrust in his direction. All identical as far as he could tell. The woman still looked up, but not at him. She looked at the milling line behind him, as if he were not there.

He took the forms and looked for a table to fill them out on. There were no tables.

~*~

He stopped at a restaurant on his way home. The robo-wait would not take his order.

~*~

He went back outside. Crowds poured from the buildings that lined the street -- the work day had ended. People crashed into him, punching him, kicking him. Almost as if they could not see him.

A hand grabbed his sleeve.

~*~

Manny felt the blood rush to his face. He had never been angry before. Never like this. He turned and lashed out, hitting again and again with his fists. Hitting the beggar.

The beggar laughed -- he knew the laugh now. It was Vincent Balincott's.

"Come on, Manny. I'm not going to hurt you," the beggar said.

It was good old Vince, who had worked at the desk across from his. Vince, who had been fired six months before.

Exhausted now, Manny shrugged and obeyed, following Vincent into an alley just like the one he had glimpsed that morning. He looked around him as they went from shadow to shadow, waiting then dashing across the streets, then into new mazes behind the next buildings.

He saw the cracked brick and peeling plaster, not just on the backs of the buildings, but even on the facades he'd passed daily when he had been working.

They reached an apartment building he knew, one on the block just across from his own, yet shabbier now than he remembered. Vincent led him back into the crowd, into a knot of translucent people -- people he could scarcely see except at a glimpse, out of the corner of his eye -- that had split from the rest.

"Careful, Manny. They can't see you either."

Manny grunted. He and Vincent rode with the knot up the cracked concrete stairs that led into the building, then let themselves be propelled into a corner of the lobby. Following Vincent's lead, he sank onto a couch that smelled of urine -- the air was scarcely better inside than it had been outside.

But outside the air was supposed to be sweet.

Thick and delicious -- wasn't that what they said on TV? When he'd had a TV?

Not rancid with smoke and stinking of garbage.

~*~

"We can talk now," Vincent said. "They can't hear us either. Once the crowd has thinned out some, if you want we can go across to your apartment. It'll be padlocked, but maybe we can break in anyway and get your stuff."

"What do you mean? I went to the housing office today. I filled out some papers. . . ."

"All of which looked the same to you, didn't they? All of them nonsense. Do you remember what you *did* when you were working?"

Manny tried his best to remember, but all that came was the image of the blonde-braided woman. Making marks and pushing out papers, none of which had to do with his problem.

"On the eviction notice they said I had three weeks," he finally said. "Three weeks before I had to leave."

"That's what they said on my notice too. They lied to you, Manny. Maybe not really lied as such, because it's not as if they wanted to deceive you. It's just that they've forgotten about you. You saw for yourself -- they can no longer even see you. They no longer care."

"But *I* still care. Why do I have trouble seeing *them* now? Why do I . . . why does *everything* seem so different?"

"Neither you nor I exist, Manny. Not in their world. Not anymore. When we lost our jobs, we lost our places."

Manny bowed his head, scarcely hearing. He thought of Vincent as he was now, then as the beggar he'd glimpsed in the morning. Then as the beggar he *didn't* see, but only sensed as he dropped five dollar coins into a cup. His anger came back. "I still don't understand," he said. "If this is a different . . . a different world . . . then which is the real one?"

"Which one is the nicer world, Manny? The other world, right? The politicians who rule on that side have gone to great pains to make sure it's nicer. That decaying buildings look shiny and new. That air that's choked with pollution smells pleasant." He stopped and smiled, giving Manny a long, thoughtful look before he went on.

"But this is the real one."

~*~

"It's not really stealing," Vincent explained a few nights later when Manny joined him on his first food raid. They'd gone into a supermarket, late at night, and, carefully keeping out of the way of the few normal shoppers still in the store, they filled their packs with items left out on the markdown shelves. "These are things that would just be thrown away," Vincent continued, pointing out the expiration date on the package Manny was holding. "These have already been counted as losses. They always hope to get something back -- a few dollars maybe -- but if they don't, who's going to notice? In any event, I will leave *some* money by the register when we go out, as if a regular customer had when the robo-cashier had been distracted."

Manny just nodded, still afraid to talk out loud in front of "normals." But when they got back to the basement they shared with six or eight others -- people who, like them, had become invisible to the society they once belonged to -- his curiosity had to be let out.

"I don't mean to pry if it's embarrassing or anything," he said. "But that money you had -- did all that come just from begging from people like me?"

Vincent laughed. "That and more, yes. Somehow, normal people feel guilty -- they may not see us, but they can sense us when we're around. And when, out of the corner of an eye, one of them sees an outstretched hand, it's nature to put money in it. But that's not the primary reason we beg. Not just to get money."

"I'm not sure I follow you."

Vincent laughed again, louder this time, and one or two of the others joined in. "The money is a convenience, yes. But remember, since we're invisible, we could just take anything we wanted, as long as we were reasonably discreet about it. The main reason most of us work the streets, though, is to keep an eye on the normals. You get a sense of who's fading out -- like I did with you. Of who should be followed and kept out of trouble when they begin to make the transition. . . ."

"You mean like recruitment?"

Again there was laughter.

"Sort of like that, yes," Vincent said. "Tell you what, Manny. You've been learning the ropes pretty quickly so far. Tomorrow, I think, we'll give you a chance to find out for yourself."

~*~

Now Manny had a new job of sorts. Every morning, after the normals had already gotten to their destinations, he picked his way through the garbage lined streets, avoiding the cracks and broken glass that only a few weeks ago he had not even realized were there. He took his post at the mouth of an alley next to the building he used to work in and, when the offices emptied for lunch, he held out his cup. And the money would come, five and ten dollar pieces, more than he had thought people like him -- like he *was* -- could have afforded.

At night, after the streets were clear of home bound commuters, he would return to what he had begun to call "the hideout." The idea amused him -- that he or Vincent or any of the other "invisibles" might need to hide. He, and whoever else had been on the outside that day, would place what they'd gotten into a pool, to be used as needed by that night's collectors. These were the ones who, as Vincent had shown him, would go to the markets and other places to take the things the colony needed.

And, throughout it all, Manny continued to be a fast learner. He no longer minded asking questions -- questions about the notion of colonies and how many others there might be.

"Hundreds," Vincent suggested when he first asked the question. "All over the city."

"All over the world, you mean," another voice cut in. This belonged to a female invisible named Bianca. "We're still a minority, far as I know. But there must be millions of us altogether."

"Maybe so," Vincent agreed. "In any event, our numbers are growing."

"That's what I still don't understand, Vince," Manny said. "You say that *our* world is the real one. That somehow the politicians are able to disguise it for the normals -- to make it seem better -- and, at the same time, somehow to make us just disappear. But how do they do it? Do they put drugs in the water or something?"

"I don't know, Manny. I doubt it's drugs -- the way the water pipes keep bursting, it'd take really massive amounts to maintain a single apartment building, much less a city. Bianca's got a theory that it's caused by TV."

"Not really caused," Bianca broke in. She was younger than Manny, with long dark hair that framed an expression of angry intenseness. "It's more a case of reinforcement. People would *rather* believe things are fine, just like the politicians tell them, and, after they've been told and shown that often enough, they tend to ignore anything they might see that contradicts what they've come to believe."

"It's like a religion, in a way," another voice said. "You're not only preached to about what to look at, but once you start looking, you're told what you see."

"Sort of like that, yeah," Bianca said. "With priest-politicians doing the telling. It's only when something shocks you out of your deepest beliefs -- something like being fired from a job that you always felt was somehow guaranteed -- that the system first begins to crumble. That having lost that first part of your faith, your eyes start to open, in pieces and snatches, to what's really been going on around you all the time."

~*~

Another week passed and Manny began to notice the auras some normals possessed. How some would suddenly seem to be visible, even if only as shadowy figures approaching his cup. How they'd seem to fade in, even when he looked at them directly, then, just as quickly, fade out again.

"Those are the ones we're looking for, Manny," Vincent said when he asked about it. "Once you see someone drift in and out like that more and more often, start to follow his or her movements. That's what I did with you. Follow him home and be ready to guide him."

"You mean those are the ones that are ready -- how did I put it that time you all laughed? -- ready for 'recruitment?' That when somebody fades in for me, he's fading out for the normals around him?"

"Absolutely, although there's nothing that has to do with recruitment about it. Nothing that we've done. Something in *his* world will have happened to cause him to doubt. The rest may come quickly -- a matter of minutes -- or, like with you, stretch out over days, but, either way, the process has started. . . ."

Manny nodded. "One of the normals I'm starting to see --I'd like to start following him tomorrow. I'm not sure yet, but I think it's someone I used to know." He paused and thought back, trying to picture the man whose desk used to be in the cubicle next to his. "I think maybe it's a guy named Dick Anton. One of my best friends when I was a normal."

~*~

The man he was following *was* Dick Anton. Manny was sure now. The aura was so strong the next time the hand thrust through smog-laden air to drop coins in his cup, that Manny almost shouted out loud. He stopped himself only because Bianca had warned him that that could be dangerous. That sometimes normals changed over too quickly as it was.

And so he just followed, watching his friend's back fade in and fade out, each time coming in focus more clearly. He followed him to the restaurant where he himself had been refused service the day he had been at the housing office. Watched Dick Anton order three times before the robo-wait took it down.

And watched his friend reappear on the sidewalk, more visible than he had been before.

His head-shaking look of disorientation as he walked -- staggered -- was buffeted -- pushed -- by his fellow pedestrians into the street.

A shriek of brakes.

A *thunk* as a car, its left front tire split when its wheel plunged into a hole in the roadway, careened through the red-lit intersection. A scream as it hit.

And Manny's own scream as he watched his friend die, wholly visible now. As he pulled the corpse off the street into an alley, cradled the bloody head in his lap, and started to feel his own blood grow hot.

He sat a long time. He thought of the old life, about the work he used to do and about his friend, the one thing he really remembered about it. He thought of a time Dick had taken him home to show off his family. Of how Dick, in the office, would argue politics, criticizing his own lack of interest.

Would argue about the mayor and governors and how it was vital that everyone voted.

And then he remembered what Vincent had said. About politicians.

He looked up and saw the huge wall poster that dominated the building directly across the street. Saw on it a picture of a man named Meredith Wexford, advertising a speech he would make to the city the next night.

Council of Governors' President Wexford.

He stared at the picture. An overweight man. He dredged more memories, one of a fat bully on a playground, who first taught him what it meant to be normal. And how, from then on, the lesson continued to be reinforced.

How he had learned to accept things just as they were presented, to fade with the other eager acceptors into the background.

How not to ask questions.

He stared at the poster, questioning now. Noting the time the speech was set for, the hall it would be in. The TV networks that would show it live.

He focused his anger.

~*~

Bianca was happy to steal the gun for him. A rapid fire, automatic rifle -- a sportsperson's weapon, from what he remembered from ads on TV.

While she was gone, the others had argued.

They argued about what good it would do, even if what he planned did start a revolution. Sure, even some invisible people still watched TV.

But what could *they* do?

\#

"Maybe they'd shoot more politicians," Bianca suggested the following night, when she and Vincent huddled with Manny in the booth overlooking the stage. "That would do some good."

"You mean if our people *were* watching TV?" Vincent asked. They spoke in whispers, even though the TV sound booth was automated. Even though, even if they shouted, they could not be heard by the normals who packed the hall below. "But that's not what you have in mind, is it, Manny?"

Manny lifted his rifle to test the sights a final time before he answered. "Not quite, Vince. It's more for the normals. Bianca, remember what you said just a few nights ago? About how normals begin to question only when something shocks them out of their deepest beliefs. When they've lost that initial piece of faith. But once *that* happens, their eyes start to open to other things too."

"Yeah," she said. "Like when you lost your job. Or when I saw the man I'd been living with disappear in front of my eyes. When no one would help me and, when I finally learned how to make myself disappear too, he'd already found someone else on this side. . . ."

"Shhh," Manny whispered. "The speech is starting." He raised his rifle to his shoulder. "See that mike swinging. Now that the introductions are over, it's moving to focus in on the main speaker. That's how I'll aim -- swing my rifle with it."

He concentrated, trying to see. Pointed his rifle at the spot the mike homed in on, above and slightly to the left of the lectern that stood at the small stage's center. Thought he heard an unseen crowd cheer.

He jerked the trigger -- felt the rifle buck.

Brought it down and fired again, holding the trigger back.

Fighting the rifle -- trying to see. Fighting to see through a spreading red haze.

"Manny, you've done it!"

He blinked his eyes. Saw blood cover the lectern. Saw an overweight form spout red, then stagger and tumble.

Felt Bianca's kisses.

"Manny, you've done it," she said again. "Look. Look at the body -- we can see it as well as normals. And look at the cameras. They're still showing pictures. . . ."

"And look at the normals in the audience," Vincent broke in. "Is that what you meant about causing a shock?"

They looked down at the rows of chairs, seeing first one, then another shimmer. Saw people fade in and out of view.

"They're trying to fight it," Bianca said. "They don't want to believe what they saw because, in *their* world, things like assassinations aren't supposed to happen. And, as for the people who saw it on TV. . . ."

Vincent whistled. "The people who saw it on TV saw more, didn't they, Manny. They would have seen Wexford die close up -- maybe even on a split screen. Seen it from two or three angles at once."

Manny nodded. He put his arm around Bianca, then pointed to the sound booth window -- through its glass, the studio audience seemed to be larger, the shimmering brighter.

"I think we'd better get back to the hideout," he finally said. "Especially because of the people who saw it on TV." He led them downstairs and onto the street where buildings were already starting to empty. "I think, tomorrow, there'll be lots of people seeing the world for the very first time. In the full light of day."

"There'll be confusion," Bianca said. A siren echoed her voice in the distance.

"Yes, there'll be confusion," Manny said. He steered them to the between-streets alleys that Vincent had shown him -- how long ago was it?

But this time it was the guide who followed.

Twenty-One Seconds

By
Ian Neack

"I think you missed a checkpoint on the way here," the shorter man said to the giant walking next to him. The two men hurried through the streets, making their way past people and camera posts.

"A checkpoint? I'm not worried. Randy can yell at me all he wants when we get back to work tomorrow. If anyone asks you, Lucas, the card reader wasn't taking my ID." The giant then reached into his inside coat pocket to make sure his card was still there.

"No, Stephen, I mean the checkpoint at the Kane Plaza train station," replied the smaller of the two, Lucas.

"Oh, then the city police can yell at me, if they want. If anyone asks you, the card reader wasn't taking my other ID." Stephen winked at his small friend and then checked to make sure he still had his second card as well. "It's not the first time I've said that to them, and it probably won't be the last."

"You're not worried about them reporting you for abusing the new transit system?" asked Lucas.

"New? Lucas, how long have they been doing the new system? Two years? The only people I have known to lose train privileges were caught drawing graffiti and breaking into shops," Stephen answered.

"The camera feed will show that you pushed in with me through the gate. That will look suspicious," Lucas pointed out.

Stephen shrugged, "Nah, they will be more amazed that a big guy like me moved that fast through. I might get picked up by a basketball team afterward. My daughter would be happy about that."

Lucas and Stephen made an abrupt turn and ducked through the worn side door of The Finnegan Tap. They dusted the snow off their coats and made their way through the room. When they made it to the bar, they dragged two stools over to their favorite spot.

Stephen sat down first and spoke, "Nice to finally be out of the office." He looked over at the far wall, but a wooden pillar blocked his view of the camera.

"That's why we do this every week. It's like the bar knows what we need: some peace," agreed Lucas.

"Hey you two, I saw you coming in." The lady behind the bar came over with two filled glasses in hand. She placed them in front of Lucas and Stephen. "Or was it going to be something different this week?"

Stephen looked at Lucas. "This bar knows what we need too well. If only they paid attention to these kind of details at work, I might actually enjoy it for once."

"Jessica, I may have said this a hundred times already, but I'd much rather have you as a boss than Randy," Lucas stated.

"Too bad they weren't hiring someone for his position when you applied. Glad to hear you got the position in Marketing, though," Stephen added.

"Thanks guys, and thanks for the recommendations. It really helped with getting the job," said Jessica.

"No problem. You should have told us sooner that you were applying. We could have sneaked you into Procurement. Then you would know why we drink so much. On second thought, Marketing is a better place for you. You'll get to use that degree you got, too," Stephen rambled.

Lucas leaned in. "Just know they watch everything, and I mean everything. They track how long you spend in the bathroom, and I wouldn't be surprised if they had records on what color it is too."

"Lucas, why would they need to know the color?" Stephen shivered. "I really didn't need the image of someone recording that, however they do track how long you're in there. It might be rough at first, getting used to be monitored all the time, but you'll pick it up as you go. You'll do fine. The worst they'll do is bring you in their office and yell at you. After that you go back to your desk and pick up where you left off."

"Thanks for the heads up, but I'm already used to being monitored." Jessica motioned with her head towards the far wall as she spoke. "I may already be in trouble for stopping and talking to you guys for too long."

"Already in trouble? We just said hello. That's a little strict. If you have to leave us for a bit, can you come back with another whiskey for me? Some of us came here to drink and not watch their beverage age more, right Lucas?" Stephen gave Lucas an elbow in the ribs as he finished talking.

Lucas fired back, "I was just seeing if my drink could catch up to you, but it has a long way to go to do that."

"Look at this guy," Stephen said to Jessica as he pointed at Lucas, "He's about to turn forty and still hasn't learned to respect his elders. At least I set a good example for those around me."

"And at least I have hair," Lucas fired again.

Stephen sat up fully and glared at Lucas. "Oh, you went there, and you're not even one drink in. Today must have been a rough day for you."

Lucas leaned toward Jessica and asked, "Can you turn the lights above the bar off? They're reflecting off his head and blinding me."

Jessica laughed, "Let me get the couple who just sat at the other end taken care of, and I'll be back. But if you two don't stop," she pointed at the two of them, pretending to be threatening, "I'll have to throw you out of here." She then turned and walked away.

"She should have thrown us out the first day we came here three years ago," Stephen stated before taking another sip of his whiskey.

"I agree, and yeah, it was a rough day. Randy made sure of that," Lucas said.

"It's almost as if it is his job. What was he doing today?" asked Stephen.

Lucas took a big drink from his beer. "He keeps asking me to recalculate the costs again for Project Lawrence."

"Project Lawrence? Who comes up with these awful names?" Stephen grimaced as he asked.

Lucas responded quickly, "Probably the same guy who wants to know what color it is." They burst into laughter for a while.

Lucas and Stephen shifted on their stools to get a better view of the TV hanging on the wall next to the bar. Highlights flashed from yesterday's game, showing the local basketball team, the Monarchs. It was the pregame show.

"Lauren wants me to take her to a game. Ever since she made the high school team she has been obsessed with the Monarchs," Stephen remarked.

"So when are you taking her there?" asked Lucas.

"When tickets aren't so damn expensive," said Stephen. "At least they serve alcohol there, unlike at her games."

"That's because it's at a high school, Stephen."

"Have you ever seen a high school basketball game? You need

alcohol just to get through the first quarter. At least it distracts you from the damn bleachers. I can't sit on those for a full game."

Jessica came walking back just in time to catch Stephen's last comment. "You can't stand the bleachers, but you come here and sit on these stools for an entire night without complaining?"

"Exactly, there's alcohol here. See what I'm saying?" Stephen lifted the new glass Jessica had just brought him to punctuate his point.

"Maybe you'd have the money for the tickets if you didn't drink so much," Lucas jabbed.

Stephen rebutted, "But Jessica wouldn't like that. That's money not coming to the bar."

"It's not going to worry me, big guy. I'm leaving shortly anyways," Jessica added.

"Speaking of that, when is your last day?" Lucas asked.

"Next Friday," she replied.

Lucas nodded, "That's great. Then the Monday after that, Stephen and I will stop by your desk and welcome you."

"No we won't," Stephen objected. "We can't. Marketing is on floor four. Our IDs won't let us off the elevator there. We're stuck on three."

"That's right. What a dumb system. What are they afraid of, the people in Procurement sneaking up a floor and stealing Marketing's coffee?" Lucas said, rolling his eyes.

Stephen leaned in towards both of them, looking around as if he had important information, "The reports I have of floor four say they have a few flavors of coffee that aren't available to us plebeians down below. If this is true, Jessica, I would be willing to offer some favors in return for some flavors."

"Well maybe they are smart to be paranoid of the unwashed masses of floor three," Lucas said before finishing his beer.

"We'll see," Jessica replied, "but now that you mention reports, did you see the one on the news this afternoon?"

Lucas and Stephen looked at her inquisitively. "No we haven't," admitted Lucas.

"Remember a few weeks ago when they caught that large group from Astrea? You know, the ones that tried to blow up the bridge downtown?"

Stephen glanced back at the pregame show on TV. Lucas nodded. "I remember. It was everywhere in the news. It would have been hard not to hear about it."

"Well," continued Jessica, "Just this afternoon they caught more a few blocks from here. They were still in the apartment planning the next attack. I think it was to be in a public square or a place like that, you know, somewhere with lots of people."

"No way." Lucas was astonished. "How many did they get?"

"About fifteen in total," answered Jessica. "They were saying…" Jessica was interrupted as the phone behind the bar started to ring. "Sorry, Lucas, I'll be back." Jessica hurried away.

Lucas looked at Stephen, who was still turned toward the TV. "Did you hear what Jessica was saying?" Lucas prompted.

"I heard. They got a few more. I don't understand why that is more exciting than the game tonight." Stephen swirled his glass.

"You're not interested in something that is happening only a couple blocks away?" questioned Lucas.

"Nah, I don't need any more worries in my life. Besides, they got the guys, and nothing happened. That's good news. We don't need to worry anymore about what could have been the first bombing in, oh I don't know, five years?" Stephen took a drink.

"And what do you think about the ones they caught weeks ago?" pushed Lucas.

"What do I think? Another group thwarted. No need to worry about them either," Stephen said. He relaxed when he saw Jessica was walking back over.

"Sorry, boss is in the room," she said in a hushed tone. Lucas and Stephen both nodded in understanding. Jessica took the empty glass in front of Stephen and moved on, busying herself with wiping down the unused bar top. Stephen frowned.

"So what do you think happened to the ones they caught a few weeks ago?" Lucas asked.

Stephen threw his hands out. "I don't know. They're probably in a cell somewhere."

Lucas narrowed his eyes at Stephen. "Yeah, but are they? There's no official record of the bust, or a court date, or even any witnesses."

"I didn't know they always reported all of that," Stephen continued to sip on his whiskey.

Lucas kept pressing the issue. "You normally can find out that information. It isn't always on TV, but it's out there. Except in this case there isn't anything. What do you make of that?"

Stephen thumped his glass on the bar top and crossed his arms, looking straight forward. "Lucas, just get to the point."

"This isn't the first group they arrested, and you can't find anything about what happened next. It only started a couple months ago," Lucas stated.

"So what you have is an omission of facts," Stephen yawned.

"Exactly. It means someone may be covering up something," Lucas concluded.

Stephen rebutted, "No, it just means you don't have facts. Do you have proof of someone actually covering up events?"

"Well, no," admitted Lucas.

"Then you don't have anything worth being worried about," Stephen said.

Lucas shook his head. "You're not seeing the problem."

Stephen raised an eyebrow, "Not seeing the problem? All I see is something that may or may not be real. I see you fussing over a hypothetical situation."

"So this doesn't disturb you? Weren't we a little worried a couple years ago when they set up all those checkpoints and issued us our cards? We had to start swiping to get on the subway, we had to swipe to get onto our floor at work, hell, there's a camera in this room on the other side of that pillar there," pressed Lucas.

Stephen leaned in and spoke in a lower tone, "Sure I was worried at first, but do you know what I see now? I'm not worried about the time of day or what part of the city I am walking in. I'm not worried about getting to my daughter's games and supporting her. I'm not worried about when I will need to take my wife in for a doctor appointment. Things are great. I don't see why you want to jump to these conclusions. There's no need to be paranoid."

"No need to be paranoid? Then why are you whispering? You're obviously afraid," Lucas said.

Stephen pursed his lips. "I'm afraid of something completely different. I don't need others thinking I'm some conspiracy theorist."

"Who don't you want thinking that? The guy on the other end of that camera feed?" Lucas pointed at the far wall.

Stephen picked his drink back up and rested it against his chin. Seconds became minutes, but he didn't answer.

"We are talking about people disappearing. People," Lucas said.

"I never said we weren't talking about people," Stephen clarified, "but rather we are talking hypothetically."

"How long though until you think this hypothetical becomes reality?" asked Lucas.

Stephen placed his glass back on the bar top, gripping it tighter. "Alright, I will play your game. Let's say some leader set up the whole sting operation. There really isn't an Astrea force out there threatening to bomb places. They were made up by the police or the government so they had a feel good story to tell us. They have our backs. No need to worry."

"You're being ridiculous," scoffed Lucas.

"Now you know how you sound to me," asserted Stephen.

"Would you be saying the same thing if someone you knew was taken? What about your family? What if you had no way to find them or contact them afterward? Would you be so quick to dismiss the situation then?" Lucas snapped.

Stephen glanced at his wedding band. "The problem with your abduction theory is they aren't going to take me or my family. They would let us live our lives. I would go to work, Lauren would go play basketball, and my wife and I would get to have a nice dinner once in a while. We would get what we want, and those in power would get what they want. There's no reason to bother me and mine."

"You're saying if everyone was like you then there would be nothing to worry about," Lucas said.

Stephen nodded. "Absolutely."

"But you know as well as I do that it would never be the case. There will always be someone who pushes back against those in control. The more people fight it, the stronger the push for control would become."

"But if all of this were true," Stephen shot back, "why would I have any reason to fight? Getting involved would only get my family in trouble. Not all of us are single, Lucas. I have to think of them, too. If we are allowed to be a family, then fighting for control only brings unnecessary conflict."

"So you're fine with forgetting a few people to keep your world as is?" Lucas asked.

"Once again," Stephen started, "do you have proof of this happening? Or are you wanting to fight something as real as the bogyman?"

"I don't think you are going to get the amount of proof you want," Lucas pointed out.

"Well," Stephen brought his glass near his lips, "sounds like you are worked up over nothing, then. Let me know when you have some evidence. I will be more willing to consider all of this then."

Lucas was shaking. His hands were bone-white from gripping his glass. Moments passed without a word. Stephen turned back to the TV to watch tip off. After a few more minutes of silent brooding, Lucas stood up and started to put his coat on.

Stephen reached out and grabbed his arm. "I know when I've made you mad. I know this all means something to you, but don't jump to conclusions. Try to relax when you get home. We have the On Time Delivery Meeting in the morning tomorrow. It will be stressful enough. No need to add any more."

Lucas took a deep breath and let it out slowly. He nodded, and Stephen released his arm. Leaving some money on the bar, Lucas turned and walked across the room and out into the evening air.

~*~

It was 7:58 when Stephen got off the elevator and swiped his card. Two large glass doors opened up to allow him into a massive room of cubicles. His coworkers were already at their desks busy working, even though it was not quite starting time. Supervisors prowled the aisles, their eyes scanning every monitor.

Stephen strolled down the main aisle to the very back of the room. "I should be just in time this morning," he mumbled to himself.

As Stephen reached his desk, though, he stopped short. Lucas' desk sat adjacent to his, but nothing was there. His friend's pictures were gone, the monitor was missing, and the desk was wiped clean. Stephen glanced around to see who else had noticed, but if they had, he couldn't tell. Their heads were down in their computer screens. It was as if Lucas had never worked here.

Stephen's eyes kept coming back to his desk and the empty one next to it. How easy was it to erase his friend? How many boxes did it take to remove any trace of Lucas? How many would it take to remove any trace of himself? Scanning his own desk, he stopped at the single picture frame he kept next to his monitor. It was a photo of his family. All three of them smiled back at him, happy.

"You were right, Lucas," Stephen hung his head, "and now we'll see if I was, too."

He moved to his desk and sat down. When he turned on his computer a voice came through its speakers.

"Welcome Stephen. You are twenty-one seconds late today."

FINDING CHIDERA

By
Dave Creek

Chidera Kapur fights his way out of exhausted sleep. Twenty-seven hours awake, most of them under interrogation. His head lolls. Strikes something hard and flat. Eyes flutter open. Beneath him, the Earth is in flames.

His mind struggles toward full awareness. Mouth feels dusty. I'm on a shuttle, he remembers. Headed through the fires of re-entry. Everyone keeps reminding me the Earth is our original home, wondering why I wouldn't want to go there for the first time. I feel like I'm returning to the womb within a veil of fire.

Around him, people ooh and ahh, their faces cast in a devilish light. Not appropriate, Chidera thinks, it's the hell of the New Lancaster Habitat that I'm leaving.

Memories of that hell sear through his consciousness despite a determined effort to cast his mind away from them. The last decade, from the time he was a newly orphaned pre-teen, has meant performing any job demanded in Gideon Markham's restaurant or a good beating followed. Sometimes it followed anyway.

Spend hours cleaning toilets and be beaten for being dirty. Report to the main dining hall and have boiling soup dumped on him by "accident" in front of paying customers, who loved "practical jokes."

Be forced to lick boots to all-around laughter. Sixteen-hour, 18-hour days, more beatings at the slightest infraction, real or imagined.

All on an Earth-orbital habitat that could've had all those duties performed by scrupulously clean, tireless tech.

But that wasn't the point. The point was being able to lord it over someone, to be privileged in a time when tech had abolished privilege throughout much of Human space.

And now I'm free, he thinks.

Of all but my own guilt.

~*~

Final approach to the city of Brussels: Chidera squints against sunlight as it mirrors off glass-walled skyscrapers, opens eyes wide again to take in constant movement — flitters zooming across the sky, monorails cruising just over street level, pedestrians scurrying ant-like among buildings.

My world is opening up, he thinks. Soon to be more than filthy back rooms and constant humiliation.

Never mind that he'd brought humiliation upon himself in his final moments back on the habitat.

Religious leaders on New Lancaster, which was primarily populated by New Order Mennonites, had discovered Markham's abuses and, with the help of Earth Unity security, shut his place down. Chidera, freed of his servitude, could choose: remain on the habitat or settle on Earth.

He chose Earth, but his best friend — only friend, Miyanda Mukela — begged him to remain. He tried, but couldn't push aside memories of all the times they'd commiserated with one other far into the night, aching for the chance to share more than a furtive kiss before the threat of the master's fists sent them to their separate rooms.

As they stood outside the restaurant within the two-kilometer wide cylinder, she threw herself into his arms, telling him, "I'll be all alone here, you gotta stay!"

Chidera closed his eyes tightly against her words, wanting to scatter them to the winds. Freedom was his only thought, and if leaving behind the misery and the pain meant also leaving behind his only source of solace and comfort, then so be it.

He held Miyanda by the shoulders until she whimpered in pain. "I can't stay here any longer," he told her. "Come with me."

Miyanda looked as frightened as she ever had beneath Gideon Markham's stern gaze. "No, I — I can't! This is...home!"

"No longer my home," Chidera told her. "No longer mine. I have to make a new life." He relaxed his grip on her shoulders, turned, and started walking, Miyanda's cries fading with every step.

~*~

Shining, sparkling all-white room within Earth Unity headquarters, inside the old European Parliament building. Silvery table, a sterile smell. Two women insist Chidera undress, no need to be embarrassed, they're doctor and nurse, medical checkup is just routine.

Bare ass on table, expect a shock of cold, but it's surprisingly warm. Maybe even calibrated to his body temp. Neither woman touches him at first. One runs a hand scanner across his body as the other checks readouts on a medical console. Chidera discretely folds his hands across his groin, and the doctor gives him a knowing grin.

Despite their professionalism and friendly manner, Chidera fears these women, as he does anyone in authority. I feel as if a trap door is about to open beneath me at any moment, he thinks.

"Mr. Kapur," the doctor says, "you're in excellent health physically. Some scarring on your back. That's something we can take care of right away, if you'd like."

"No," is all he says, and doesn't choose to elaborate. I'll wear those scars as a badge of honor, he thinks. Though he wonders if eventually he may change his mind.

The doctor continues: "Psychologically, I expect you should be able to adjust well enough to Earth. It's very different from what you're used to, of course. But it's also better in every way. Replicator economy. Essential needs taken care of. Housing, food, clothing, all that."

"I've heard. Sounds like paradise."

"You might want to schedule some counseling, all the same. This can be a rough transition."

"I'll consider that."

One final procedure, he's told. They will insert a device called a datalink just under his skin. It's a microscopic implant that, as far as he can tell, serves as a combination communications device and tracking system. It can even translate the speech of the Galactic intelligences that Humanity has regular contact with.

The doctor asks him to stand still as she places the barrel of a device that looks disturbingly like a pistol just behind his left ear. She pulls the trigger. Chidera flinches, as much from anticipation as anything; the sting is minimal.

The examination ends. Chidera's given a clean bill of health and a new set of clothing. His old dirty and, no doubt, unfashionable work shirt and durable pants have been discarded. His new shirt is shiny and white, with a tall collar. It abrades his skin, and his hand keeps rising without thinking to rub the back of his neck. His pants appear to conform themselves to his waistline; he has no belt.

And no pockets. Where do I keep my stuff, he wonders.

~*~

Chidera's departure from the medical unit is unremarkable; he's told his new home, at least for now, will be a town called Encinitas, which is apparently in a North American province called California, which he believes he's heard of.

He's guided to a large elevator crammed with a couple dozen or so people, and heads downward to the Brussels-Luxembourg Railway Station beneath Unity HQ. The people all around him waiting to go about their business, whatever that might be, seem happy and healthy enough, and some nod in friendly acknowledgement as the elevator descends.

Elevator doors slide open. A whiff of air enters the elevator car. Oddly, it smells fresher than the air outside or in the medical unit.

Chidera pauses. The wave of people from the elevator car parts and flows around him. This station doesn't resemble anything he expected. He sees nothing resembling a rail line, no metal rails over an endless string of wooden ties. He wonders if his impression of such a place is too informed by historical documentaries and dramas.

Immediately before him, people are lined up against a solid wall beneath a gray domed roof. He can make out conversations in French and what he imagines to be Dutch as well as in English. Long corridors to his right and left terminate in similar walls. Escalators and elevators take people to levels above and below this one. On a whim, he takes a right to investigate down that corridor.

And hears a voice inside his head!

"Chidera Kapur — the maglev train you are scheduled to use lies straight ahead," the voice tells him.

He stops cold. Pivots slowly on one heel to face forward again. Of course. The datalink. Sees all. Knows his every move. No escape, any more than he could escape his captivity back in the habitat. What would happen, he wonders, if he were to continue to the right?

Anyway. Stand stock still. Face forward. Wait.

Within moments, he feels a low rumble beneath his feet, but doesn't hear the train's approach. Wouldn't such a train make its very mass, its substance, more apparent?

Perhaps not. Certainly people around Chidera seem expectant. Around him, here's a man rolling his shoulders, a woman checking her wrist readout, another man bouncing slightly on his heels, impatient to get going.

The rumbling fades. A pause, as if to add drama. Then the wall raises, and the maglev train is revealed. After all the buildup, it's rather a mundane vehicle, a row of seats two across on either side of a single aisle. Chidera travels along with the flow of people and quickly finds a seat. No windows. Then he remembers — of course, there are no windows, because all there would be to see is the inside of a tube. And within that tube, a vacuum, which gives the train its great speed. It's also, he realizes, why he didn't hear the train's approach — sound wouldn't travel within that vacuum.

No one sits next to him. He wonders if he's somehow marked, somehow obviously different from those around him, and they're spurning him. His next thought is how ludicrous the previous thought was; it's simply not crowded on this train, and people tend to create their own private spaces, given the opportunity.

How far away is California? Chidera realizes there's a fold-down comp on the seat in front of him. Fold it down. Ask a question, in a low voice: "How far is it from Brussels to Encinitas?"

The comp, in a pleasant female voice, replies, "Nine thousand, ninety-three point one kilometers."

Chidera's eyes widen and he fidgets in his seat. Over nine thousand K! This trip could take days, he realizes, and wonders if he should have stocked up on provisions for this trip.

But I have no money, is his next thought, and then he remembers most places on Earth, unlike New Lancaster Habitat, do not have a market economy. Replicators are everywhere, and to Chidera it's as if magic has become real.

Calm down. Ask the obvious question. "How long will this trip take?"

"Approximately one and one-half hours."

How is that possible, Chidera asks himself. I haven't even felt the train start to move. "Has this train started up yet?"

"We are nearing our first stop — London."

Chidera took a deep breath. "How far have we come in this trip?"

"Approximately 360 kilometers."

"How long did that take us?"

"Approximately five minutes, including acceleration and deceleration."

Chidera gripped his seat's armrests in anger. Someone believes I'm a fool, he thought. I'm sitting in a stationary train car, denied windows, and expected to think I'm shooting across the European continent.

The car's doors open. Passengers file out as others wait to enter. The station beyond those doors is different from the one he supposedly left in Brussels, the roof still a dome, but lower, and an odd shade of beige rather than gray. Now all the conversations around him are in English, and these new passengers' mode of dress and even their gestures have subtly changed.

Chidera slumps into his seat, his anger rising. Arms folded, jaw set. He can't imagine someone would create all the stage sets needed to deceive him in this way, or create a virtual reality program for that purpose.

But something has happened, he thinks as the doors shut him off from "London." And although he intends to ride this trip out, once he arrives in "Encinitas," he intends to demand answers.

~*~

New York City. St. Louis. Denver. Beyond the first city, Chidera has little concept of the exact location of the others, but he knows they are placed across the width of the North American continent. Yet each trip takes only minutes to achieve. At San Diego, California, the stop is a bit longer than at the others.

Chidera reasons that if he is already in California, the trip to Encinitas cannot take much longer. Sure enough, when the doors finally close at San Diego, it's only a matter of about half a minute before they open again.

Chidera's datalink tells him: "You have reached your destination. Welcome to Encinitas, California." The doors open onto a smaller station than he's seen before, this being the only track visible. A pale woman who looks to be in her late twenties or early thirties comes up to him. "Chidera Kapur?" Her smile appears sincere to Chidera, but it doesn't seem to extend to the lines at the corners of her eyes.

"Yes." He draws close to the woman, thrusting a finger toward her face. "I demand to know what's going on."

The woman's expression doesn't change. "I'm Helena Penner. I'm to be your guide during your first days here."

Chidera takes another step toward Helena. "And just where is 'here?' Am I still in Brussels?"

Helena takes a deep breath. "Another centimeter closer, and I can put you on the floor. Then police officers will take you away."

Chidera realizes his breathing is rapid. He fears he may be hyperventilating. Between breaths, he manages to say, "Already, the threats have begun."

"You made the first one. Now, come with me or get on the next train back to Brussels."

Chidera stood, eyes closed tight, breath huffing, fists clenched.

Helena continued: "If you'll just come outside with me, I can prove you're really in California."

With effort, fists unclench. Breathing slows. Eyes open. "All right. Take me."

Helena turns and starts up a short flight of stairs. Chidera rushes to follow her. As they near the top of the stairs, Chidera's eyes narrow and he raises a hand against bright sunlight. They emerge on a cliff about a hundred meters above a beach that stretches as far as he can see in either direction. Surfers perform their balancing acts upon the more challenging waves. Directly below, children scream in delight.

The ocean breeze is salty and cool.

Chidera nearly staggers from an overload of sights and sounds. Ocean and sky seem to reach toward infinity. Chidera realizes in a flash how accustomed he is to being enclosed and secure within the comforting curve of a habitat's interior.

Helena asks, "Have you ever seen a virt this good?"

"I've hardly ever been in one."

"Pick up a rock. Any good-sized rock."

"What the hell are you — "

"Pick it up, goddam it!"

Habit and instinct kick in, and, hating himself for it, Chidera picks up a fist-sized rock.

Helena gives him a hard stare. "Hit yourself in the head with it."

"What the hell?"

"I'm proving you're not in a virt. Knock some sense into your own brain."

Chidera taps the rock against his head.

"Harder!"

Again, a tap.

"Harder!"

He knocks himself on the head, harder this time. "Damn!" he says, and drops the rock. "I should'a tossed that at your head."

"Which wouldn't prove anything if I was a virt just like everything else you saw. Have you ever heard of a virt where you can hurt yourself?"

"I guess I haven't." Chidera folds his hands and performs a slight bow. "I apologize. Please forgive me."

"No trouble at all," Helena says. "This is my job."

"I thought people on Earth didn't have jobs."

"Most of us don't have to. Some of us want to."

"And you're one of those people."

"I'm also from New Lancaster Habitat. I got out a couple of years ago."

"I never knew you from Gideon Markham's restaurant."

"I was never there," Helena says. "I was in the majority area — the Mennonite area. I worked in the fields on my parents' farm. I knew Malcolm Vicari."

"Oh," is all Chidera can say at first. Vicari was a sexual predator who misused medical biotech to steal others' emotions and relive them anytime he wanted, often leaving his victims empty shells mentally. "I'm sorry."

"I was actually one of the luckier ones. No permanent physical harm. My mind's still intact. But unfortunately, so are all the memories of what he did to me. Yeah. Damn lucky."

"I don't know what to say. I don't know which is worse. The beatings I took or...."

"Let's not make it a competition, OK? Lemme get you settled into your house."

Helena starts walking away, realizes Chidera isn't following, and turns. "What?" she asks.

Chidera can only say, "House?"

~*~

Helena opens her arms wide in front of a small, plain, single-story concrete home overlooking a nearly deserted stretch of beach. To Chidera, it may as well have been a palace.

"I...live here?" he asks. "All by myself?"

Helena turns, and this time her smile is more impressive. "All by yourself! Let's go inside."

Through the reinforced doorway. House is completely furnished, with hand-crafted furniture, many items made of wood. Living room gives way to kitchen, hallway to the right has doorways leading to two bedrooms and a bath.

The entire time, Helena enthuses over the home, showing him the environmental controls, the replicator, how the house can detect severe weather and harden itself against any threat, even a hurricane. There's even a nanodoc module that can detect a medical emergency and send for help even as it's treating you.

I might need that doc in a minute, Chidera thinks, as the room starts to spin and he grabs the back of a chair.

Helena, not noticing his distress, throws open the doors to the back of the house, which boasts a deck that looks out upon the ocean. He takes a tentative step onto the deck, and the air, still cool, settles his senses. The dizziness fades.

The sun is lower in the sky now, looking down on a section of beach that isn't nearly as busy as the area near the maglev station. The waves caress the beach with less force here. "Looks like I can have a lot of privacy," Chidera tells Helena.

"You sure can."

"Why does anyone live anywhere else than Earth?"

Helena looks out across the waters. Chidera suspects she isn't paying much attention to them. "Earth isn't perfect, by any means. You might find that freedom has its own traps."

"I think I could name you more than one person who would just sit around drunk all day."

Helena leans against the deck's sturdy railing. "Sad thing is, you really could do that, and your home's nanodoc would just clear out all the toxins the next day, and send out some biotech to prevent cardiomyopathy and cirrhosis of the liver. And it wouldn't let you leave while you're impaired. Second attempt brings help."

"Help? You mean the police."

"No. Counseling if you want it. If underlying psychological factors are making you drink, they can let you talk through it until you're cured. If that won't work, they might even be able to do a snip in your brain."

Chidera's horrified. "They'd operate on your brain?"

"Only if that's what you wanted, and only if you had parts you wanted to forget — stuff that was leading you to the drinking or drug use or becoming a virthead, or whatever."

"There's nothing like that happening with me."

Helena stares out at the ocean for a long moment, then asks Chidera, "Did you receive an offer of psychological counseling?"

"Yes."

"Yes, and — ?"

"I turned it down."

"Typical."

"What?"

"Chidera, I'm just remembering having to tell you to back off. There's anger there that could become dangerous to someone. Maybe even yourself. Maybe especially yourself."

"I'll...I'll be fine."

Helena's mischievous smile impresses Chidera; he's impressed by her range. She tells him, "Just wait. It's easy to think you've arrived in paradise. But even watching the waves roll in and drinking margaritas can get boring after awhile."

"Is that why you have this job?"

"It's one reason. That, and wanting to help people who've escaped from New Lancaster. Or any number of other places where they've been beaten, abused...raped. You know."

"Yeah."

"Some of those places are still right here on Earth."

"Standing in this house, that's hard to believe."

"Believe it. Well, then, I guess I'll leave you to enjoy your home."

Chidera looks around. "That's it?"

"That's it. If you need anything, you can give me a call on your datalink."

"I guess I'm confused."

"It's common. My first week on Earth, I stayed curled up in my bed for a week."

Chidera takes a step. "I — " Now he does stagger.

Helena starts to reach for him, but stills her hand just short of touching him. "Whoa, hold up! You all right?"

"Yeah. Just...sleepy. Hungry."

"I've been a fool. Of course you are. Lemme get you started on a meal."

Chidera follows her toward the kitchen.

Helena asks, "What do you want?"

Sit at the table. Time to test the home's capabilities. Willingness. "Well...steak would be nice. If we have it."

"We have whatever you can dream up," Helena says. Works the replicator unit. "How'd you like it?"

"Well done. Baked potato?"

"Coming right up."

"Tea?"

"Tea, we got as well."

Chidera's eyelids flutter. Chin sinks toward chest. Then: sharp aroma of cooked meat. Earthy, salty smell of potato. Clinking sound of tea pouring against ice.

Helena sets the plate before him, and Chidera can barely believe the sight. It's as fantastic as the shuttle flight downward to the Earth or the crashing of the waves against the California shore.

He devours his food, savoring the easy way his knife slides through the steak as much as the flavor of the meat itself. The interior of the potato is as fluffy as freshly-fallen snow, the butter melted within it just arrived from heaven. The tea is beyond nectar.

This is how all those I served for so many years lived, he thinks. All the food they wanted, live where they like, have as many friends as they wanted.

He holds up a finger to capture Helena's attention. Swallows a too-big, though delicious, lump of food. "Show me again how to work that. You know, for in the morning."

Helena shows him, then says, "I'll leave you alone to enjoy your meal. Some more people are coming in over the next few days, and I'll be their guide as well. But I'll try to see how you're doing."

"Thanks," Chidera says, food muffling his voice. Helena leaves. He finishes his meal. Sits back, rubs his stomach.

Gets up. Goes to the replicator. Calls up the same thing again. It's just as good the second time.

Double feast done. Chidera lumbers into bed, not even turning it down, wearing all his new clothes. Sleep is immediate, but in his dreams he throws up his arms against the brutal fists of Gideon Markham one moment, and reaches for the gentle hand of Miyanda the next. As far as he can extend his hand, though, it's not far enough actually to touch her.

~*~

Rising from sleep. A slow process. Chidera's lying on his back. Urge to pee is great, but so's urge to keep from having to get up. He realizes only after a few moments that the light cast against the ceiling is natural light — sunshine!

That's right, he recalls. I'm on Earth. I'm free.

To do what?

For now, he decides, to resign myself to getting up. Gotta pee pretty bad. That pressure's not going away.

After that, and other morning rituals in the pristine bathroom, time to plan the day.

First things first. Breakfast? Chidera rubs his stomach, recalls making the same gesture last night after stuffing himself. Still. Go to the replicator.   Order up a glass of orange juice and a cinnamon pastry. Then to the deck.

Chidera looks toward the sunrise, realizes he has to have slept about twelve hours. Quite a luxury.

A sip of juice, and his body finally seems to get the message that it has to move today. I should go into town, Chidera thinks. Engage with people. After all, I'm all alone here.

He pushes thoughts of Miyanda aside as he heads out the door.

~*~

The town, it turns out, isn't far from Chidera's home. Though the air is still, the morning's still cool. Even as he flags down a transit bubble, though, he can feel the sun asserting itself, making it clear that the day will keep growing warmer. While boarding the single-passenger bubble, he makes a mental note to find out how to access a weather forecast, something unneeded within the habitat. He thinks, I'd also better check what kind of variation in weather this province has. My home can harden itself against hurricanes, Helena told me. Should I expect one to arrive in the next few days? What else might I have to endure? Floods? Snow? Earthquakes?

As the bubble glides along the center of a grassy roadway, he encounters joggers, most of whom give him a friendly nod. He begins to get a feel for which people are probably locals and which are most likely tourists.

One couple — or is it a foursome? — Chidera sees walking toward the ocean are certainly tourists. The two are Cetronen paired symbionts. Each consists of two beings. The "major" is the about two-and-a-half meters tall, with thick fur and muscular arms. They have wide pointed ears, a thin mouth, and no nose. The "minors" are smaller, thinner versions of the same species who sit on a hump on the major's belly. The majors provide the strength, the minors bring the brains.

Chidera has never seen an alien — oops, can't use that word! — before. He openly stares. He's tempted to speak to them, to give his datalink a workout, to see if they could understand him, and he, them. But he doesn't, and isn't sure why.

Both majors ignore him, intent upon carrying along their minors. One of the minors gives Chidera a stare from deep-set eyes beneath a jutting brow. He wishes he could read the emotional content of that stare.

Who thought I'd ever live in a tourist spot, he thinks.

Somewhere a person, even someone from another planet, of another species, would want to go to.

And tourist spots, he thinks, will have restaurants. The idea has an immediate appeal. From stuffing himself the night before, he already knows how enjoyable the food here on Earth can be.

What would it be like to be waited on, rather than being the servant?

His heart races with excitement at the prospect — he could be the one giving the orders, he could be the one looking down upon someone, forcing them to —

No.

Shame washes over him, and he hopes it isn't visible on his face to the people he's passing. How could I even consider that? he wonders. I know what humiliating someone else is like. I know how I felt about those who made me lick their boots or who watched when I became the butt of a so-called joke.

Why would I ever want to be that person?

He continues toward town, the very idea, and the shame associated with it, fading only slowly.

When he arrives in the town proper, he's confused. He approaches what appears to be the main street, judging by the large overhead sign reminding him he's in ENCINITAS. The street is mostly a wide pedestrian walkway, but he sees tracks that imply trolley cars also run here.

But he has to wonder where all the businesses are. To his right, he sees residential buildings that could be either large homes or small hotels. To the left, what appears to be a public swimming pool. This close to the beach? Plenty of people are walking around, but where the hell are they going?

Where are the restaurants? Where are the gift shops?

Then Chidera realizes: I'm taking my cues from living on the habitat, and from watching historical cube dramas. No market economy here.

Damn. A world without restaurants? Hard to imagine.

Chidera continues down the street. People passing the other way flash a smile or say, "Hello," and he reciprocates. A trolley, sure enough, rounds a corner, gliding almost soundlessly down the tracks until its bell sounds out with repeated dings as its operator gives Chidera a big wave.

Finally! He approaches a storefront with tables and chairs out front. Outside seating for a restaurant?

He exits the bubble and looks at a sign overhead. Turn the Key is apparently the name of the place. Chidera leans toward the front window and cups his hands against the glass to see inside. Plenty of tables, chairs, and booths indicating a restaurant. He sees a menu attached to the store's glass front. He takes a look: various pizzas, antipasto, chicken and veal dishes. "Oh — Italian," he says aloud without realizing it.

A voice behind him: "You'll have to come join us sometime."

Chidera turns and finds himself facing a man in his fifties, dark hair going gray, with clear blue eyes and a broad smile.

Perplexed at being caught talking to himself, Chidera can only say, "What?"

"You'll have to join us sometime for a meal. I promise you the best."

"Are you...the owner?"

The man shakes Chidera's hand. "I have that honor. "Tremaine Keyes."

Chidera indicates the overhead sign. "But you're not open?"

"Not right now."

"When are you open?"

Tremaine shrugs. "I don't know. I have to get in the mood, maybe come up with some dishes I haven't done before."

"You mean — "

Tremaine snapped his fingers. "You haven't been to Earth before. I bet you came from a market economy."

"You'd be right about that," Chidera says, grateful that he didn't have to go into the full explanation.

"Well, the fortunate thing is that I can set my own working hours. The hard part is getting some help. I love making food for people, but I can't do all the preparation by myself. And someone has to be wait staff, and it can be hard to find volunteers for that."

"Well, Mr. Keyes — "

"Please, make it Tremaine."

"Very well. Tremaine. I'll be sure to check back sometime to see when you might be open."

"You do that. I'll look forward to it."

As he walks away, Chidera thinks, I heard the implied recruitment pitch, but I'll be damned if I'll volunteer to do something that used to pay me in beatings and humiliation.

~*~

Chidera wanders through much of the town but doesn't find another restaurant. Small public food replicator facilities are scattered throughout the community, some even with seating, but they seem impersonal, sterile to him.

But safe, he realizes. It also occurs to him he's seen no police officers, no security guards, no officials of any sort the entire time. These people can't be that goddam perfect, he thinks. Someone has to beat the shit out of someone every once in a while. Someone has to...well, I guess they don't have theft in a place where you can have anything you want.

Maybe Helena's right. Maybe paradise gets boring.

As if thinking of her conjured her up, Helena's voice comes over Chidera's datalink. "How's your first full day on Earth?"

"Thinking about what you said yesterday. How'd you like a margarita?"

"Sounds great, actually."

"I'm headed back to my house. Let's meet on the beach."

"See you soon," Helena says, and signs off.

~*~

Back to the house. Set the replicator for a couple of margaritas. Head down to the beach. He's intrigued by the inexorable rhythm of the waves, by the idea that Earth's moon is their main engine. I thought I was at the mercy of a habitat for most of my life, he thinks, but these waves are at the mercy of an entire world.

Chidera takes only a couple sips of his drink before Helena catches up to him. He hands her the other drink and she thanks him.

"So how did your day go?"

"I met a restaurant owner."

Helena stops in mid-sip. "Tell me you didn't go looking for restaurants."

"Not as such. But it occurred to me once I got into town."

"This is my fault. That was a rookie mistake on my part."

"I shouldn't go to a restaurant?"

"You shouldn't go to a place that evokes bad memories just because it's something familiar."

"I wanted to be the person being waited on for once."

Helena sighs. "That's just as bad. That's reversing the concept instead of avoiding it. A common pattern."

"Shouldn't I be facing these issues instead of avoiding them?"

183

Helena takes a long sip. "That's one theory."

"You're not a trained psychologist."

"I'm someone who's been down a lot of the same paths you have."

Chidera takes in a long breath of sea air, watches a phalanx of clouds advancing over the waves. "I don't feel as if I'm entitled to such beauty."

"You're entitled to whatever you can grab. Without hurting someone else."

"Yeah. A new concept to me."

"Paradise isn't for the weak. It can defeat you sure as being a slave or a prisoner can. It fools you because it feels good while it's doing it."

"How do I keep that from happening?"

"Reach out. Create your own community. Find people with common interests. Did you have people you counted on back in New Lancaster?"

(Miyanda's gentle hands wash his wounds after a particularly severe beating.)

He can barely hear his own voice say, "Yes."

"You have to find people like that here."

"Our common interests back there were not getting beaten. I'm sure here you're talking about art or music or something."

"The people you became close to were the ones that just happened to be thrown together with you."

"Yeah."

(Miyanda wraps his wounds and makes sure he gets into bed so he can return to work in four hours.)

Chidera reaches for Helena's hand. She squeezes it in return. Pulls it slowly away.

Chidera looks questioningly at her. Helena says, "I'm sorry. I'm still in the middle of my own recovery."

He understands. Emotional abuse. Sexual abuse.

Helena continues: "I'm leaving here soon, anyway."

Blood pulses at Chidera's neck. "Where are you going?"

"Just away. You have your common pattern. I have mine. I'm going to travel all around North America. Maybe even other continents."

"And that's common among — "

"Among people who get the hell out of habitats to make a better life down here. Yes."

"I...hope it goes well for you."

Helena smiles. "I do, too. You'll get another guide."

"But you'll come back?"

Helena looks at Chidera. Her expression reveals little. "I hope so. But it has to be what's best for me."

"That's how it should be. And maybe something I need to learn, too."

Helena hands Chidera the margarita glass. She turns away from the beach, and Chidera starts to follow, but she holds up a hand and he stops. "No," she tells him. "You'll see me before I go. Right now, I think it's best for you to stand right here and convince yourself you deserve this beauty."

Chidera faces the ocean again. He hears Helena padding away. He only turns to look back at her a couple of times before she's gone.

~*~

The next three days: Chidera watches the entire 18-hour-long cube saga A SHADOW OF HONOR, based on Rosa Sandage's classic work on the Great Human War, which was fought nearly a half-century earlier. Tires of steak. Tries Chinese, Somali, Thai, and Guatemalan dishes. Stands on the beach for hours at at a time, watching the advance of the sun across the sky, the arrival of the waves. Drinks more margaritas.

He doesn't shower for two of those days.

Helena calls once, but the conversation is short; Chidera doesn't feel like talking, and she's obviously busy getting ready to leave on her journey, or quest, or however she thinks of it.

Perhaps I don't deserve paradise, he thinks on the fourth morning. I certainly haven't been doing much with it.

Decision. Time for a shower, first. Then head back toward the town. Destination: exactly where Helena advised him he shouldn't go.

Turn the Key, this time, is apparently open. No customers visible through the front window, but at least he can see movement inside.

His hand hesitates mere centimeters from the front door handle. I don't know why the hell I'm here, he realizes. I don't want to work here. And Helena says I shouldn't want to be waited on.

Chidera pulls his hand back. How the hell did I get so confused? How the hell can there be too much that's good in my life?

Helena was right, he decides. He starts to walk away. Behind him, the restaurant door opens. Tremaine Keyes' voice: "Chidera, where you goin'? We're not quite open yet, but com'on in."

The desire not to be rude overrules all of Chidera's objections. And his smile for Tremaine is genuine, and he's quick to accept his handshake.

Tremaine holds the door open for Chidera, slaps his back as Chidera passes through the doorway. "Good to see you. You won't believe what I've come up with for my next dishes." He indicates the rear of the restaurant. "I even lined up some help. In fact, she just came here from some habitat or another, just like you did."

The dining room is only dimly lit. Tremaine motions for him to head toward the rear of the restaurant. A door back there swings open and a woman wearing an apron comes out from the kitchen.

Chidera stops breathing. It's Miyanda!

He's rushing toward her, a detached part of his mind wondering why. Miyanda's eyes go wide as she looks up and sees him. He reads fear on her face. He realizes he must be silhouetted in this dark room against the stark light from the street, she may not even recognize him.

A chair stands in his way. He casts it aside. It overturns onto the floor. A table is next, its legs scooting with a screeching sound against the floor.

He reaches Miyanda. That detached part of his mind can't understand why he's ripping the apron off her when he should be sweeping her up in an affectionate embrace. "What the hell are you doing here?" he demands.

A hand clasps his shoulder. Tremaine says, "Get away from her!"

Chidera throws his arm back, thrusting Tremaine's hand away. His unexpected anger still commands him, but he can't allow it to harm Miyanda. The overturned chair is handy. He picks it up, tosses it against the nearest wall. A crash and a clatter, and all his anger is in play as a table becomes his next target, and a couple more chairs go flying, and then he feels a pounding on his face and head and he realizes his wrath has turned against himself and in the next instant the floor rises up to slam against his body.

~*~

Chidera's first awareness: the voices around him as he lies on the floor, but with someone cradling his bruised and pounding head.

He hears Tremaine: "I've called the medics. They'll be here within a minute."

Miyanda: "What happened to him? I've never seen him like

this."

Chidera's eyelids open only reluctantly. It's Miyanda who's holding his head in her lap. "Oh, thank God," she says, "you're awake."

His voice is a painful croak. "I'm...I'm sorry. I don't know why I....no, wait a minute. That's not true. I know why. I just didn't want to admit it to myself."

"Don't worry about any of that now."

"I have to. I saw you in a position where I'd only seen you abused. I didn't want that to happen anymore. But this is a different place."

"Everybody says it's paradise."

"It is. But it isn't perfect. And neither am I."

The medics, a man and a woman, arrive. They ask Tremaine to step back but tell Miyanda she can continue to hold Chidera. Both run hand scanners over him. Chidera recalls the medical checkup upon first arriving on Earth. At least they didn't make me get naked, he thinks.

As the female medic runs another instrument over him, Chidera asks Miyanda, "How did you even get here?"

"I wanted to surprise you." Tears flow down Miyanda's cheeks. "I guess I did."

"And in the first moment I see you...I do this."

"You didn't hurt me. I was scared for you. But I wasn't scared of you."

Chidera's pain subsides. He touches his face, expecting it to be swollen and tender, but it's not. "You'll be fine, Mr. Kapur," the male medic tells him. "But I see Helena Penner is your guide. I think it'd be best if you have a long talk with her, whether here or, well, in custody."

Tremaine speaks up: "I'm not pressing any charges."

"Very well, then." He tells Chidera, "Take it easy for a couple of days."

The medics leave. Chidera tells Tremaine, "Thanks for not...you know."

Tremaine kneels next to him. Touches his arm. "Don't worry about it. I'm just glad you weren't more seriously hurt."

"It's your restaurant that took all the damage," Chidera says.

"And I'm going to insist that you help clean up."

Chidera sits up, rubs his head. "I'll do that gladly."

"Good. Then I don't want to see either you or Miyanda in here for a long time."

Miyanda's jaw drops. "But, Mr. Keyes, I need this job."

"It's Tremaine. And no, you don't. Not here. And part of this is my fault. If I'd looked into your background, Miyanda, I'd never have let you in here. For your own good."

Chidera rises. He pulls Miyanda up. She asks, "But what'll we do?"

Chidera says, "I think I know."

Tremaine looks into Chidera's face and nods. "I can see you've figured it out."

Chidera slaps Tremaine on the shoulder. "Let's start cleaning up."

~*~

Afterward, Chidera takes Miyanda to show off his home. She stands in the middle of his living room and spins around. "All this is yours?"

"Didn't they give you a home yet?"

Miyanda stops spinning. Her expression turns serious. "I just got here from Brussels. I...told them I hoped I didn't need a home."

Chidera goes to her. "Because you wanted to come here."

"I do," Miyanda says, and they embrace. After a moment, they kiss.

Chidera, smiling, looks all around. Miyanda, seeing that, looks worried. "What is it?"

Chidera laughs. "No one to look out for. We're free."

Another embrace. Miyanda pulls him into the bedroom.

Chidera's hand trembles as he touches her bare skin for the first time. "Just take it slow," Miyanda tells him.

Finding the proper positioning of arms and legs is awkward at first. Laughter cures that. What follows is tentative, then frantic, then joyous.

The second time is ever better and becomes the template for the rest of the night.

~*~

Chidera, Miyanda, and Helena stand in the Encinitas maglev station, in front of the wide doorway behind which the maglev train will arrive soon. They await the arrival of several people who have just arrived on Earth from orbiting habitats or from other worlds, other star systems.

Helena tells Chidera, "I don't think this could've worked out better."

Chidera's holding Miyanda's hand. "Someone had to take your place."

Helena grasps Miyanda's arm. "It looks like it's taking two of you to replace me."

"We work better as a team," Miyanda says. "We found that out the hard way."

Helena tells Chidera, "I should've insisted upon counseling for you from the beginning."

"I had to make my own decision in my own way," Chidera says. "I had some rough spots. I'll probably have more." He looks at Miyanda. "But I have some help now."

"All I can do is wish you the best of luck today. You're on your own from here on out."

"You're leaving?"

"I've taught you as much as I know. You've learned how to cope with the same things these folks are going to be dealing with. I have faith in you both." Helena embraces Chidera, then Miyanda. "I may see you in a few months." A final wave, and Helena leaves.

Miyanda squeezes Chidera's hand. Chidera feels a familiar low rumble beneath his feet. "Ready?" he asks.

Miyanda says, "I guess this is what our life will be, at least for now. A door opens, and we cope with whatever comes through it."

"Helena said it. Living in paradise isn't for the weak," Chidera says. "Take away the need to work. Take away the abuse. The humiliation. You find out who you really are."

Miyanda says, "I think we're both exactly who we need to be right now."

The wide door rises. Chidera and Miyanda step forward.